HESITATION

Avery drove by the shop after dinner. His shop, a converted depot. The sign said MARS MARSHALL, WOODRIGHT. Her hand trembled on the steering wheel. Her breath caught in her throat. Twenty-one years since she'd seen him. She'd spent all those years looking for life, while Mars had gone on and lived it. Avery wanted to stop, but couldn't.

She would sleep. Prepare herself. Avery fought for a balance between caution and harebrained recklessness. She would see Mars tomorrow.

Crowfoot Ridge

A NOVEL

ANN BRANDT

HarperPaperbacks

A Division of HarperCollins*Publishers*

📕HarperPaperbacks
A Division of HarperCollins*Publishers*
10 East 53rd Street, New York, NY 10022–5299

This is a work of fiction. The characters, incidents, and dialogues
are products of the author's imagination and are not to be
construed as real. Any resemblance to actual events or
persons, living or dead, is entirely coincidental.

ISBN 0–06–109709–8

HarperCollins®, 📕®, and HarperPaperbacks™ are
trademarks of HarperCollins Publishers Inc.

Cover illustration © 1999 by Wendell Minor

A hardcover edition of this book was published in 1999
by HarperCollins*Publishers*, and was previously
published in 1997 by Alexander Books.

First HarperPaperbacks printing: March 2000

Printed in the United States of America

Visit HarperPaperbacks on the World Wide Web at
http://www.harpercollins.com

10 9 8 7 6 5 4 3 2 1

for Charlie and Jimmy

Crowfoot, crowfoot, evergreen
Shall good luck forever bring.
Find it on the forest floor,
Keep it with you ever more.

Appalachian Folklore

ACKNOWLEDGMENTS

An amazing crew joined me on this voyage to guide me around the storms and rescue me from the doldrums. Their skills and generosity of spirit meant the world to me.

My agent, Jillian Manus, and my editor at Harper-Collins, Carolyn Marino, came aboard and charted a new course for this adventure. Peter Cooper taught me to believe first in the journey, not the destination. Ross Browne, Toby Heaton, and Janet Kent's writers' group helped man the lines. My Lotspeich relatives and my loyal friends came along for the ride, no matter where we landed. Most amazing of all were my sons, Charlie and Jimmy Brandt, who kept me on an even keel.

PART
ONE

1

Ken Kessler stood alert and prepared at the podium, ready to deliver the future. His infantry assembled in the company's new conference center. The sales team chatted in the aisle, dressed for business, not Florida's subtropical heat. Planners, accountants, and the others had taken their seats. He tapped a pointer on the lectern and waited for everyone to settle down.

"Friends and colleagues." He leaned into the mike and flashed his quick smile. "Welcome to the 1985 Kessler Properties annual meeting. You all have made this a banner year for us, and I want to thank you." He began the applause. When it subsided, he continued, "Some exciting projects are in the planning stages. To start with, we are advertising lots in Pelican Estates. Gina, the phase-two map, please." He waited while his assistant displayed the plan. "We expect to revitalize the project, kick it in the ass, as they say. My wife handles sales there, so contact Avery if you have any questions or need any brochures." He gestured toward her.

Avery, sitting at the far end of the second row, waved an acknowledgment. The last place she wanted to be was trapped for two hours on a plastic chair listening to her husband. She imagined him naked at the podium, a ploy to diminish his stature.

"The Tequesta project is under way," Ken said as Gina slipped the development map into position. "The entrance has been changed because the county had a problem with traffic congestion around a school." He indicated the change with the pointer.

Ken's voice had the sound of a late-night disc jockey, all optimism drenched with seduction. And so casual in his expensive tweed jacket. Avery tuned him out; she'd heard it all before. The company thought they owned the Treasure Coast and conducted their slash-and-burn conspiracy as if they were irreproachable. The world-famous diver Mel Fisher searched offshore for the wrecks of Spanish galleons with treasure spilled across the ocean floor, while Kessler Properties found their treasure onshore, leaving the land wrecked. Avery shared the bounty and the blame.

Gina had the prodigious task of changing the maps on the easels. She'd been hired to answer phones not so long ago. Advanced fast, from receptionist to secretary, to office manager, and now assistant to the double-tanned vice president, first from golf and then from sailing. She positioned a new schematic plan, and Ken began to talk about it. With her brooding Latin eyes and enough black hair for two people, she was Avery's opposite. And Gina was ambitious.

During the seventies, Ken and Avery had been drenched with ambition, hope, and responsibility. His ambition was alive still, while Avery was left with the responsibility and a growing sense of catastrophe.

She wished she'd grabbed a glass of water before the meeting started. She heard the words "deer pond" and began to listen.

". . . exciting project," Ken was saying. "Deer Pond Garill be an exclusive community with a security entrance. A guard house here," *tap*. "As you can see, we are leaving park land, drainage ponds, wooded areas," *tap, tap, tap*, "here, here, and here."

"Deer pond?" Avery asked. "Excuse me for interrupting, but there aren't any deer left in this part of Florida."

"Statues of deer, Avery, not real deer." Everyone laughed.

"Life-sized statues will be scattered around in the green areas and especially at the various drainage ponds. We still have deer in Florida, don't we?"

"Price range, Ken?" someone asked from the back. Everyone was still chuckling.

"Quarter mil and up." Ken circled the map with his pointer indicating the boundary fencing.

Avery couldn't remember the last deer she'd seen in this overpopulated region, and tried to think when she'd ever seen wild deer. On one of her family's vacations to North Carolina, a doe, a buck, and a little spotted fawn had come to drink from the pond at Sylva's house. She and Sylva were both seven years old, and it was the first time she'd ever been allowed to spend the night with Sylva. Hard to believe thirty years had passed. She chased the thought away by running her locket along its chain.

The caterers were brewing coffee at the back of the room. The aroma of French roast blended with perfume, aftershave, and the formaldehyde of new carpet. Avery took a glass of white wine after the meeting and nibbled a Swedish flatbread spread with crab-laced cream cheese. She hung back, away from the giddy award winners, away from the rabble of doting accomplices around Ken. He was in his element at these functions. His casual confidence, the company's success, their gilded future, attracted people to him.

"Avery, hi. Where have you been hiding?" Two

prim-figured women from accounting joined her.

"Ladies, how's it going?"

"Pretty darn good for Gina, if you ask me," one said. "I heard she's taking over Golden Sands."

"Not Golden Sands." The other snapped her fingers as if trying to come up with a name. "It's those new condos over on Jensen Beach."

"Taking over?" Avery asked. "As property manager?"

"Interesting, isn't it?" The woman's eyes were elusive behind bifocals. "Funny it wasn't announced today."

Avery nodded and felt ambushed by innuendo.

"We just thought you'd like to know. Ken has mapped out a grand year for 1985. He's terrific, isn't he?"

"Yes, terrific. What would I do without him?"

The two women looked puzzled; they waved and moved back into the crowd of eager employees.

Avery wormed her way through the big-boned contractors and divorced realtors, speaking to people she hadn't seen in a while, nodding to others.

"There you are," Ken said.

"I don't mean to intrude. I see you're busy."

"Not at all," he said to the others. "Avery's done a great job with Pelican Estates." He put his arm around her, drawing her into the circle. "Ten years she's been running the project."

"Thanks, but I don't run anything, Ken." Avery smiled a tenuous smile. "I just wanted you to know

I'm getting ready to leave. I'll see you at home."

"I'll be late, we have the corporate meeting here tonight."

Ken kissed her forehead.

Avery slipped out the side door and walked to her car. The afternoon had turned dark as twilight. She glanced around at the active sky, smelled a shower on its way, felt a hint of moisture on her skin. She pulled out of the landscaped grounds surrounding the corporate headquarters, passed a decaying strip mall with a row of rusting newspaper racks out front. Plastic bags were caught in their feet.

Avery was heading home on the old two-lane parallel to I-95. Rush hour snarled the interstate on Fridays, but the secondary road stretched out mostly deserted, flanked by the marsh on the left and the canal on the right. She drove fifty miles an hour on a collision course with the storm, watching it inventing itself until thunderheads boiled above the horizon.

Deer Pond Gardens? She laughed and tried to imagine statues of deer all over the place. They would put Bambi on the letterhead, no doubt. She wondered about Kessler Properties, but everything they touched turned to treasure.

The wine had left her mouth dry. She blind-searched her bag for a Life Saver, fingered the roll, and loosened the candy with her fingernail. It tasted of lime. She turned on the radio to help erase thoughts of the new projects and the natural places they would destroy. The creamy sleeve lapped at her wrist, and her gold ring caught a glint of dashboard light. On public radio a local debate about the endangered wetlands reassured her. Someone cared.

Lightning flashed way off in the distance, framed against a reddened sky. Raindrops beaded and slid sideways off the windshield. She flipped on the wipers, watched the blades hesitate on the downbeat.

Avery switched on the headlights, accelerated, pulled out to pass an old man in a compact, wondering how he could see over the steering wheel, and left him diminished in the rearview. The storm eclipsed the sunset and blackened the sky.

The wipers struggled against the increasing deluge. Headlights reflected the lonely spirits of highway, leaving Avery defenseless. The center-line Morse code faded out of sight while gale-force wind buffeted the car. Pea-sized hail danced on the hood and bounced on the asphalt. Storms like this were usually contained to small areas, furious and fast; the trick was to move through it.

The BMW fishtailed and recovered.

Her measure of apprehension rose a notch, and she slowed down.

A deer appeared out of nowhere, stranded in the rain, paralyzed in the Beemer's headlights. Avery thought it must be an apparition, a vision, a figment of fantasy.

The animal's fear-frozen eyes penetrated the night in the glare of her lights.

Every fiber of Avery's body filled with the dread of killing it, with an overwhelming premonition of guilt. She slammed the brake pedal down and swerved. The wheels lost traction on treacherous Florida ice. The deer vanished.

The car aquaplaned into a slow-motion spin. Avery fought to regain control by steering into the spin. Panic seized her.

Steering lost function.

Brakes failed.

Strange parts of the landscape were illuminated and then blurred in the helpless slide. The car careened into the black canal. Her forehead slammed against the steering wheel. Lights flashed in her eyes and went out, short-circuited.

The water exploded with the impact. A tidal wave erupted and flew out in every direction. The canal began to settle back, seeping into the car. The musky scent trapped her as she plunged into the cold spongy void of limbo.

Brackish memories swirled, images spiraled. Old guilt washed in. Another time, another deer.

The family of deer had stopped to drink at the

pond and then moved into the meadow. The buck looked around, his white tail standing straight up. The doe followed with her spotted fawn. From the window in Sylva's house, Avery watched them foraging. She looked out over a lawn they mowed with a big orange ride-on mower. She could see across the meadow from her position at the breakfast table. The forest beyond mounted a steep rise up Crowfoot Ridge, thick with laurel and bottle-green undergrowth, misty with summer fog.

Hunter Marshall sliced a giant cathead biscuit on his palm with a menacing butcher knife. Sylva's daddy scared Avery. His wife, Kitty, sat opposite. Sylva's brothers and sister crowded together on the benches. Wayne speared a piece of ham. Charlotte unscrewed a jar of homemade apple butter. The room was quiet, except for the sounds of chewing, forks and knives hitting plates. Mars scraped a mound of eggs onto his plate and spooned applesauce over them. A place had been left for Franklin, even though he wasn't there.

Avery pointed to the window and told Sylva to look at the deer family. Sylva frowned and punched Avery with her elbow.

Hunter bolted from his chair and snatched a gun from a rack on the wall. The screen door squeaked but he closed it without slamming. He took aim.

"Papa, no," Sylva screamed, brave for a seven-year-old.

The shot rang out, stunned them, made everyone jump.

Brought them up cold.

Sylva's brother Mars covered his ears with his hands.

The blast of the gun exploded, cracked, rang, and splintered the serenity of the morning, the mood, the meal, and the meadow. The ear-splitting shock of it bounced off the mountains, through the garden, through the henhouse and echoed back again. It ricocheted through Avery's body.

The buck fell.

The doe and her baby fled into the forest.

Hunter returned to the table to finish his breakfast. No one said a word. They sat, stunned and silent, watching him shovel one forkful after another into his mouth. His wiry beard and mustache made his mouth a grizzly hole into which the food disappeared.

Sylva's eyes had a look of defeat.

Avery sat frozen in shock, looking across the once quiet meadow, too dumbfounded to cry, too young to protest. Mars's eyes told her not to speak. He shook his head with just one tiny, almost imperceptible motion, showing a wisdom beyond his nine years. A blanched fog curled over the meadow.

The buck had fallen near the woods where tall grass concealed his body. They knew he was there.

If he'd jumped up, run into the kitchen, and danced a jig on top of the table, Avery wouldn't have been any more aware of his presence.

His death.

Wayne leaned forward and took a biscuit. His bitten fingernails looked sore. He swiveled around on the bench, balancing to get his long legs out, and stood to his full height, tall for fifteen, built thick like his daddy. His hair fell across his face.

"I'll start to dress it," he said, and went out the door. The screen door slapped against the wooden frame.

"Get them scent glands first, son," Hunter called after him.

Then Hunter stood and lit a cigarette. Smoke came out of his nose, circled his head, formed a ring, and hung in the air. He followed his son out without another word.

The smoke ring disintegrated.

"Don't go frettin' none about the deer," Kitty said. "He'd be starvin' to death come winter anyway. Y'all go pick us some pole beans now, hear?" Sylva's mama spoke with a southern music like the rest of them.

They didn't want to go out to the garden, afraid of what they might see, but more afraid not to mind Sylva's mother. They took the basket and went out the back door.

"Close your eyes and take hold my hand." Sylva's voice was sweet and rich like hot fudge melting on vanilla ice cream.

"How can you stand to look?"

"I ain't lookin', only watchin' the ground with squinty eyes."

"Why did he kill the deer, Sylva?"

"He kills everything," she said. They ignored the tomatoes and the yellow squash hiding under the leaves, and filled the basket with beans. The garden smelled of damp green. The sun cast no heat, too early in the morning yet.

"Where's Franklin?" Avery asked when they carried the basket back.

"Gone off to fight the war," Sylva said.

Avery stopped at the pond and tossed a pebble into the tea-dark water, remembering the deer family. She stood watching the wavelets bleed from tight-controlled to loose-disjointed circles fanning out in expanding patterns under the mist. Bees buzzed around the daylilies.

Mars was in the barn sitting with his back against a post, knees up, sketchbook in his lap. Avery sat down next to him and leaned close to see his drawing of the deer. Its eyes were blackened with the tip of the pencil, and tiny lines made the hair look real. Mars held the pencil with long, thin fingers.

"It's all my fault," she said, fighting tears.

"Avery Baldwin, it wasn't your fault." Mars concentrated on his work.

"If I hadn't said anything, your daddy wouldn't have even seen them. This is the worst thing I ever did in my whole life."

She got up and ran all the way down the path to the cabin her family rented every summer. Trapped forever with the shame of the dead deer.

2

Oranges ripened on the tree outside Avery's office window. Dense to suffocation, the fruit obscured the dark lacquered leaves. The calculated location of the tree and massive doses of fertilizer ensured the desired, if deceptive, effect during the prime buying frenzy. The oranges looked juicy and sweet, but the tree produced sour oranges.

The ugly wound on Avery's forehead had faded to a pale violet. The goose-egg lump had receded. Ever since her plunge into the canal, disillusion nagged her. Her life seemed sweet enough on the surface, but the deception was as real as the orange tree outside the window with its bitter fruit.

The phone at her elbow rang.

"Avery Kessler."

"How are you, dear? I didn't think you'd be back at work so soon." Her mother's voice was tinged with concern.

"I'm fine, really. Sorry you and Daddy were dragged out to the hospital in the middle of the night."

"Ken called us. He's such a gem. You're lucky, Avery."

"I know. Thanks for the flowers."

"You're welcome. We're just glad you are all right."

"Give Daddy my love. I'll see you soon, Mother. Thanks for calling."

Avery sat looking out at her neighborhood. Pelican Estates had replaced a natural inlet off the Indian River. Bulldozing, dredging, laying in of roadbeds, building seawalls, and clearing for the houses had destroyed everything. Part of old Florida, the part the Seminole had cherished, vanished. Concrete-block stuccoed houses with pastel shutters and matching garage doors mushroomed out of the marsh. Driveways and sidewalks replaced cabbage palm. The houses backed up to man-made canals where speedboats cradled in the arms of boat lifts, fishing skiffs rocked in the waves, and sailboat halyards clanged against the masts all night.

Avery's life played out in white-washed ritual. Her mother's dream for her had come true, but Avery wasn't living the dream. She wasn't even present most of the time; she was gone, lost in grumbling memories.

A car pulled into the driveway. She glanced up and then turned back to her work, unable to focus.

Easy and Mark Buyer, neither taller than five six, both eager, both twenty-five pounds overweight, commented about the oranges when they came in.

"I'll be with you in a minute," Avery said. She took a sip of coffee, gone cold. She would let them familiarize themselves with the layout of the development, then drive them around to see the completed area.

They stood studying the phase-two map on the wall. They were squeezing the juice out of sixty. A thousand couples just like them had stood in front of the maps over the years. Mark pointed out the golf course to Easy. She noticed most of the lots backed up on canals and said he could have the fishing skiff he'd always wanted. They might have been New Yorkers, Minnesotans, Jerseyites, Ohioans, but Avery could tell by their accents they were southern. She did not want to talk to them.

"I'm Avery Kessler." She got up and circled her desk. "How may I help you?"

Their name, too hard to pronounce or remember, flew right over her head. Polianski? They were from Durham, North Carolina. Ah yes, Easy had retired from teaching, Mark would be retiring from the post office in two years.

"Two and a half, dear," Easy said just under her breath.

"So, this trip is to buy land. Then we'll build later," he said, ignoring her.

"We can't take the hard winters anymore," Easy said. They all said the same thing. "No point staying locked inside five months of the year when we can move here." Not when they could stay locked inside twelve months of the year to avoid the heat. Even May could be hot in southern Florida.

"No point," Mark agreed.

Avery ushered them into the backseat of her new car. She kept the passenger seat cluttered with papers to maintain some separation, and always kept the air conditioner set on freezing. Eye contact with them would be through the rearview mirror.

She chauffeured them through the seasoned and mature neighborhood past her own house on Gull Circle, off Sea Grape Drive. They'd bought one of the models when Ken took over Pelican Estates twelve years before. Nothing Avery learned in college had prepared her for a job, so she took the six-week real estate course and went to work selling for Kessler Properties.

"There's my house." It helped to let prospects know she lived in the subdivision. "I see our gardener is here today." Skeeter was bent into the viburnum hedge, pulling weeds. She usually stayed home on the days he worked in the yard or the garden.

Green manicured lawns surrounded stuccoed

houses painted pastel colors. Sidewalks were swept clean—the epitome of isolation. A boy squirted his sister with a hose in front of one house. They passed a lone jogger.

"Friendly neighborhood?" Easy asked.

"Very," Avery lied. She'd sold most of the houses in the development; intimacy with her neighbors was a wave to a passing car.

"How long have you been here, dear?"

"I was born in Stuart."

"Oh, a native Floridian. I thought everybody in Florida came from somewhere else."

"I'm not the only one," Avery said. "Adam, my brother, was born here as well."

She stopped in front of lot 340 on Tidewater Drive. They walked across the denuded, sand-covered ground. A stiff breeze slapped them. One long strand of hair on Mark's balding head stood on end. Easy's short graying hair wasn't disturbed, so tight was the perm.

"The seawall is finished, just waiting for you to put your dock in." Her words were blown away on the scalding wind as they followed Avery toward the mosquito-infested canal.

"We've come to Florida on vacation for years." Easy held Mark's hand to avoid tripping on the concrete flat lot. "We drive down from Durham, you know."

"My mother always hated the heat so much we went to North Carolina every single summer all the years I was growing up."

"Might have passed on the highway," Easy said.

"Might have."

They stood on the seawall looking at the quiet canal and the empty land across the way. Prospective buyers didn't realize this lot would be surrounded by houses some day, with speedboats racing up and down the canal, and lawn mowers grinding through grass all around them.

"We have alligators so big they can swallow a dog in one bite." Mark and Easy laughed at Avery's deadpan joke.

"What part?" Easy asked. "Of North Carolina?"

"The mountains. We always went to the same place, Crowfoot Ridge. My father used to go trout fishing. We stayed at MacKinsey's Farm near Asheville, in one of Mr. Mac's rental cabins."

"Lots of farmers found ways to increase their income by renting rooms or cabins. The mountains are beautiful," Mark said. "Floridians retire in North Carolina and we all come to Florida."

"Grass is always greener," Easy said. "You could put a bigger boat in here than a fishing skiff."

"We have a twenty-eight-foot sailboat moored at our dock." Avery pointed up the canal. "It's called the *Bald Wind*."

Mark was looking at the waterway. Avery could see his wheels were turning; his boat was in the canal. A sale was assured.

"My best friend lived about a mile down the road from MacKinsey's place," Avery said. "Her name was Sylva Marshall. Her father kept a loaded rifle right by the door, hard to believe. I saw him kill a deer one time."

"Not uncommon at all," Mark said. "The Appalachian farmers were trappers and mountain men to start with, you know. They still keep loaded guns around. I suppose the practice may seem surprising to some."

"Do you ever go back?" Easy asked.

"No, it's been a long time. We never did go back."

"Whatever happened to your friend? Do you keep in touch?"

"I don't know where she is now. She meant so much to me, her brother too, but the years pass. I should go back." So many things were left unfinished. But no, she couldn't. She wanted to see them, but it just wasn't possible. Avery knew she didn't have the courage to face Sylva. "Someday maybe."

How could she have let Sylva take the blame? How could she ever face such shame? As far as Avery knew, Mars didn't know the truth, or would Sylva have told him? Either way, they didn't know everything. She should go back and tell them. At least have the courage to face it and lay it out once and for all. Just the thought of it halted normal functions; blood stopped flowing in her veins, and her heart slowed. Breathing, hearing, seeing, all shut down.

"Is MacKinsey's Farm still there?" Easy asked.

"I don't really know if it is or not. I remember the guy who owned it." Avery had never forgotten old Mr. Mac. "I'll give you some time to think about the lot," she said as she walked back to lean against the car.

Avery could picture MacKinsey's Farm, distinctive in late afternoon when the ridge cast a long shadow over the land. The shadow shaded the barn, crawled over rolling pastures, deepened the green of the ragged-leafed corn growing between old Mr. Mac's place and the sorry excuse of a farm Hunter Marshall kept. And in those long afternoon shadows, Crowfoot Ridge was the life blood of her restless youth. Fizgig lightning flickered in the sky before a shower, and marble-smooth watermelons cooled in the creek. Fireflies darted in the zinnias or were trapped in a mason jar. As a child, Avery waited all year for their summer vacations with wild anticipation.

One day Mr. Mac saddled Moonshine and Lightning so Avery and Adam could ride up the ridge to pick blackberries. If they got enough, the Cherokee cook would make cobbler for dessert. Her name was Neco-wee. Avery had almost forgotten.

Avery's bucket had been half full when Mr. Mac walked up the path with his thumb hooked in his leather suspenders.

"Neco-wee says you'd better bring a bucket down now, sent me up to tell you," he said. "Go ahead and take a bucket down, Adam. I'll stay with Avery."

Adam combined the berries into one bucket. Avery started all over again. He climbed on Lightning, and the horse took off at a trot. Mr. Mac sat on the grass watching Avery pick berries. He made her feel funny.

"You want to see my Indian?" he asked after Adam was out of sight.

"What Indian?"

"My special Indian. I'll let you hold it." Avery walked toward him, curious. He held it in his lap with one hand, a stick covered with polished leather stained to look like real skin. But not a toy Indian.

Avery said, "Cowgirls shoot Indians."

He was stroking it, goading her. "It's a toy, Avery. Something to play with."

She sensed danger, smelled it like the dead burnt fume of a fire gone to smolder. Her feet stopped moving, froze her to the spot.

He jumped up in one quick motion and grabbed her.

She screamed, twisted, slippery as a skinny eel, and ran for Moonshine. She pushed the horse, slapped the reins down, and grabbed for the saddle horn. The horse went back to the barn with her dangling at its side.

At the age of eight, she'd been quick. She'd been clever. And she'd gotten away.

This was the first of the Crowfoot Ridge secrets.

Cowgirls don't tattle.

"Yoo-hoo, Mrs. Kessler, we've made a decision."

The Buyers joined her by the car and said they'd decided to purchase the lot. Avery drove them back to the office and prepared the contract. Just a lot, but the small sale would lead to a contract for a house in the future, worth the hour she'd spent. Their names were John and Edith Polianski, nice couple. Avery thought she'd grown too cynical over the years.

In the afternoon, Avery drove out to see the land Ken was just starting to clear for a new development. Orange bulldozers with Kessler printed on the doors were busy clearing another tract of land. She couldn't hear the seabirds above the racket of the earth movers, dredgers, and trucks.

Metal washboard waves chopped the surface of green water. She tasted the salt air. Clouds sailed along white highways in the sky. Avery felt responsible for their invasion of this land. The color of destruction was orange.

Ken pulled up in front of her car and parked. He

walked toward her, hidden behind aviator sun-glasses.

"What are you doing out here?" he asked. "Are you all right? Shouldn't you stay home a while longer?"

"I'm fine. I sold a lot on Tidewater this morning."

"Avery, I'm worried about you." He brushed her bangs away and examined the bruise on her fore-head.

"Don't be. Looks like they killed something out there, a snake maybe. The men are gathered around looking. I feel responsible for it."

Avery felt heartsick watching another landscape surrender to the demands of suburbia. What would it be replaced with? Three-bedroom, two-bath night-mares on the streets of screams that encroached like a blight on the wetlands and the natural places. Everything would be replaced with blacktop and stucco painted yellow. Yellow was the color of lies.

"Why? That's crazy." Ken cocked his head, looking at her as if she'd gone mad. "Maybe getting knocked unconscious messed you up more than we thought."

"Knocked conscious." Avery wondered what had been killed but turned away, knowing she was too late. The chatter in her mind darted like the sound-less seabirds, hiding real thought. She wanted to drive into the work area, blow her horn, and stop them somehow. Nothing she could do would stop this progress.

Whatever happened to Avery Baldwin? Had she

been killed too, like the marshes? Whatever had died out on the marsh had no meaning. One more thing to feel guilty about.

"This is what we do, Avery, what we've been doing for twelve years. Why does it bother you now?"

"Because, don't you remember when we were hell-bent on saving the environment, the turtles, everything?" Avery turned to face him, stood with her hands on her hips. "We are taking too much. The business is too big. Will one of the bulldozers be ravaging land on judgment day?"

Ken looked at her. "You'd better hope a Kessler bulldozer is still working out there. You work for the company too, you know."

"There will always be just one more project to build." She looked away.

"Oh, Avery, I walked Deer Pond this morning, great land. I was thinking about doing a house for us there."

Avery flinched.

"Why does Deer Pond bother you?"

"I don't know. It doesn't, no more than the others. The name is a lie."

"What would you think about moving? The clubhouse will have an Olympic-sized pool. You could start swimming again. You always say the one at home is too small."

"Too small for serious lap swimming," Avery said.

"I swam in high school, Ken, twenty years ago."

Ken turned away. "I gotta go. I'll see you at home tonight." He waved. "Don't think about stuff too much, Avery. Enjoy it."

She watched him leave and then looked out over the site.

When all the wilderness was tamed, when condos and subdivisions smothered the state, when mangroves and manatees, conch and coquina, were remembered only by the old-timers, the Crackers, and the 'gators, when the black ink of their balance sheets owned the balance of Florida, and red tide claimed the water, a Kessler bulldozer would still be belching soot out on the flats.

Ken had his own truth, clear, simple, and direct. Truth seemed to be the one thing that couldn't be corrected or changed or colored. Truth had no color. Her mind was cluttered with trivia and tadpoles and terrible tales. Lost, out-of-focus, jumbled thoughts danced around on crazy quilts, gave colors to everything like jelly beans in a mason jar, and often replayed the Technicolor pictures of childhood memories.

Avery's truth was buried deep in lies, too deep ever to uncover.

3

Skeeter had aged graceless but not confused. He'd leathered like a shipwreck's timber. He drew convictions from wasps and ethics from ants, though failed to become a relentless machine. He could predict the slightest change in the monotonous stewing weather. He called the four seasons hot, rainy, humid, and buggy. Seagulls screeching meant a squall was brewing out in the marsh under jaundiced skies, nappy clouds spin-drifting west to east. And a storm would hit a couple hours later. Never failed.

Avery once went out to Skeeter's shack with him in his boat. He lived in Martin County on the St. Lucie. Marsh rabbits slept in a cage. An iguana lolled in the sun. A diamondback terrapin peeked out from under its shell. Scrub pine and cabbage palm grew on the quaggy marsh, same as always.

At Avery's house, they had turned the side yard into a native garden using plants Skeeter brought from the marshes. They'd been working on it for years. Ken hadn't been thrilled with the idea of using part of the yard as a native Florida landscape. He thought everything should look the same, with grass carpets and specimen plants. In fact, he'd refused to allow it. Avery fought for her garden, so Ken gave in, then fenced the whole area in with a six-foot-high privacy fence. Her garden embarrassed him, but Skeeter and Avery loved it, and Skeeter brought new plants every week. In two years they had it looking like it had before the developers destroyed it. The maypop vines and climbing asters flourished on the fence.

Avery and Skeeter had been working in the garden for three hours in the June heat when he stood and shook stiffness out of his old bones. With his narrow Seminole nose, he sniffed the salt air, watching some brown pelicans fly in formation. His hair, peppered with gray, was caught here and there with long thin braids.

"Sky looks funny, don't you think, Skeeter?" Avery asked.

"Storm's coming." He looked all around at the swirling clouds. A stiff breeze blew cooler than usual. "Could be a bad one."

"Do you remember when hurricane Diane hit here?"

"I do, but can't remember when. In the fifties?"

"Daddy let me mark the coordinates on the map when I was little. I thought it was a big deal." Avery sat down to rest and poured each of them a glass of water from the jug. "He said the same words you just said . . . could be a bad one."

"Well, we might get a thunderstorm, but no hurricane."

Skeeter scratched his head. Long raw muscles rippled under his skin.

"Hurricanes must be bad for the Seminoles, living out the way they do," Avery said.

"Naw, we don't build anything we can't do without. We just put up another shack. We stay close to the ground when a bad storm comes."

"My grandmother died right soon after the hurricane," Avery said. "This was her locket." She held the heart-shaped locket away from her neck so he could see. "My mother gave it to me."

"What's inside?"

"Old pictures, one of me and one of my brother." She ran the locket back and forth on its chain. "I wore my best dress to her funeral, a pinafore with yellow butterflies, the straps never stayed put, bow in back never stayed tied. My shoes were black patent leather. I sat still as a rock next to my mother and listened to the words, but I didn't understand."

Her grandmother used to put Ovaltine in their milk, which left brown smears around the glass and a glob at the bottom.

Funny, the things she remembered.

Skeeter got up and looked through his bag. "I brought some seeds I wanted to plant before I leave."

"I'll do it. Hand them to me."

Skeeter gave Avery the seeds, and she began preparing a place for them while he went about his other work.

"One time when I was little, we were at Crowfoot Ridge, we planted Mary Jane seeds for Sylva's older brother." Avery didn't look up. Skeeter took a hoe and loosened the soil for her.

"What's Mary Jane?"

"We thought they were flowers. We were only about eight years old. By the next summer they had turned into real pretty bushes. Later, we found out her brother Wayne was growing marijuana." Avery laughed. "Took us a long time to figure everything out. There was a ridge behind the farm, we used to climb around up there. The ridge was covered with a plant they called crowfoot. If you kept a sprig, it would bring good luck."

"I never heard of it," Skeeter said. "What'd it look like?"

"Sort of a vinelike ground cover. The little branches looked like bird toes."

"Might have been creeping cypress, sometimes called ground pine."

"Crowfoot Ridge was named for the plant. There was some Appalachian folklore poem or rhyme about it bringing good luck, but I don't remember how it went."

"It was probably some type of lycopodium." Skeeter began to gather his things, getting ready to leave for the day.

"My best friend in those days knew all the names of the plants, just like you do. She showed me bluets, foxglove, golden sundrops, black-eyed Susans, and one called jack-in-the-pulpit. Another one was old-man's beard. Sylva taught me to recognize poison ivy and poison oak, so I wouldn't break out with an itchy rash. I don't know how she knew so many plants."

Avery walked with him down to the dock where he tied his skiff.

"You know, Skeeter, ever since the accident, I've been thinking about all the damage we're doing to everything. Kessler Properties seems too ambitious, all of a sudden."

"No more than normal, I wouldn't say." He put his things in the boat, ready to leave.

"And these childhood memories come flooding in my mind, some like they happened yesterday."

Skeeter yanked the cord on the outboard. It sputtered and then roared. He hollered, "See you next week."

Avery untied the line and tossed it on the bow, waving as he left, hoping he'd make it home before the rain.

Two hours later the storm hit. The pool shimmied under torrents of rain. Water ran down the windows in sheets. Lightning flashed and the lights flickered. Thunder shook the house, making Avery jumpy and cold, so she turned in early.

Ken came in slamming into things, whistling, noisier than usual. He switched on the hall light and staggered into their bedroom.

In the half-light, Avery saw he was disheveled. The clock by the bed showed two in the morning. He shook out of wet clothes, draped a towel over his head, and fought to keep his balance.

"You asleep? Some storm, huh?"

Ken hadn't been drinking much lately, so it surprised Avery to see him staggering around.

"Did you hear the news? Good ol' Mel Fisher finally scored. He's the treasure hunter, you know."

"I know who Mel Fisher is," she said.

"He found the Spanish galleon he's been looking for. Sixteen years, he's been searching off the coast of Florida for the *Atocha.*" Ken's voice was harsh, louder than necessary. "He scored big too. Millions."

"So you were out celebrating Mel Fisher's good fortune?"

"No, we're finished with the damned art center. We deserved a drink after that mess. Try to do something nice for people and see what you get? The bitch Myrtle Talkathon, or whatever her name is, nearly drove me insane. Anyway, our part is done. The interiors people and the landscape architects take over now. Then Myrtle and her crew will fill it with a bunch of dead stuff. They can have it." He chugged from an open pint. The towel sailed to the floor.

He flopped down on the bed, sweaty, smelling of fish and whiskey. His boxer shorts were bunched up. He lifted his leg and pulled off his sock. One off, one on. He grabbed Avery and pulled her on top of him, tearing her nightshirt open in the process. The buttons flew off.

"What are you doing?" Avery struggled to get away. "Leave me alone."

He tightened his grip on her.

"You're hurting me, Ken."

"What's the matter, Avery? You're not glad to see me?" He spit these words right in her face. She smelled his acidic breath. He had an abrasive hold on her. She felt his erection. She squirmed free but he grabbed her again. She swiped at his face with fingernails, made contact, and gouged.

"Jesus, shit, what are you doing?" He covered his eye.

He threw her off the bed, got up, and went into the bathroom. The light switched on.

"Jesus, look what you did. You almost scratched my eye out. What on earth is the matter with you?"

Avery pulled herself up and ran out of the bedroom, down the hall, and let herself into her garden room, closed the door and locked it. She curled up on the daybed facing the sliding glass door, looking out over the moonlit garden. Leaves sparkled with lingering drizzle. He was lucky she didn't kill him, she thought, and knew for the first time she didn't trust herself.

Ken apologized when he came in the kitchen for coffee the next morning, but it was too late. The scratches on his face were red and ugly. He'd have to explain them away somehow.

He sneezed, blew his nose, coughed.

"I guess I'm getting a cold," he said. "I feel like I died."

Avery pressed her palm against his forehead. "You have a fever. You'd better stay home today."

"Will you stay with me?"

"I can't, Ken, I've got to meet the termite inspector at the Logan house. I have a closing at ten, then a showing at Tequesta this afternoon. In fact, I'm late now."

"Avery, you know I wouldn't ever hurt you, don't you? I'm sorry about last night."

"You should put something on those scratches," Avery said as she left.

They had devoted themselves to work. No time for children. In what little free time they had, they sailed the *Bald Wind* out of their canal, into the inland waterway, across the bay, and sometimes out into the ocean. They had died and gone to paradise, fool's paradise.

The painful and obvious reality for Avery was Ken didn't have a creative thought. He wasn't sensitive, perceptive, or intuitive. He didn't listen even when he was sober. His highs and lows were always dead center. No matter what happened in business or at home, he kept his keel even. Sometimes Avery wanted to shake him to make sure he was alive.

They were both doing the right things. Everybody was happy. Slaphappy. And the years sailed by. The war in Vietnam had raged on, while the flower children danced to The Doors, worshiped Bob Dylan, sang along with Roger Daltrey, The Who, and Neil Young. Students protested, higher than heaven, everybody else died and went to heaven, the soldiers, the children, the villagers. America had gone to hell in a Honda or to Woodstock in a Volkswagen van.

In Avery's opinion, while all the world seemed on the brink of disaster, Ken flamed steaks on the grill by the pool without one flaming thought. He grilled Hibachi hamburgers on the aft deck of the *Bald Wind*, oblivious and numb to shame. Listening to

Jimmy Buffett, Avery straddled the bowsprit and watched dive-bombing pelicans and racing porpoises and dreamed her childhood dreams caught forever in the feathers of a dream catcher.

Skeeter came to work in the garden on Friday. Avery was quiet. They worked together for two hours before he asked her what was wrong.

"You're usually pretty chipper," he said.

"I'm thinking too much about what used to be or what might have been. I think I'm drowning in the past."

"The only way to survive, Avery, is to live every minute in the present. Let the past go. Forgive yourself and forget it."

"Forgive myself? What do you do if that's not possible?"

"You identify your own truth and then you live your own truth, but you have to know what it is first."

"What's this, some old Seminole wisdom?" Avery sat back and stretched. "I don't know how to face my truth."

"Do you know what the truth is?"

"Maybe some."

"Seek it all. Don't stop until you find it. You can't live without it."

Skeeter stood, satisfied he'd pulled every weed in

the bed. He was near seventy, or past, yet as compact as a Swiss army knife.

"When I was a boy," he said, "sometimes we'd find castaway snake skins. We collected them and decorated the walls because we thought they were pretty. I asked my father one time why the snakes shed their skin. He said they had to shed the old skin to grow bigger. Many lessons are taught in nature; many truths we forget. Be still and listen, and you will learn many things."

"But, Skeeter, the problem is, I'm torn between the past and the present."

"Give the present your full attention. Shed the old skin, make room to grow. The present deserves all your energy, otherwise you are divided between two worlds, a time of dreaming, which is sleep, and a time of being, which is awake."

"And it tears me apart?"

"You know it does." Skeeter smiled down at her.

"You know, Skeeter, I'm lucky to have you."

When he left, she went down to sit on the dock and stayed until the sunset faded away.

Ken was waiting for her when she went in. He'd been nursing a bad cold all week, no doubt caught when he closed down the bars with his construction guys.

"How long have you been here?" she asked.

"A while. I didn't want to disturb you."

"Used to be a time when you would have just hollered at me and I'd come running. Anyway, you're not disturbing me."

"I brought a bottle of wine. Would you like some?"

"Yes, thanks, why not? How's your cold?" She followed him to the kitchen where he had the bottle chilling in the freezer. The scratches had healed a little but were still noticeable.

"Better," he said. "Jack called today." Ken uncorked the wine. "He and Lissa are coming down. I had to respond on the spur of the moment. I said it was okay. Do you think we can manage it?"

"I'm delighted. We haven't seen them for a long time. We'll take the boat out. We haven't sailed in a long time either."

"But you're sleeping in the garden room."

"And?" Avery took the first sip from her glass, realized he'd gotten an excellent wine. "They can have the guest room. I don't see a problem. Unless, of course, you're embarrassed for them to know."

"No," he said, and looked at Avery. "You know I'm sorry about everything."

"It's not your fault, not alone, anyway. It takes two. I overreacted. I always seem to overreact. I'm sorry I've been so awful, bitching at you about everything."

Avery walked out by the pool. He followed. They sat on the deck chairs.

"But I shouldn't have come home drunk."

"And I shouldn't have tried to scratch your eyes out. When will they be here anyway?" Avery asked.

"Any time, now."

"You mean they're coming in tonight? Jeez, Ken. You didn't say they were coming right now. You never say the whole of anything." Avery jumped up. "I've been in the garden with Skeeter all day. I need a shower."

"Sorry. I thought I was perfectly clear," he called to her as she left.

Half the problem was communication, Avery thought as she ran the water for the shower.

Fifteen minutes later, she came back to the pool, clean and changed, her hair still damp. Lissa and Jack were sitting with Ken. Avery kissed Jack on the cheek and gathered Lissa in a bear hug, rocking her side to side.

"I'm so glad to see you. So glad you could come down. We let too much time slip by, Lissa. I miss you."

"We finally got a break and just decided to come at the last minute." Lissa held her friend's hand. "I hope you didn't go to any trouble for us."

"Ken gave me about two minutes' notice, enough time for a shower. We'll go out to eat. But I wouldn't have cooked anyway, it's getting to be my lost art. Anybody up for Craggy Joe's?"

"I don't cook much anymore either," Lissa said. "Ken says we're going sailing tomorrow. Glad I brought a bathing suit."

Avery wanted to be alone with Lissa but enjoyed the foursome as they'd been friends since college. If anyone noticed the new sleeping arrangements, nothing was said.

The next morning everyone helped get the boat ready, and Ken motored out the canal. He was at his most efficient on the boat. Avery liked the way his tanned bare feet looked in Docksiders. Once they were under sail, Lissa and Avery went to sunbathe on the bow. Ken and Jack were aft handling the lines. They sailed in a light breeze on a broad reach in the St. Lucie River.

"We don't get together near enough. How are you, Lissa? How are the kids? Tell me everything."

"Not much to tell. Everything's the same. I want to hear about you." Lissa smeared sun lotion on her legs. It smelled of coconut oil.

"I've been wanting to talk to you. Ever since the accident I had in the car, things have been so strange for me. First of all, I think Ken's having an affair."

"What? Are you sure? With whom?"

"It's been little things. He works all the time. Night meetings."

"That's not new."

"No. We've been seeing each other two nights a week maybe, watch TV, don't talk, go to bed early. When we do talk, I end up berating him about the business. A couple nights ago, he came home drunk and grabbed me. I went berserk, Lissa, I mean really wild. I nearly scratched his eyes out. I smelled the whiskey on him and, man, I don't know what to say. I lost it. God, I could have killed him. It was so bad it scared me. I mean to say, I scared myself. Then, I started sleeping in the garden room. I've turned it into my private space. He hasn't said anything. Never comes near me."

"I saw the scratches on his face. What do you want? Do you want it back the way it was?"

"I want to be left alone."

"What makes you think he has a lover?"

"I think it's Gina. He stays out all night sometimes. Of course, he has places—the condos, friends, family in Ft. Pierce. But we can't go on this way. We're living a lie."

"What do you mean?"

"He's not who I thought he was. Remember in college when we met? We used to love Florida. We were all so intent upon saving the turtles, the dunes, all of it. We cherished old Florida."

"I know. I introduced you two, remember?"

"Of course. Look at him now. They're starting another project called Deer Pond, for God's sake. They're going to put deer statues all over the place. He's talking about moving there so I'll have a pool to swim laps in. It's been twenty years since I swam laps. I think it's the last comment I made that he actually remembers."

"You married him in sixty-seven, Avery. Everybody was like that. Most of us had to move on, to make our living, to support our children. He's a developer. What do you expect?"

"Some sensitivity to the environment. Is that too much to ask? In the past I wanted to go to the mountains in the fall to see the autumn leaves, or in the winter, but no, never once did we go. Ken wants to go sailing. We go sailing. My garden? He fought against the idea. Such a simple thing. I think he resents the time I spend working with Skeeter."

"They build what sells."

"I know. Hell, I help. I sell the lots, the houses, and the condos."

"You make a good living selling real estate too."

"I don't give a damn if they buy anything or not. I give them no pressure. Some of them, I don't even want in my neighborhood. I figure my success has something to do with job security. Maybe it had to do with investment. I made no investment in getting the job, keeping it, or advancing in it. I like the freedom and I can put up with the buyers for short periods of time."

"Tough work but somebody's got to do it, right?"

"I tell them we've got mosquitoes carrying diseases they haven't even discovered yet. And alligators big enough to eat a dog. You can't discourage them. They can't sign the papers fast enough. But I'm not living. Lissa, I'm buried in memories, hating him half the time for what we do. I can't change any of this."

"Oh yeah, this is just awful." She gestured wide to include the boat, the bay, and the sky.

"Hey, you two," Jack said as he shinnied along avoiding the genoa and came forward. "Where's lunch?"

They anchored in Manatee Pocket and ate the sandwiches and potato salad picked up at a deli earlier. Ken and Jack dove off the aft deck to cool off. When the galley was cleared away, Lissa and Avery went back to the bow. The guys got under way again sailing toward Port Salerno.

The breeze freshened as Ken headed back tacking on a close haul, calling "ready about" every fifteen minutes. Lissa and Avery dodged the genoa and clutched the stanchion to keep from being knocked overboard by the flying jib. Finally they gave up and went below.

Lissa said, "I think Holly is involved."

"How seriously?" Avery laughed at her old friend.

"I'm pretty sure she's having sex."

"And she just graduated from high school?"

"Yes, she starts college in two months. I know, Avery, I'm not surprised, it's just different when it's your daughter."

"Talk to her."

"It's easier to say than to do."

"Why?"

"What did your mother have to say about it?"

"Absolutely nothing. Everything I ever needed to know about life I learned at Crowfoot Ridge with the Marshall kids. One time we were sitting around under a tree, and the dogs came running out in the meadow and were humping on each other. So I asked what they were doing. Mars said I didn't need to know."

"Well, you learned a lot from the experience."

"I'm not finished. So later Sylva told me the dogs were making babies. Then a couple days later I see this pregnant woman, and I asked her where her dog was, because I thought she had to have a dog to get pregnant. The woman said her dog was in a kennel and asked how in the world I knew she even had a dog. I said I figured she did."

Lissa laughed at Avery.

"I thought for a long time you had to dance around with a dog to get a baby."

"And it's not far from the truth." Lissa almost fell over laughing. "Holly isn't so confused about things," Lissa said, still giggling.

"I'm sure she'll be okay," Avery said. "You should talk to her though, try to anyway. Find out how serious she is with her boyfriend, what she wants from the relationship."

"Avery, I thought something horrible happened on one of those vacations."

"The place was magical. The best times of my life were spent at Crowfoot Ridge. I fell in love with the mountains, the waterfalls, the extraordinary scenery. I learned all the important childhood lessons, some hard life lessons, shared every new idea, every painful discovery, every joy with Mars and Sylva. And I loved them both with all my heart. Then, it ended. And it was over. We never went back."

"You've never forgotten?"

"As a matter of fact, I haven't thought about it in a long time, years really. But ever since the accident . . . I hit my head really hard, you know, and something was jarred loose. The memories play like movies in my mind."

"Why didn't you ever go back?"

"Couldn't go back, no way." Avery looked out over the bay. "I loved Ken when I married him, didn't I, Lissa?"

"You seemed so wounded back when we were in college. I thought you loved him, but maybe you needed him. Big difference between needing and loving somebody. You know he's a good man, Avery. An affair is no reason to end your marriage."

"You're right. I know he's a lot better than some, anyway. But I heard he was moving Gina into one of the condos."

"Sounds convenient," Lissa said.

"Yes, very."

"I still don't think you learned much about sex at Crowfoot Ridge." Lissa shoved Avery to make the point.

"Well, I didn't tell everything, now did I?"

4

Three gruesome gashes on the back of one manatee had been inflicted by an outboard motor propeller. Avery held the hose for the manatees, squirting fresh water in their gaping mouths. They were her little elephants of the opaque canal. Skeeter sat in his skiff trying to free a crab trap from the *Bald Wind*'s anchor. Crab traps demoralized anchors and outboards.

"How hard would it be to outlaw boats without propeller guards?" Avery wondered aloud.

"Wouldn't be hard if anybody cared. They outlaw everything else," Skeeter said as he took the hose from her and filled the twenty-gallon water jugs in his boat.

"It's a wonder he lived." Skeeter pointed to the manatee with the long diagonal scars across its back.

She dropped a pebble into the espresso water, watched the circles ripple into threads of oblivion, the only constant was the inconstancy. Balance a penny spinning on its rim, watch it wobble, watch it fall.

"What you dreaming about?" Skeeter's question startled her.

"I was thinking about the manatee drifting along just beneath the surface, and wham, a speed boat's propeller chops those gashes into its back. It's horrible, you know. They're so innocent. I drift off thinking, connecting the dots, looking for the truth, I guess."

"The dreamer knows no truth, Avery. You have to be awake to see the truth." Skeeter turned, started to leave, then he paused and said, "Go and face whatever destiny has in store for you." He left the dock and wandered back to his work.

Avery watched the manatees glide and dip, surface and dive, often touching, always close.

> *Three long scars.*
> *Three scarred lives.*
> *Three blind mice.*
> *See how they run.*

In the daydream, Avery and Sylva were nine years old again, crouching midway on the stairs at the Marshall farm.

"Did you hear that?" Sylva asked Mars, who was standing in the kitchen doorway.

"Just the dogs." He looked up at them and adjusted the only thing he was wearing, rumpled pajama bottoms.

Their new baby brother, just eight months old, was in the playpen over by the Buck stove. The shower splashed in the downstairs bathroom. Something big crashed on the porch. Avery huddled closer to Sylva. They heard a snarling roar, and the dogs were barking their heads off.

A black bear lifted itself up on its hind legs right outside the front door. Its body filled the whole doorway. When it pushed at the door, the door exploded off its hinges. Screen and wood flew into the room. The bear dropped to its four paws and just walked in.

Avery felt the vibration in the stairs as the floor absorbed its weight. She was paralyzed and grabbed hold of Sylva.

The bear padded two steps into the room, moved its whole head to look at Mars with small pig eyes, then rolled its head and looked toward baby Shelby. Avery heard its raspy, choppy breath through its yawning mouth.

The bear lurched toward the playpen with teeth bared, toppled a small table, stopped, distracted by a breaking vase. Muscles of great power bulged under its thick rippling coat when it moved.

Shelby howled.

"Hey, bear," Mars yelled, jumping up and down, "over here." He waved his arms.

The bear was between Mars and the playpen. It moved in slow motion, sniffed the vase, swiped at the table, looked at Mars. Its claws tapped on the hardwood floor when it took a labored step toward the kitchen.

Avery bolted down the steps, flew across the room, snatched Shelby out of the playpen, and ran back to Sylva.

The bear watched her, pushed off with its front paws, stood, and roared. Fear crawled up Avery's spine, lodged in her throat in a soundless scream.

When it dropped back to the floor, the windows rattled.

The water running in the shower shut off.

The bear lumbered toward Mars, wagging its head back and forth. Avery smelled the horrible reek of death when it passed by the stairs.

"Run, Mars," Sylva screamed. "Papa, Papa."

Mars darted back into the kitchen. Sylva took the baby from Avery.

The bear lunged with astonishing speed and strength into the kitchen chasing after Mars.

Mars let out a blood-curdling wail.

Hunter ran out from the shower, dripping wet, wrapped in a towel.

"What?" He looked up at the girls on the stairs.

"A bear's in the kitchen," Sylva shouted. "He's after Mars."

Hunter grabbed the rifle off the wall and crossed

back to the kitchen with two quick steps.

He fired.

The shot was a loud clap, a cracking sound that reverberated inside Avery's head. A bellow and unearthly growling sounds caused tentacles of fear to rise on Avery's neck. She heard crashes, the bear staggering and thrashing, knocking over chairs. Hunter fired the gun again, and the bear fell, vibrating the whole house. The smell of gunpowder waffled up the stairs.

Mars was silent.

Shelby cuddled in Sylva's arms.

Avery moved down three more steps so she could see. Unspeakable anxiety silenced everyone.

The bear lay on the kitchen floor, twitching. Shards of bone, bear brains, and blood had splattered on the chairs and on the wall by the refrigerator.

Mars was stretched out on top of the upper kitchen cabinets lying with his back plastered against the wall. Blood flowed out of gashes on his side. His eyes were glazed; his face, drained of all color. His blood dripped on the cabinet door and on the counter.

Hunter placed the gun on the counter. He grabbed a chair, stepped on the seat, then up on the counter. He lifted Mars down in his arms. He stepped back to the chair, then to the floor. He carried Mars to the sofa as the family gathered around in shock.

"Wayne," he shouted, "back the truck up to the front

door. Kitty, bring my clothes. Sylva, get a blanket. Charlotte, run get Mac. The boy's bleeding to death."

Sylva passed the baby to Avery and bolted up the stairs.

Charlotte ran like a deer out the doorless front door.

Sylva's mother handed Hunter his overalls, then bent over her son. Blood was gushing out of him. Hunter pulled his overalls on while Sylva helped Kitty wrap the blanket around Mars.

Then the blanket turned red.

Hunter collected Mars, bloody blanket and all, into his arms and stepped barefooted over the remains of screen and shattered wood. He slid into the truck holding Mars in his lap. Wayne screeched away.

Avery didn't think anybody could live if all their blood was on the counter in the kitchen, and soaked into the blanket.

Mr. Mac arrived moments later with Mr. Baldwin. Adam and Charlotte were in the back of the truck.

"Good Lord," Mr. Baldwin said, shocked to see the dead bear, blood all over the floor and dripping off the cabinet. He ushered Sylva and Avery away, but they watched from the hall.

Adam and the two men tied the bear with a rope and dragged it out the back door to the porch. They lifted the bear onto the tailgate of the truck and rolled it into the bed. They drove away with Adam sitting between his father and Mr. Mac.

Charlotte swabbed down the floor in the kitchen with a wet mop. Her feet anchored as she swayed.

Kitty stood on the chair to clean the blood off the upper cabinet. She put the gun back on the rack and then cleaned the counter.

Hours later, Avery still felt trampled, as if an elephant had crushed her. She and Sylva thought Mars must have died or they'd be back already. They waited, walked in the meadow, but mostly they watched the road.

They pulled the shattered screen door out to the porch and swept wood splinters out of the living room.

They paced on the porch.

Then they settled on the steps and watched a hummingbird hover above the honeysuckle, wings a-blur.

They waited.

"I love you more than anybody, Sylva, more than if we were real-live sisters."

"We are more than sisters, Avery. We're friends. That's the best thing," Sylva whispered.

Avery remembered when Hunter killed the deer. She'd seen her grandmother's casket lowered into the ground. She knew when people died they didn't come back anymore.

Avery had a lump of fear in her throat.

Mars and Sylva were her best friends and she loved them.

Avery didn't say anything else. She just kept on watching the road.

Waiting.

Hours later, Wayne's truck pulled into the driveway, inched up to the house, and stopped. Hunter carried Mars straight in without a word and took him up to his room. Kitty followed.

Avery and Sylva watched the empty stairs.

"Can we go up?" Avery asked.

"We better wait," Sylva said.

Sylva's daddy finally came down the stairs and said, "He had over a hundred stitches. He'll live." Sylva and Avery breathed the first sigh of relief.

Hunter retrieved a jar of clear liquid from atop the bookcase and drank deep. Then he went out, got in the truck, and left.

Wayne went to the porch to see if he could fix the door, then took the broken mess out to the barn.

"Here comes your daddy, Avery," Sylva whispered, as Mr. Baldwin pulled into the drive.

Mr. Baldwin came up to the porch and called for his daughter. Avery met him at the door.

"How's Mars?" he asked.

Avery told him what she knew.

"Come on with me, Budlet. We've missed lunch, but Neco-wee fixed something for us."

Avery hugged Sylva tight and said, "Take Mars something to eat, some soup, maybe."

A few days later, Wayne asked Sylva and Avery to help fix the Mary Jane plants he'd cut earlier, bundled, and left drying in the barn. He showed them how to do Mars's job. They clipped each dried leaf off the stems and crushed it with their fingers into plastic sandwich bags. They separated all the seeds out and put them in a jar. The work was tedious, made their fingers sore, but they didn't care. When Wayne paid them for their efforts, they gave the money to Mars.

When Mars was better, the Baldwins took everybody to the Cherokee Indian Reservation on the hottest day in all history. The heat irritated his wounds, but he wanted to go anyway. The shops sold plastic tomahawks with feathers tied on them, moccasins with little beads on the toes, toy bows and arrows. The place was run by the Cherokee Nation. Avery would have thought they'd want to present a more authentic picture to the tourists. The road burned right through her sandals, and all she wanted was to go home and drink a gallon of lemonade.

Heading back toward the car, they came upon a cage. Sylva saw it first, jumped back, gasped, and grabbed Avery. A live black bear pawed at the bars shaking its huge head.

Mars almost fainted dead away.

When they returned to Crowfoot Ridge, Mr. Baldwin dropped them off at the Marshall farm. Mars walked into the living room, stopped short, and the girls ran into his backside. He pointed to the wall, and there hung the bear hide stretched out on the living room wall with its shaggy fur, its beady eyes, and even its claws.

Mars went limp when he saw the wretched thing and looked away fast.

Did this mean he would have to live the rest of his life looking at the same bear that had almost killed him? Avery couldn't imagine a more horrible existence. Mars didn't say a word. They followed him upstairs.

"How could Papa do such a thing?" Sylva asked.

"It wasn't a good idea to put it on the wall," Avery said.

"It's okay. Just shows yet another way how Hunter is."

"None of us wants the horrible thing hanging on the wall," Sylva said.

"It's Hunter's house. It's Hunter's bear," Mars said with a helpless sort of expression. "All I want to do is get old enough to leave this place."

Avery hoped for his sake the time went fast. They were growing up at lightning speed in this house. She spent only one month a year with them and couldn't imagine what it was like twelve months running, year in and year out.

Time accelerated during the summer vacation. They were on a roller-coaster ride, speeding toward something, but Avery couldn't see what the something was.

Avery and Ken took sandwiches and a couple of beers down to the dock to watch the sun set on the horizon beyond their canal and wait for the Fourth of July fireworks display.

"We could have taken the boat over and been closer to the show."

"You want to?" Avery asked. "We still have time."

"Naw, it's too much trouble. We can see okay from here, don't you think?"

"Whatever."

"You've been acting strange, Avery. What's going on?"

"I think my clock is screwed up. Time seems to stand still one day, then the next day it rushes by. We never see each other anymore since you spend so many nights away. We really need to talk."

"We talk plenty. I don't have time to worry about things."

"I didn't say I was worried, Ken. I'm just, what should I say, reflective."

He slipped his arm around her and said, "Avery, you think too much about stuff." She wondered if they could still salvage something of their lives.

The first gigantic dandelion of colored lights flared in the dark sky. Rockets shot up and bloomed like minigalaxies.

"Daddy used to call those fizgig sparkles when I

was little. He called the spidery kind of lightning fizgig too." She leaned against him.

"He has a way with words, like calling you Budlet and Adam, Bud. Yep, he makes me laugh."

Avery thought her daddy had very few words.

Explosions set the night ablaze, parachutes of glitter cascaded, and then disintegrated.

5

Florida blistered under a relentless sun all through August. Avery hibernated most days in her air-conditioned lair, drinking iced tea or lemonade. Skeeter hadn't been around in two weeks. The garden suffered from his absence and from the heat. Ken employed many gardeners for many projects, so Avery thought Skeeter was working elsewhere. She parked the car in the driveway next to Ken's, went into the kitchen, and put the bag on the counter.

"Can you believe this heat?" she asked Ken, who was making himself a drink at the sink.

"What did you expect, snow in August?"

"I haven't seen Skeeter in ages. Do you know where he's been working?" Avery unpacked the bag, lined the little white buckets of Chinese food up in a row.

"Hello to you too," Ken said. He half filled a low-ball glass with scotch, dropped a fistful of ice in it. "Ol' Skeeter died."

A socked-in-the-stomach feeling assaulted Avery. "Died? No, you can't mean that. What do you mean? When? How? Why didn't you tell me?" She was immobilized.

"We were informed at the office. I guess I forgot to mention it." He put a drop of water in his scotch, jiggled the ice.

"You forgot? You mean he's dead? Skeeter? And you never told me? Skeeter was my best friend. We've been working on the garden together for years. You didn't think to tell me he died? I can't believe this, Ken." Tears welled in her eyes. She was more hurt by the immediate realization of Ken's insensitivity than the shock of the news, which she could not yet comprehend or assimilate.

"I'm sorry." He looked into his glass as if to see if a fly had landed on the scotch. "I forgot. I didn't think you'd care."

"Not care? Ken, Skeeter was my . . . I'll miss him more than you'll ever know. You don't know me at all. I can't believe you didn't tell me. When did he die? What happened?"

"I don't know, a week or so ago," he said. Then after a slight hesitation, "I'm sorry, I just wasn't thinking. I'm so busy with work and getting ready to start dredging at Palm City for the canals."

"How? What happened to him? He hasn't been sick. Oh God, poor Skeeter. What will I do without him?" Avery felt rage building, wanted to kick the wall. How could she live without Skeeter?

"I don't know what happened to him, Avery. I didn't actually take the call."

"I could have helped him. I didn't know he was sick or hurt or anything. I could have done something. Who told you? When was the funeral?"

"His brother called the office. The Seminoles, they take care of their own. He said Skeeter had died. He didn't say anything else. Skeeter was old anyway, maybe seventy. I'll send someone else to do the yard."

"Do the yard? You are unbelievable." She grabbed the front of his shirt and pulled him close. "Do you think I care about the damned yard? What were you thinking? You have no idea who he was, what he meant to me. Not an inkling," Avery shouted in his face. She slammed her fist into his chest, then shoved him hard, back, away from her. She began to pace, running the locket back and forth on its chain.

"Beat me up, why don't you?" He straightened his shirt, smoothed it flat with his hand. "And what would you have done about it?"

"Something. I could have helped him, gotten him to a doctor. He probably didn't even go to a doctor. He could have stayed here. At least, I would have gone to the funeral. He was full of wisdom and hope. He knew all the plants and the wilderness and the weather. He was my connection to reality, to the past, to everything we've lost."

"I guess I should have told you."

She grabbed his shirt again, wadded a handful on his chest. "You don't have a clue, Ken. Do you?" she screamed and shook him hard. "Not a fucking clue." His drink spilled. "Are you conscious at all?" She released him with a backward shove.

"What the devil?"

"Just leave me alone." Avery stormed out of the kitchen. She went into her room and closed the door. The garden needed water. She went outside and set the sprinkler with trembling hands and watched it rotate right to left.

An hour later, Ken tapped the door with a fingernail. "I'm going to eat. You want yours heated up?"

"I'm not hungry," she said through the door, still too shocked to cry.

"Come on Avery, eat with me. I'm sorry I forgot to tell you about Skeeter."

She opened the door and stared at him. "Shit," she said as she pushed by him. "I'll get dinner ready."

She went back to the kitchen, put the dishes on the counter, slammed the cabinet door. Ken poured a glass of wine for her, offered it with a timid unspoken question in his eyes, like setting a bone out for a wild dog.

"You won't stop until everything's gone, will you?"

"Stop what?" The ice cube moiled in his mouth.

"Stop killing the marshes, dunes, bays, everything. All of old Florida."

Avery couldn't believe Skeeter would not be poking around the yard, bringing marsh plants for the garden, tying his skiff to the dock. She didn't know how she would manage without him. She opened the containers she'd picked up on the way home, spooned the slimy stuff on plastic plates. She put a plate into the microwave, punched the time in.

"You're going ahead with the land out west of Palm City?" she asked.

"We've got six hundred houses planned."

"Skeeter lived out there. Can't you find a way to protect those marshes? I've always loved that area. It's the last bit of our wilderness."

"The Everglades are protected." He drained the glass and captured an ice cube. He tried to ignore her, but she held her eyes on him.

The oven beeped. She served the meal.

"People don't want to live in swamps," Ken said. "We mold the land and make it livable."

"We've destroyed everything. Look at Port St. Lucie and its reeking rows of tract houses. The suburbanites chase the crabgrass, fish the last of the snook, nothing will be left. One day it'll all be gone."

"It's better, not gone." He spooned rice over his cashew chicken. "Wouldn't be livable without us. Anyway, we have a problem with the land abstract, so we're not starting right away. The lawyers are messing with it."

"The Seminoles lived here and didn't harm the first palmetto." Avery toyed with the lo mein. "We used to love Florida, remember? What happened to us?"

"A bit of reality set in, I guess. A handful of Indians used to live here. Now we're preparing for the largest population growth in the nation. Anyway, hell, it pays the mortgage." He fished an egg roll out of the bag, ate it in three big bites.

A splinter of pain lodged in Avery's heart for her lost friend, and for Florida. She looked at Ken as if she'd never seen him before. How could she have accepted this? How in the world could she have accepted, participated in, and even worked for the company?

"I hate all of this," Avery said after a long silence.

"You should be counting your blessings, Avery."

"Yes, Mother says the same thing."

Ken Kessler, husband of too many years, businessman, community leader, Optimist, tanned golfer, windblown sailor, sat before her eating Chinese food, a complete stranger. His secretive eyes were familiar. His shaggy, sun-bleached hair was recognizable. His mouth turned down in a frown. His appearance seemed reckless somehow.

"What're you looking at?" His voice was familiar

too. "What do you have to bitch about? I provide the house, the pool, the boat, the cars."

Avery's chilled silence irritated him. Her eyes picked holes in him.

"What?" he asked without curiosity, head cocked.

"So, this is your house, your pool, your boat. Why am I not surprised?" Avery turned away because she couldn't see him. He had vanished in one small colorless realization of truth.

"And my business contacts, my golfing friends, my involvement with the Optimists. My contacts give us the social status we have. I've built half the houses on the coast, half the condos. You don't think this counts for something? What have you contributed? Your only friend is a wacky old Seminole Indian."

"Was."

"Was what?" Ken looked at her as if they weren't involved in the same conversation.

"My only friend was Skeeter."

Avery began to cry. Ken tried to hold her, but she bolted. She went down to the dock and stayed there almost all night.

The iguana was gone when Avery drove out to Skeeter's shack a couple days later. The terrapin was gone. The rabbits were gone. Worst of all, Skeeter was gone. Plants he'd been propagating for their garden stood in a row. The wilderness was already reclaiming his space. She kept expecting him to appear from around back or chug up to his little dock in his skiff.

She'd been crying for three days. Collecting the plants and putting them in the car brought tears again. She knew Skeeter would have wanted her to take them, but her heart was no longer in the garden. She didn't even know if she could plant them. The garden had been theirs, not hers.

By some wild chance, their little native garden had become famous. Avery had shown a neighbor one time, God, when? A long time ago. The woman worked for the local newspaper and came around several days later asking if she could photograph the garden and do an article. Avery was astonished something so simple, so natural, could attract attention, but it had. Not long after the article appeared, garden clubs started calling and asking if they could see it. And then a television station called wanting to feature it on a gardening show. Avery always invited Skeeter to be present when these interviews happened. He knew the names of all the plants, and she didn't trust herself to remember them. He'd dress up and stand tall and be so proud. She couldn't believe she'd never see Skeeter again.

How had she let him go without telling him how much his friendship meant to her? How had she let him go without telling him all her secrets? Skeeter had been the one person she trusted. She allowed the opportunities to fly away when she could have told him everything. He might have understood. Someday she would have to face her own truth, as Skeeter had said so many times.

Ken spent his evenings at zoning meetings in Martin, St. Lucie, or Palm Beach counties. He met with subcontractors, architects, dock designers, landscapers. Avery's days were spent floating on a raft in the pool, sitting on the dock, or moving the sprinkler around in the garden. She didn't go to the office much anymore.

She drove out to see Kessler Property's new site. Months of burning, clearing, and excavating, using cats, dozers, backhoes, and dredging machinery had leveled the marsh, reshaped the wetlands, cut in canals and roadbeds, churned through the habitats of every living thing. Avery watched with tears in her heart.

She had to stop at least her part of the destruction. She decided to sell no houses, no lots, nor answer a single question, ever again.

"I'm going to quit, Ken," Avery said as she stood at the kitchen counter opening the mail.

"Quit what?"

"Everything. Selling houses. Work, supporting this program of ours."

"Why?" he asked. "You're good, you know. Why would you want to quit? You've had your cushy job all these years. Where do you think you'd get another job? Who would hire you?"

"I've had a job, now I want a life."

She stared into the eyes of a stranger.

"So? What are you going to do instead?"

"Do?" She cocked her head.

"With your life, what are you going to do with your life?" Ken waited for an answer. Avery ignored him, letting minutes pass.

"You're a thousand miles away," he said.

Skeeter had accused her of the same thing more than once. He'd be talking away about the weather or the garden or whatever, and she'd be gone.

"A thousand miles?" Avery turned to face Ken. "I'm right here, dear, drowning."

He switched on the television while Avery flipped through the bills. She came upon a wedding invitation and opened the envelope.

"Lissa and Jack's daughter is getting married," she told him. She sat down holding the invitation, ran her fingertips across the raised lettering.

Ken watched the news. Another plane crash. A Delta plane had crashed at Dallas–Fort Worth earlier in the month. Now, 517 were dead in another crash in Japan.

"I didn't know five hundred people could fit on one plane."

"Five hundred and seventeen. When is Holly's wedding?"

"Next Saturday, in St. Augustine. You'd better make reservations at a hotel. Their house will be full of relatives, I imagine."

"Sorta quick, don't you think?" he asked.

"Lissa had her reasons."

An uneventful week passed while Avery cleared her office out. On Friday morning, Ken and Avery packed the car for the drive to St. Augustine.

"You made reservations?" Avery asked, as Ken put his golf clubs in the trunk. "You're not going to have time to play golf, Ken."

"We're staying three days," he said, "I like the course at Saw Grass."

He followed her back into the house. The television reported yet another August plane crash. Avery went into the bedroom.

"Tragedy always comes in threes," Ken said when she passed in front of the television again. "This time a British charter plane went down. Burst into flames on takeoff from Manchester."

"You reserved two rooms?"

"Jesus, Avery, we've been married forever, for Christ's sake. Two rooms? They're a hundred bucks a night."

"You mistake me for someone who cares how much the damned rooms are. Were they full?" Avery stopped and glared at him.

"How the hell should I know. I called, I asked for a

room. I got one." He shook his head. "I didn't ask for two rooms."

"Hadn't you noticed we no longer share a room?"

"I noticed." He rubbed his forehead. "I noticed all right."

"What made you think I'd share a room with you in St. Augustine?"

"I don't know, I must have lost my mind."

Avery went to the phone, called the hotel, and reserved another room.

"Avery, I'm up to here with you," Ken said, leveling his hand above his eyes. "What are we supposed to do? Drive up and pretend everything is fine?"

"This is Holly's wedding. Lissa is my friend. I am going. Don't go if you don't want to."

"Jack is my best friend."

"Well, Ken, why don't we go and just make the best of things."

"I wish I could go with someone I liked," Ken said under his breath.

"I heard that. You want to take your girlfriend? I assume you like her."

He stopped and stared at her.

"Do you think I'm stupid?"

"Avery, we need to talk," Ken said. "We need some resolution here. We can't go on like this."

"In my opinion, we need some dissolution."

They drove to St. Augustine in three and a half

awkward hours of silence. Avery let herself miss Skeeter, watching the roadside monotony.

She sat beside her husband at Holly's wedding, presenting a united and peaceful front. She kept thinking about Neco-wee's daughter. The girl's name was Echo-la, another exotic Cherokee name, but everyone called her Echo. Her wedding was the first Avery had ever seen. Echo was also Sylva's sister Charlotte's best friend. And Echo married Sylva's brother Wayne. Neco-wee did not hide her disapproval. The wedding was extraordinary and Avery had never forgotten it. While Lissa and Jack escorted Holly down the aisle, Avery was watching Echo-la in her mind. And to this day, Echo was the most beautiful bride Avery had ever seen.

Echo had worn her hair loose, not braided, and had woven tiny white flowers into a crown with ribbons hanging down into her long black hair. Her creamy leather dress moved with her steps just like satin. Tiny beads were sewn on the bodice in meticulous patterns. Her violet eyes shown bright in her dark complexion. Her steps were silent in soft leather boots. A Cherokee princess.

Neco-wee had worn a hat and a fancy dress to the wedding. Avery had never seen her dressed up before. Neco-wee told Avery she saw a black cloud over Wayne and thought the union was a bad one. Avery thought so as well and had to think everyone knew. Maybe Echo knew too. She wondered why they went ahead anyway.

Wayne wore a witless smile, a cheap suit, and dirty shoes. His hair, whacked and misshapen, was colorless just like his personality. For one instant, Avery saw the black cloud Neco-wee saw and knew Wayne was doomed. How could he dare take such a girl to be his bride? He squared his shoulders.

Neco-wee fanned herself with a cardboard fan. No fledgling of hope.

Echo-la should have married a Cherokee man, tall and straight, and proud. She should have married a man with the same tanned skin and had babies with pure Cherokee blood. A man with acres of black hair who could dance with fire and ride through blizzards. A man who could stand on top of a waterfall. A man with a name like Standing Feather.

Avery's dreaming the images of what should have been did not change what was, but at least, she lived through the wedding from a long mental distance, filled with confusion, filled with a clarity she'd never been capable of before.

Sylva and Mars used to make dream catchers out of feathers and jute. A dream catcher was kept by the bed so good dreams could float through it into the universe, and bad dreams would catch in the feathers. Watching Holly's married life begin, knowing her own would soon end, brought Avery intense sadness. She wondered if Echo and Wayne were still together twenty years after their wedding day. She doubted it very much.

Ken and Avery drove halfway back to Stuart in silence.

Skeeter's death in early August had jolted Avery into even more of an acute awareness of how bad things had gotten. She'd thrown her life away. She didn't know what she might have done differently, but she knew this wasn't right.

Finally, Avery folded the newspaper she'd been reading, looked at Ken and asked, "Do you want a divorce?"

"No." His eyes were on the road.

"Why not?"

"Because."

"You can't tell me you're happy in this marriage."

"Avery, I'm comfortable," Ken said. "I don't want to go through it. I won't see Gina any more if it bothers you."

"If it bothers me? Your affair neither bothers nor surprises me. It's stupid to stay together, Ken."

"It's not. We'll get past this. You'll see."

Avery felt dead. She wondered how much his dullness affected her. Or was her apathy affecting him? Ken was a good man, had been a good husband. She hadn't been a wife to him for a long time. She was the one who pulled away, who never said the whole of anything, who gave so little. Who would blame him?

She didn't say anything.

"So just because I had an affair, you want a divorce? It's not like our sex life has been perfect. It was never much. Now it's nonexistent. I don't know a single man who hasn't had affairs."

"Single men are free to do whatever they please."

"That's not what I meant. Shit, Avery. Most of my married friends have strayed, one time or another. And their wives, too."

"So, because they do it, it's okay for you to do it?" Avery realized she wasn't saying what she meant to say, again. "This doesn't matter, the problem started with us. It may have ended in your seeking companionship elsewhere, but it started right here."

"You've never loved me. That's where the whole mess started." Ken glanced at her and returned his attention to the highway. "You've never gotten over that guy from your childhood. I don't know what happened to you back then, and Avery, I don't want to know, but that's where it started, and that's where it'll finish."

He didn't know how close he'd come to the truth.

"I have loved you," Avery said. "We started out wanting the same things out of life. We had visions and goals and mutual interests. I don't know what went wrong."

"I just told you what went wrong—you never got over your old flame."

"I haven't thought about him in years," Avery lied. "Things didn't work out. We were too young, too geographically undesirable, as they say. I have no idea where he is, what he's doing. There was never one word from him. It's been years since I saw him." Exactly twenty-one years this summer, Avery knew.

"Doesn't mean you forgot."

"Whatever memory I may have has nothing to do with our marriage in any case."

"You live in absolute denial, Avery. You don't think I know you at all, but I know you only too well. Don't you think I can tell the difference between a woman who puts up with me and a woman who is desperate for me? There may have been a time when I didn't know the difference, but by God, I know now."

"Gina is desperate for you?"

"She's in love with me and you're not."

"Then why don't you want a divorce?"

"Because, God help me, I still love you. I keep thinking we'll work things out. I've always felt so responsible for you, Avery. I always thought you'd fall in love with me someday."

"Don't lay that on me. Let's just try to honor the commitments we have, and get through the next couple weeks. The wedding is over, but Lissa and Jack are coming down for the Fish Fry."

"And we have the opening ceremony thing at the art center," Ken said. "You promised you'd go. Did you send in the donation?"

"I sent the donation, and I'll go to the thing at the art center with you." Avery nodded.

Theirs was not a dream destined to float off through the hole of a Cherokee dream catcher. Too many dreams got caught in the feathers.

6

People swarmed around the serving line at the Labor Day Fish Fry held on Hutchinson Island. Ken and Jack worked the crowd like politicians, glad-handing the businessmen, kissing their wives.

Clouds out over the ocean were sucking the light away, confusing the sky. Alternating stripes bled from rose to tangerine across the horizon. Lissa and Avery stayed to themselves at a picnic bench under a shelter. Last year they'd both had their hair cut short, this year they were letting it grow out, comparing notes on what to do with the awkward length.

"I like your hair this length, Avery, but the color needs something, maybe a little frosting would brighten it, add highlights, show off those funny-colored eyes of yours," Lissa said, smiling at her old friend.

"Funny?" Avery questioned. "They're green."

"Sometimes they're green," Lissa said. "Sometimes they're funny."

"Holly's wedding was beautiful, Lissa. You put it together fast, didn't you?"

"I knew she was involved, I just didn't know to what degree. She was three months' pregnant on her wedding day. Things escalated rather quickly once she admitted everything. I hope they'll be okay."

"They seem to be in love."

"Aren't we all on our wedding days?" Lissa knocked sand out of her sandal. "What's new with you and Ken?"

"We're starting to talk some. It's hard because neither of us hates the other. I almost wish for a fight of some kind to push us over the edge. He told me he knew I'd never loved him and Gina did love him."

"Oh, so it's in the open now."

Avery waved to one of her neighbors. "I knew it was Gina, I've known for a long time. It's hard to blame him. He thinks I never got over Mars, but God, Lissa, that was a lifetime ago. He thinks I'm in denial about it. I had two summers with Mars, one good and one bad. I'd known him since we were children, but our romance, if you could call it a romance, was no more than two months with a year of separation in between. I admit it had a lasting impact. Ken and I have eighteen years together."

"The separation may have caused your relationship with Mars to escalate out of proportion, especially in the eyes of naive teenagers and considering the intensity of first love."

"Puppy love. Nothing more. Lissa, believe me."

"Still, the question is, how was it resolved? When things are cut off, snatched away somehow, for whatever reason, and there's no resolution, then you get messed up."

"It was resolved. Believe me, no resolution to anything was ever more final."

"I don't think so. This isn't the first conversation we've had about him over the years." Lissa knew some of it, certainly not all of it. Certainly not the recondite truths.

"I admit I think about him. I think about those summers at Crowfoot Ridge, probably too much. Doesn't everybody think about their childhood years?"

"Most of us have passing thoughts," Lissa said.

"Guess I'm crazy. Movies play in my mind all the time, night and day."

"Something has remained unresolved, Avery."

"No doubt."

The country band took the stage, speakers cranked up loud enough to be heard in the Bahamas. Avery and Lissa couldn't hear themselves think, let alone continue the conversation. Ken and Jack joined them. The square dances were starting.

"He played the guitar, even had a small country band."

"Who did, Avery?" Lissa asked.

"Mars."

After the Fish Fry, Ken and Avery saw little of each other. Ken changed, seemed to lose hope. Avery thought his affair had escalated, maybe some outside pressure was being applied. One night they settled on the dock to talk. Sheet lightning flashed way off in the black sky. First cool night they'd had in six months of endless summer.

"Okay, you win," Ken began. "Let's put an end to this."

"It's best, I think."

Ken leaned forward, elbows on knees, eyes searching the canal. The *Bald Wind* rocked in the black water. "What is it you hate so much about me?"

"I don't hate you, Ken, I hate what we've become. I hate myself for going along with it all these years. I loved Florida and the beauty in these wetlands and waterways. All my life I've seen such wonder here. Sometimes it's a beauty you have to look hard to see. You shared these feelings, once. I didn't realize the projects would grow so big, take over so much of our lives."

"I don't think my work on Kessler projects is the issue here. The problem starts with your inability to give yourself to me, to our marriage, to our lives. I trusted you, wanted to know you, to know everything about you. I get so close, then the barricades go up. Whatever happened, Avery, whatever it was, must have been devastating."

"You've known something happened?"

"What do you think? Do you believe I'm so dense that I thought the whole story was some teenage hillbilly gave you the slip? The same scenario happened to everybody. Most of us forgot about it. If you haven't opened up in all these years, my guess is you never will."

"So now this is all my fault? Nothing to do with your affair?"

"Exactly. The affair happened because the marriage failed. So you can dance around your poor lost Florida while you live in one of the nicest subdivisions in the state, and you can blame Skeeter's death, or me for not telling you fast enough, or the weather, or anything under the sun. But you need to look inside to find your answers."

"What do we really have together, Ken? We're not even friends."

"You need to see a psychiatrist," he said, dead level. "The fact is, you're thirty-six years old, and you've never grown up."

"I'm thirty-seven, I'll be thirty-eight in December. See, you don't even know how old I am." And suddenly tears were streaming down her face.

"I only missed by one year." He wrapped his arms around her, held her, let her cry.

"It doesn't matter anyway. We *are* friends, Ken. That's why this is going to be so hard."

"But you have to leave, don't you?"

"Losing a friend is a great tragedy," she said, and she knew that better than anyone.

Avery's parents had lived in the same house for thirty-five years. Every time Avery walked up to the front door to visit them, her shoulders knotted. Every time she sat in the living room where Adam's trophy case had been, she remembered feeling unworthy, second-rate. Her old room, transformed now into a decorator den, reminded her of rejection, humiliation, and disapproval. This house of pinch-pleated draperies with matching throw pillows, color-coordinated plaids and prints, silk florals, and mall art, was the house of her nightmares.

"Leave Ken?" Avery's mother's eyes were wide. "Why, Avery?"

"I don't know why. It's over, what can I say?"

"What will you do without him?"

"I'll live, I guess. Start to live."

"Your marriage hasn't been bad. Ken has been a wonderful husband."

"I know, Mother, it hasn't been so bad. It's been sad, though. I need to be free to live my own life," Avery told her. "We've grown apart. Things happen.

We used to have the same goals, mutual interests, but not anymore. I hate living in this air-conditioned illusion. Ken is a fine man, it's not his fault."

"Avery, where is this coming from?"

"From the past, from lies, from manipulation, from lost love, and lost hope, and ruined lives."

"What melodramatic nonsense! Avery, you must think about what you're going to do. Where are you going to go?" Her mother did not want to hear about the past. Sweep it out the door like sand blown in from a storm.

"I don't want to do anything. I've already done enough damage, don't you think?" Avery said. "I want to go somewhere cool. I want to open the windows. I want fresh air. I never want to see another bulldozer scrape the life out of this land. I want to go far away where I have no address."

"Oh, Avery, speaking of addresses, a letter came for you yesterday. Can't imagine how anyone could still have this address for you." She went to her desk and retrieved the letter. She handed it to her daughter.

The return address sticker on the envelope was from D. R. Thornsberry with a Brevard, North Carolina, address. Didn't take a minute to figure out it was from Sylva.

"Thanks, Mother." Avery tucked the letter in her pocket. "I think it's from Sylva Marshall."

"My, my, you haven't heard from her in years, have you?"

"It's been a long time."

Avery kissed her mother's cheek, an obligatory gesture.

Her father, returning from a golf game, pulled in just as she was leaving. She couldn't ever look at him, not in his eyes. She couldn't talk to him apart from pleasantries. She waved as he unfolded from his car.

"You leaving already, Budlet?"

"Hi, Daddy, sorry I can't stay, but I'll see you soon." Avery's eyes bypassed his, aware only that a looming mist separated them in the brilliant Florida midday sun. "How was the game?"

"Fine. Fine. I shot a seventy-seven." He bent to a breezy kiss of her cheek as he passed.

Sylva's unread letter felt alive in her pocket, obvious and competing for Avery's attention. She opened her car door, watched him walk up the walk, aging and graying, stooped a little, but still tall, still tanned, still slender. Good genes, she thought.

"Daddy, I'll see you soon," she called even as she knew she couldn't see him and he couldn't see her. A blindness existed for them, cutting Avery and leaving open wounds. The distance began when reality overwhelmed father and daughter and moved them both out of the realm of communication. She wondered if he'd died when he learned he couldn't protect her or when she was damaged beyond his love. The void had been so sudden, so complete, they had found comfort there and stayed forever.

She drove to the ocean, parked, and opened the handwritten letter.

Dear Avery:

Where do the years go? I've been thinking about you, just all of a sudden like. Wondering where life has taken you. Wondering who you are now. Wondering what you're doing. How many kids you have. Where you're living. Who you married. What your life is like.

Me? Same ol', same ol'. I married Donald, guess you figured. I worked as a secretary a few years, until the babies came. We have three kids, two boys and a girl. Mostly grown up now. We sit on the porch at night, rocking, watching the fireflies, wondering if there might have been something more.

Why haven't we kept in touch?

Mars got married about ten years ago. They have a boy. Mars is a carpenter and still plays his music in coffeehouses around Asheville. He restored an old depot, has a cabinet shop there now. Built himself a darling house. We don't see them too much anymore.

Whatever happened to Adam? He was my first love, not a good first love to remember.

I hope this letter reaches you, somehow. It's been a long time. If so, please, please write back. I never forgot you.

Love,
Sylva

Tears welled in Avery's eyes, burned her face as they fell. She wept as seagulls circled the beach. Her tears seemed close to the surface these days. She reread the letter a dozen times through blurry vision.

So, Sylva married Donald. Good. Sylva with three children. Not a word about Charlotte, Wayne, or Echo. Mars married? A shard of pain crawled slowly into her heart. What on earth had she expected? In Avery's mind, Sylva was still sixteen and Mars a stringy eighteen-year-old. Was Sylva's hair still thick and long and strawberry blond? Did Mars wear jeans and boots and keep his hair long in the style of the sixties? Their lives were unchanged in her mind, but Mars would be forty. Why, indeed, hadn't they kept in touch? The years went slip-sliding over the smooth stones of time.

Ken was right—she had been living in absolute denial.

Late that night, Avery sat down in the garden room to write to Sylva. She held her pen positioned over the paper for an hour and found she had nothing to say. Had she stopped feeling? Anything? Sylva's letter arriving just then was providence, but Avery couldn't write a single word.

One more Kessler Properties obligation was left to fulfill. Avery hated these business functions. As perhaps the one last favor for Ken, she agreed to attend the opening of the new art center. Cultural Center, they called it. Ken and Avery were supposed to meet before the dedication ceremony and sit together. Avery wandered through the exhibit of American Indian arts and crafts. She nodded to acquaintances.

Ken was late.

She leaned close to examine a collection of dolls in the Cherokee section. The native costumes were exquisite, executed with extraordinary detail. The tallest was no more than twelve inches in height. Minute and intricate beading on a tiny suede shirt amazed her. The skin of each doll seemed to be of polished leather, stained with such perfection they appeared natural, alive. They were beautiful, yet she stared at them as one gawks at an accident. Her breath caught in her throat. The warmth in her hands drained away. A primal fear swelled in Avery's chest, and as she studied the dolls, she began to tremble.

"Avery, come on. It's six-thirty, Myrtle Talkathon is about to begin." Ken's voice intruded from behind her. "What's the matter? I called you three times."

Avery turned to face him, and said, "I didn't hear you."

"You look like you saw a damned ghost."

"It's nothing," she said.

"Now try not to be so distant."

They walked toward the lobby, "Don't tell me how to be," she said. Her shoulders bunched up from chill or disgust. Anger. One obligation too many.

"Just act normal, Avery."

"What do you want me to do? Talk more?" Her voice resounded with curdled fury, pent-up and explosive.

"Yes, talk more." Ken didn't notice the change in her voice. "Be sociable. Participate."

They found seats in the chamber of drywall. The director, a woman who made a career out of promoting the arts, had already begun and was saying, "And so on this the twentieth of September, nineteen eighty-five, and with great pride, we are here to dedicate our splendid new cultural center. We want to thank Kessler Properties for donating the land for this project and also for their expert and timely construction. Ken Kessler . . ." The crowd applauded.

"Excuse me," Avery said loud enough for everyone to hear, "Mrs. Tarkenson, I don't see any of the masons here, no carpenters, no painters, plumbers, electricians. Weren't they invited? This is their achievement, don't you think? And what about the exhibit? None of the American Indian artists seem to be here. For that matter I see no Indians, no ethnic groups, not a person of color. This is a celebration for the cultural center, is it not? Are we here to applaud bad architecture surrounded by a landscape without a single native Florida plant?"

"Mrs. Kessler, if you'll forgive me," the director said. "We do have an agenda."

"Oh, sorry." Avery smiled at Ken. He looked as if he'd be happier at the bottom of a sinkhole full of alligators.

The speech continued another few minutes, "And now I'll read the names of our patrons, each of whom has made generous donations. Mr. and Mrs. Adam Baldwin, Senior . . ."

During the applause for Avery's parents, Ken said, "What do you think you're doing?"

"Just talking more, dear."

"Well, shut up, then."

More names were read in alphabetical order, then, "Ken and Avery Kessler, patrons and friends of the center . . ." Applause erupted again.

"Ah, Mrs. Tarkenson, excuse me please. I'm afraid a mistake has been made. The donation was made in the name of Osceola Oscipee, not ours."

"We can straighten it out later, Mrs. Kessler, thank you." The director, visibly unglued, went on with the list of patrons, all of whom had made tax-deductible donations.

Avery turned to Ken and asked, "Happy, dear?"

His expression dissolved in despair. "You made the donation in Skeeter's name?"

She held a finger in front of her lips to quiet him. He glared at her with chilled eyes.

When the speech ended, Avery slipped away while Ken was distracted with his business associates. She went to the bar and got a glass of wine.

"What was that all about?" Avery's mother asked. "You were rude and you embarrassed Ken."

"I should know better, right?"

"People will think you were raised by lizards."

"You and Ken make a couple, Mother. All you care about is what people think."

Across the room Gina had Ken cornered, and their conversation appeared intense. They both held wineglasses. He glanced around with nervous eyes. Avery wedged her way through the crowd and stood next to them. Gina's black hair was tinged with blue under the fluorescent lights.

"Avery, this is Gina," Ken said, his voice tense.

"I know who Gina is, dear. Hello, Gina." Avery smiled.

Someone jostled Ken from behind. His wine splashed onto Gina's blouse.

"What the hell?" He turned to the apologetic man, who was already dabbing at her.

"So sorry. Oh dear me," the man said.

Gina's stunned look made the effort of attending the event worthwhile for Avery.

"I'm going now, Ken. I enjoyed being sociable."

He glared at her and said through clenched teeth, "I have a meeting in Palm Beach tonight."

Avery finished the last of the wine in her glass. Then out of nowhere said, "Cowgirls shoot Indians."

Ken looked dumbfounded.

She waved to her parents from across the room as she left with an evasive, if not contemptuous, smile and went out to her car.

Free, at last.

7

The letters were in a shoe box along with some ribbons Avery had won in high school for swimming and a napkin from a long-forgotten party. The rubber band around the letters disintegrated when she touched it. She sat on the floor and read what Mars and Sylva had written more than twenty years ago. She hadn't even known she'd kept them. The first one she opened was from Mars. A sprig of crowfoot, now brown, dried, and fragile, fell out. The writing was block printing:

Dear Avery,

Here's a piece of crowfoot for you to keep. It will bring you good luck.

Love, Mars

Crowfoot, crowfoot, evergreen
Shall good luck forever bring
Find it on the forest floor
Keep it with you ever more

Avery folded it and slipped it back into the envelope with the plant. The next one was from Sylva, written in pencil, in a faded, immature printing.

Dear Avery,

I take care of Shelby all the time now. I miss so much school I afrad they won't let me go back—not in my own grade anyway. Franklin got hisself killed in the war. They shipped his body home. We buried him up to the church.

How are you I am fine. Do you still swim in the meat. Are you coming next summer. I want to see you. My sister, Charlotte, tried to kill herself. She cut her arms and bleed all over the place. Wayne carried her off to get sewed up. Now she's living in a trailer in Brevard with a guy named Wiley. Mr. Mac got put in jail for pulling some little girls pants off. Made her daddy real mad. They call him a prevert.

Avery remembered reading this before and thinking it hadn't been just her. She should have realized. She should have told. She could have stopped him years ago. How many girls? Avery wondered. Guilt rode up into the empty place her heart left—she shouldn't have kept the secret. She had protected him, a child molester, thinking she was protecting her father's friendship with the old man, the old pervert.

Poor Sylva had had such a tragic childhood. Everything hurt her. Avery could not remember which summer was which anymore. As a child, Avery had never known what to believe. The Marshall house was small, crowded with many people, a breeding ground.

The big house Avery had grown up in with few people had bred isolation.

Avery sat on the floor with the letter in her lap. She pictured the coffin Mars had built to bury Charlotte's dead baby in. He knew how to do so many things. He'd let her help him sand it. Avery couldn't believe they were going to bury the baby in their yard, but they did. Right next to where they had buried the deer Hunter had killed so long ago and where the marijuana plants grew.

Avery looked for a date on the envelope, but it was too faded. She remembered when baby Janie died. Wayne had carried the coffin down to the edge of the meadow. The Marshalls followed. Echo, with her hair hanging loose to her waist, walked with Wayne. Kitty shuffled between Hunter and the preacher, carrying a fistful of daisies. Avery followed holding Sylva's hand. Mars carried Shelby. Like windup toys, the family paraded down the meadow.

Charlotte's face had been lined with broken dreams. Mars stood by Avery. His eyes were pools of sanity in the midst of ignorance and delusion. When she was really young, she used to envy the Marshall family. She envied the farm, the animals, the lives they led in the magical mountains; autumn leaves in the fall, snow in the winter, blossoms in the spring. They had each other. Or did they? Mars was utterly alone. Sylva too. Echo had married into the family with Cherokee blood coursing through her. Could she hear the old spirits, stanzas of solitude from her heritage? Did she have an allegiance of grief, shared in stoic denial?

Sylva's mother hadn't been well, Avery remembered. Her face was fragile, lined by age, by her own harmful choice, by tedium, by failure. Her breath came in shallow wheezing. Hunter and Wayne stood like wooden men, repressing any emotion they might have felt, too indifferent to feel shame. Sylva had been trapped in her own history, the awful luck of selection.

When the funeral was over, Wayne dropped a shovelful of dirt into the hole. The sound of dirt splattering over the coffin was the sound of loss.

Then later the family lined up on the porch as if they were watching a horseshoe pitch and just stared at the meadow. Avery saw Charlotte kneeling by the new grave down at the bottom of the lawn. She rocked forward and back, then stretched out flat on the earth. Her brunette hair crazed, glossy in the final amber glow of the day. She hurled dirt, daisies, dandelions over herself, began to claw with her hands. Jagged moans waffled up the tarnished light, followed by delirious shrieks. She sat up and began to dig up her baby's grave. Then she jumped up and screamed into the forest. She fled up the slope into the thick twilight, thrashing through the laurel. Wayne leapt off the porch and ran after her. His white shirt flashed in the darkened woods like a lantern swaying from a ship's rigging tossed by the dipping sea.

Another summer Sylva and Mars were sharing the upstairs with their grandfather. He had an old still up on the mountain. Sylva showed it to Avery once. He died sometime during the year and left Mars a large assortment of woodcarvings and his old banjo, maybe the guitar too. No, the guitar had been Franklin's. Echo and Wayne had had a new baby they named Bobby. They had put a trailer on the farm and moved into it, but Avery couldn't remember when.

Her memories were a bit confused.

A news bulletin on the television attracted her attention. An earthquake had hit Mexico City the night before. The devastating pictures flashed across the screen. A portion of the city was gone, hundreds of people killed. Buildings were reduced to rubble. Their lives, sane and secure yesterday, today were blowing in the wind. The very ground they trusted had twisted into danger.

"Avery?" Ken asked from the door. "Did the truck come yet?"

"No, sorry. I didn't hear you come in." She folded Sylva's letter and put it back in the box with the others. She wiped tears away, tears she hadn't remembered shedding.

"What's the matter?"

"It's just everything." She gestured to the boxes, their house torn apart. She switched the television off. "The truck came for the furniture you wanted in the condo. That truck came." She felt tears heating behind her eyelids. Dabbed her eyes with a tissue.

Ken put his arms around her and held her. She relaxed in his embrace and clung to him.

"Oh God, Avery, I'm going to miss you. I tried to make our marriage work, I did. I know how much you've suffered. My poor darling, you've always been so lost."

"I'm sorry about the thing at the art center, Ken. Honestly, I don't know what got into me. I'm so ashamed of myself."

"Don't be."

Avery wept then, the last thing she needed was sympathy. She looked into Ken's face and tears were in his eyes.

"Ken, I'm so sorry, so very sorry. I never should have married you." She stopped to blow her nose. "I need another tissue." She turned away and got one from the box on the counter.

"Look at this. Are you putting all this in storage?" he asked. Ken wiped his face on his sleeve.

"I guess." She blew her nose again. "Some of it goes to the Salvation Army. God, that's what I need, an army to come to my salvation. By the way, I called Mrs. Tarkenson about putting the donation in Skeeter's name. Okay?"

"I don't care." He smiled then, and chuckled. "It's like we're dividing up twenty years. You take seventy-eight, I'll take eighty-two."

"You take Tuesday, I'll take Thursday," Avery said in a whisper.

"This is awful, Avery. I don't know how to say good-bye to you. You've been my life for so long. Where are you going? What are you going to do? Will you write? Call? Keep in touch?"

Avery crumbled. Her legs didn't want to hold her. She sat among the boxes on the floor and Ken joined her.

"Should we keep in touch?" he asked. He took her hand in his and held it.

"I need a little time. I'm going to North Carolina, Ken. Skeeter always said I had to go find my own truth. I know now I won't find any peace in this world until I tell the truth. It wouldn't help to tell you, wouldn't have helped to tell Skeeter, either. Mars and Sylva need to hear it, if I can muster the courage to tell it. I'm going to see them."

"What happened to you, my darling? Please tell me."

Avery shook her head.

"It isn't what happened to me as much as what happened to all of us. Mars and Sylva and I were so close during those summers. The three of us were like one spirit dancing around on six legs. There are no words to explain how it was. My folks were oblivious to us growing up, Adam and me. And Adam betrayed me time and again, or at least I conceived his behavior as betrayal. I had no connection with them, but I connected with Mars and Sylva. I admit none of these relationships were realistic, but they were real to me." Tears welled again. "Ken, I loved them right through to my bones, and then I was snatched away. I didn't know where they were, no addresses, no more letters, no news, no word. They vanished. It's possible the separation hurt them too. Whatever it is, we have to face it."

Ken had been holding her hand, running his thumb across the knuckles.

"Why didn't you go back years ago?" he asked.

She shook her head, took her hand away, and wiped tears from her face.

"I must go now." Avery looked into his eyes. "I'm so sorry I've hurt you."

A horn honked out front.

"It's the Salvation Army," Avery said as she got up and unplugged the television set. "I'm giving this one to them, okay? You took the big one, didn't you? I'm glad you're here so I don't give away anything you want to keep."

The workers came in. Together, Ken and Avery directed the final destruction of their home. Books, a few paintings, her records, and some kitchen things were wrapped, packed, and waiting for the storage truck. Clothes hung in cardboard wardrobes. Ken waited with her until the storage truck came and loaded everything else.

Avery began packing the six-month-old BMW. Ken had insisted she keep it. She watched him walk down to the dock and look at the empty space where the *Bald Wind* had been for so many years. He'd sold it and bought a bigger boat, moored it at the marina.

He came back up to the house.

Avery stood in the empty room.

"I have a cleaning crew coming tomorrow," Ken said. "New carpet will be installed."

"How much are you asking for it?"

"Two hundred. We only paid forty-two thousand, remember? Nice profit. We'll split it, okay?"

"Are you going to be all right? Is the condo okay?"

"No, Avery, I'm not going to be all right. I'm going to miss you with all my heart. Hell, I love you and I don't have any idea how to make it go away."

"I love you, too, Ken. You've been good to me. You deserved so much better."

"You take care of yourself, Avery." He embraced her, wrapped his arms around her, held her for a long time. "Well, my dearest, I guess this is it. The lawyers will handle the rest. There's nothing more we can do."

He led her out the door with his arm around her. She turned into him for one last hug, and he kissed her forehead and then her eyes. Avery held his face in her hands and said, "Please be all right. I will be in touch."

Ken watched her climb into the car.

Avery backed out of the driveway with eyes so filled with tears she couldn't see the curb, just knew where it was. She maneuvered through the neighborhood, passed the house she'd used as an office for so many years, saw a gardener in someone's yard, leaning into a hedge pulling weeds.

She headed north on I-95.

PART
TWO

8

Sylva might as well have been a fuzzy ripe peach for all the drooling she inspired during the summer vacation of sixty-two. Because Adam, all of a sudden, became enraptured with her. He had always ignored Sylva, Mars, and Avery during the family vacations. He'd gone trout fishing with his father, and when he started playing golf, they spent their days at various nearby courses. But during this summer, Adam lost interest in fishing and in golfing. He even forgot all about his girlfriends back home.

"You're a nuisance," Avery told Adam more than once. "Can't you leave us alone? Don't you have something better to do than follow us around?"

"I don't mind having Adam around." Sylva looked at him with goo-goo eyes.

Oh, brother, Avery could see exactly where this was going, and she resented it. She thought Sylva might turn out to be like the girls back home who pretended to be her friend but only used her to meet Adam. It wasn't just Adam. Mars seemed to have a different sort of interest in Avery. She figured something weird was going on. She'd always been crazy about Mars, so she was glad he was hanging around with them.

Mr. Mac's son was still running the farm. They'd gotten two more horses, Calico and Skunky. Avery figured Mr. Mac was still in jail, but nobody talked about it.

The four of them rode almost every day. Avery still rode Moonshine. By then, Mars was sixteen and Adam was seventeen. The horses gave them freedom they'd never had before, and the guys were more adventurous than Avery and Sylva would have been alone. Together, they rode up to the ridge, beyond it to the other side, and down into a mossy forest valley. They tied the horses to the gnarly laurel branches and climbed down the cliff to play in a waterfall. The waterfall plunged down the boulders, surrounded by steep banks filled with rhododendron in full summer bloom. They named the place AMAS Falls.

The pool at the bottom flowed into a rocky stream, racing over pure gold nuggets. The boulders provided places for them to sit in the sun thawing after icy wading. Neco-wee made picnic lunches of hard-boiled eggs and sandwiches, and they cupped stream water in their hands to drink.

Adam dared them to strip naked and jump in the deep pool. He and Mars went behind an outcropping of rock, took their clothes off, and jumped in. Sylva and Avery watched with envy, too shy to follow.

After a long time, Sylva said, "I'm gonna do it."

"Sylva, you can't."

"Why not?" She pulled her shirt off over her head, let her long hair fall loose. "Come on, Avery."

Avery sat on a rock holding her knees. Sylva jumped in without knowing the depth and didn't come up fast enough to suit Avery.

She surfaced struggling, slapping the water, in over her head, unable to get a footing.

Avery dove, fully clothed, and took strong sure strokes to reach Sylva. She grabbed her, turned her over, held her head out of the water with one arm, and swam to the nearest rocks.

Adam saw what had happened and swam over to them. He pulled Sylva up on the boulder.

Mars couldn't swim either, but he stayed where he could touch the bottom or hang on to vines.

Sylva coughed and choked. Adam, who had taken advanced life-saving classes, determined she didn't need respiration and would recover.

Avery got Sylva's shirt and helped her into it. Her shorts were all wet, and Sylva was shivering but okay. Avery moved into the sun to warm herself. She could sit all day looking at the water tumbling over the rocks. She had never climbed up to the top, so for her, this was where the river began. The kingdom at the bottom. She wondered if the river remembered its life before the fall. Was it the same or changed somehow by the plunge? Did rhododendrons bloom on the upper shore? Had the river ever seen these cotton-candy blossoms before? Why did it rush past in such a hurry?

The waters lingered a moment, swirled and circled under the mist, eager though to race on down the mountain, eager to hop and jump over fallen trunks, to dance before the rapids, to explode against the boulders. Would the journey end in a glorious place? The river knew to stand still was to fail. Stop the anxious momentum of life, and the pool would stagnate.

Avery and Adam began to teach Mars and Sylva how to swim, in part playfully, but they realized how serious the lessons were. Adam intended to teach Sylva more than swimming and made no secret of it. Mars and Avery watched them from a rock, then lay back and looked up through the canopy of green to clouds ever changing the canvas of an abstract sky.

Mars watched and then said, "I'd bet anything they do it this summer."

"Wouldn't surprise me," Avery said. "Would you care?"

"None of my business. She's old enough to decide what she wants to do."

"I'd think you'd want to kill him. He'd probably kill you if you tried with me."

"I doubt it," Mars said. And Avery knew he was right. Adam wouldn't give a rat's ass.

The stone warmed Avery's skin. Mars leaned over her and brushed a little butterfly kiss across her lips. His hair dripped icy water on her chest, made goosebumps rise on her. Avery liked his kisses but she pushed him away anyway.

"Wonder where the river goes?" she asked.

"I don't know. It just keeps moving."

"Maybe it flows into a lake, imagine how peaceful it would be. If it goes to the ocean it'd be lost, destroyed. Swallowed up. Then it would be afraid."

"The river doesn't get afraid, it would still be there, changed, part of something bigger, but it's forever. It's endless."

Avery never followed to see where it went and never consulted a map. She listened to its language, clear as the water, and received its message with wonder.

Mars took a chisel and mallet to the falls one day and labored over the words he carved into the boulder.

AMAS FALLS
ADAM, MARS, AVERY, SYLVA
JULY 1962

Sylva spent her extra time with Adam, insisting on going off alone with him. Mars had chores to do and wasn't around much. So, Avery had been abandoned. Adam had more friends than he knew what to do with back in Florida. Alone and miserable, Avery spent her days seething. Adam played golf with their daddy a couple times a week and those were the only times Avery had alone with Sylva. But the friendship strained against the intruder. Sylva's loyalty was divided and conversations became guarded.

"Well?" Avery asked when they were settled down by the creek one day.

"Well what?"

"Well? Do you have anything to tell me, Sylva?"

Sylva started giggling.

"I want to hear," Avery said.

"We did it, almost," she said. "Did Adam tell you?"

"No, of course not, he doesn't talk to me," Avery said. "Well, what's it like?"

Sylva shrugged. "I can't explain it."

Avery figured the reason she couldn't explain it was because it wasn't true.

"Are you going to do it with Mars?"

"No."

"Why not?"

"Because."

"You don't want to?" she asked.

"Neither of us wants to."

"I love Adam. I'm gonna marry him. I know he loves

me too. He's the most handsome boy I ever saw. And it's me he wants."

Avery couldn't imagine. "You'll have a long wait," Avery said. "He's graduating this coming year, then he's going to college. He wants to be a doctor, so college will last for eight years or more. I know Mother and Daddy won't let him get married until he finishes."

"He's so dreamy." Sylva ignored her. "I never thought I'd have a boyfriend like Adam. Don't you think he's handsome?"

"Believe me, I know what he's like. I live in his shadow, remember?" She knew him but couldn't imagine what Adam was doing with Sylva. And what about his girlfriend from school? Avery knew Adam wasn't serious about Sylva.

"He's not going to stay with you," Avery said.

"He will. He loves me."

"Sylva, you don't know him at all. I know how he is. You're going to get hurt if you keep this up."

"You don't know anything about it, Avery. I don't want to hear it. You're just jealous."

"I am not," Avery said. "First, he's too old for you. Second, he has ambition. Third, you aren't right for each other."

"Stop it, Avery. I don't want to hear it. You're just mean and spiteful."

"He has a girlfriend in Stuart."

"He does not," she said. "Anyway, he'll break up with her. Just shut up about it, Avery."

"You'll see." Avery changed the subject, knowing she had crossed some line. "Charlotte looks like she swallowed a watermelon, whole."

"Won't be long now."

"It's inconceivable to me how it gets out. You'd think it would kill you."

"Must not hurt too bad. This is the second time Charlotte's doing it," Sylva said. "I'd be too scared."

"Me too."

Eventually, Avery's mother realized Avery was alone, moping around the cabin, and asked what was going on.

"It's Adam, as usual, what else?" Avery said. "He's decided he wants Sylva for his girlfriend this summer. Now she spends all her time with him. I think she's going to get hurt. I told her so."

"I think you are hurt. What did you tell her?"

"I told her Adam wasn't serious. He's just using her. And he has a dozen girlfriends at home."

"She didn't want to hear it, did she?"

"Now she's mad at me."

"It's a case of killing the messenger."

"What?" Avery asked, cocked her head.

"An old saying. If you tell somebody things they don't want to hear, they don't like you for it. They'd rather kill the messenger than hear the truth."

"This is the worst summer of my life. I never thought Sylva would like Adam better than me. I didn't think she was like the other girls. I thought we'd be best friends forever. He has no right to butt in. He's mean and selfish and she's all starry-eyed about it."

"I'm sorry. Do you want me to talk to Adam?"

"What good would it do? If they want to be together, they'll be together. Nothing we say will matter to them."

"I guess you're right." Avery's mother stroked her hair, looked at her with sad eyes. "I am sorry, Avery."

Adam was in the barn when Avery wandered in later in the afternoon. He was brushing Lightning. She leaned against the stall and watched him.

"What are you looking at?" Always indignant.

"Do you have any idea how Sylva feels about you?"

"It's no secret. She's crazy about me." Always smug, always a jerk.

"And?"

"And what?"

"You aren't crazy about her," Avery said.

"Am so," he said. "Anyway, what business is it of yours?"

"You like her for now just because she's here. What do you think you're doing with her?"

"She's willing enough. I'm not forcing her to do anything."

"Adam, she's only fourteen." Avery climbed up on the gate to Lightning's stall.

"So? She's pretty mature for her age."

"Adam, think about it. You're going to be a doctor. Are you going to keep Sylva with you forever, to be a doctor's wife?"

"Wife? Of course not."

"Then tell her. Be honest for once in your sorry life."

"She couldn't possibly think . . ." he paused. "I doubt she'll even finish high school."

"That's the whole point, stupid. She isn't right for you. And what if you get her pregnant?"

"And what do you know about that?" Adam was filling a water bucket for the horse.

"Not much for sure. But enough to know it would be awful, for Sylva." Avery thought for a minute and added, "And for you."

"We didn't do anything anyway."

"Sylva has a different version. Whether or not, my guess is it's just a matter of time," Avery said. "I hope she wouldn't let you, but she's all crazy thinking you're going to be her boyfriend forever, and I think she might let you. It scares me to death. Adam, she's a country girl. She doesn't have the same advantages you have."

"I thought you liked her."

"I do. Saying true things doesn't mean I don't like her. I accept her the way she is."

"I've got nothing to do with it anyway."

"You do too, Adam." Avery sat down in the straw, thinking in spite of his advantages, looks, personality, skills, and abilities, he was shortchanged in the brain department. Mars wasn't as good-looking, but he was sweet, sensitive, and honest—much more important.

"Well, if we do it, I'll use protection," he said.

"You have to protect Sylva in other ways. The fact is, you've taken her away from me. She was my friend first. You have a million friends. You don't need Sylva. Now she spends all her time with you and doesn't even like me anymore. How do you think it makes me feel?"

"Hey, is it my fault she'd rather be with me?" Adam stopped brushing the horse and looked at his sister. "What are you? Jealous? Don't tell me what to do anyway." Now, Adam was cleaning the stall, pitching dirty straw out.

"This isn't a competition," Avery said. "I can't compete with you for my very own best friend when you have all the advantage. She thinks you love her. She's thinking you're having some sick romance here. You shouldn't mess with my friends, I should say my one and only friend. Not that you haven't messed up other friendships I might have had."

"So you blame me because you're not popular? Just mind your own business, Avery."

Avery stared up into his dark eyes, freezing with intelligence, yet he was hollow somehow. His hair was the color of mahogany. He'd managed to get through puberty without a zit to mar his complexion.

"Daddy joined the country club just so you could play golf. They put all your trophies on a shelf in the living room. Stuff I won gets to stay in my room, tacked up on a cork board."

"You get to swim because we joined the country club."

"I know, but it's not why he joined."

"All you ever won was a couple ribbons. Anyway you're only on the junior team. Why don't you brush Moonshine? You know we're supposed to help if we use the horses."

"So? I still won something, didn't I? Worst of all, you're always butting in on my friends, Adam." Avery found another brush and went into Moonshine's stall. "Why don't you leave my friends alone?" She stroked the horse, petted its velvet nose. Moonshine's eyes looked like plums with eyelashes.

"You don't have any friends."

"I try to make friends at school, but when they come around they just use it as an excuse to see you. Then you go flirting and jumping around like a chimpanzee and they fall over dead."

"I do not."

"You do too, Adam. You flirt and joke and prance around like a colt. Then everybody treats me like a mosquito. They treat you like some teenage idol. Every time the phone rings, it's for you. Whenever we have Thanksgiving or Christmas or anything, all anybody can talk about is how great you are. Oh, you're so smart, so cute as a bug."

"Shut up, Avery."

"I'm telling you to leave Sylva alone. She's my friend. You don't need her and you're going to hurt her."

"And who are you to talk anyway? You're probably going all the way with Mars."

"I am not." Avery was shocked he thought such a thing. "We aren't going to either. We don't even know how."

"Mars knows how." Adam had finished with his horse chores, Avery guessed, because he closed the gate and left.

"Leave Sylva alone. Do you hear me?" Avery shouted after him. "She's my friend," Avery whispered to Moonshine. "My only friend."

Someone said once, Avery couldn't remember who, a man will be judged by how he treats his sister. She thought if Adam was judged that way, he wouldn't score very high.

The last day of vacation always threatened and then was upon them like a quick summer shower. Avery said good-bye to Mars. He gave her a little hug, restrained by parental presence. Sylva was hanging on Adam as if the world was ending, parents or no. Adam promised to write to her. Avery knew better.

Sylva was crying then. She said good-bye to Avery as if she didn't even know her. Avery's heart was filled with bricks. She hated Adam for causing this particular trouble. She didn't know how to act, what to feel, what to say. Couldn't believe he could be so cruel.

Avery ran up to the kitchen to say good-bye to Neco-wee. She sat on the stoop with Neco-wee outside the kitchen door for a minute.

"Another summer ending," Neco-wee said with her arm around Avery's shoulder.

"This was a sad summer."

"How so?"

"Because it just was." Avery twirled a dandelion.

"You had the horses."

"I know. We found a valley way up across the ridge where we rode. There's a waterfall up there. We took the picnics you made and ate on the rocks. It was beautiful."

"Wasn't that fun?"

"No," Avery said. "Sylva and Adam, they, I don't know. It's too hard to explain."

Avery hugged her tight. Mr. Baldwin honked the horn.

"I love you, Neco-wee. See you next year," Avery shouted as she ran down the hill. She climbed into the backseat next to Adam.

Mr. Baldwin started the engine and asked, "All set, Bud, Budlet? Everybody go to the bathroom?"

"We're all set," Adam said.

"Sylva was sure upset," their mother said. "You shouldn't have led her on, Adam."

"She'll get over it." He was always smug. He opened a magazine to read. Avery kicked him.

"Stop it, Avery."

"You're a monster," she whispered, and turned her back on him. She looked out the window memorizing the shape of the ridge, hating to be trapped in the backseat.

"Next summer everything will be back to normal, you'll see," their mother said from the front seat, always optimistic.

"Anyway, this is my last summer coming to Crowfoot Ridge," Adam said. "Next summer I'll be working at the hospital."

"Emptying bedpans, no doubt, a fitting occupation for you," Avery said under her breath.

Mrs. Baldwin reached over the seat and handed each of them a box of Milk Duds. Avery thought her illusions about them bordered on delusion. Like they needed Milk Duds.

Sylva's childish pleading letters to Adam had arrived all during the fall. She sent cards, poems, and love letters calculated, Avery thought, to keep him from forgetting her. He'd made such fun of her. He didn't even open half of them. Avery hated him for it. He was so busy with his senior year of high school, his activities, golf, swimming, girlfriends, parties, dances, and Sylva wasn't the only girl chasing after him.

Sylva's only letter to Avery arrived after Thanksgiving saying her mother was too sick to do anything. She had quit school to take care of Shelby and Bobby, who was Echo's baby. School had offered Sylva the only possible ticket out of her situation. Mars had formed a band with another guitarist, a fiddler, and a mandolin player. She said they played at high school dances around the small mountain communities. At least he would finish school and pursue his music. And Wayne went into the army, leaving Echo home alone and pregnant.

She'd asked Avery to tell Adam to write to her. Like Avery had any influence with him. She thought the only reason Sylva even wrote to her was to get a message to Adam, which didn't get delivered.

Anyway, Adam had a new girlfriend. Tammy was the daughter of one of their father's golf partners.

Avery wrote to both Sylva and Mars. She told Sylva she didn't think Adam would be making the trip to North Carolina in the future, as he was going to college. Maybe she'd get the picture. Writing to Mars presented a problem, since she hadn't heard from him. She didn't say anything she wanted to say, only asked about his band and told him about swimming with the school team.

Once the door was open, though, letters flew between Avery and Mars during the year. Sylva never wrote another letter, and Avery feared she'd lost her very best friend forever.

When Adam graduated from high school in June, Avery thought the whole family would put a crown on his head or something.

All she could think about was going to Crowfoot Ridge.

9

The Baldwins made the trip to North Carolina without Adam in the summer of sixty-three. Mr. Baldwin arranged for Adam to stay with a friend. Avery had the backseat all to herself, making the trip seem much longer and strange.

When the car was unpacked Avery walked the path between MacKinsey's Farm and Sylva's house, worrying what her reaction would be when she found out Adam had stayed in Florida. But Sylva had other things on her mind and didn't even ask about him.

"Mama's in the hospital," Sylva said giving Avery a hug. "She's been there so long now, and she doesn't seem to be getting any better."

"Sylva, they can fix anything. The doctors will make her well. You'll see."

"I have three kids to take care of. Thank goodness Shelby starts school in the fall. Then there's Bobby, Echo's three-year-old."

"Did Wayne ever come back?"

"No. He's somewhere in Vietnam. Then, I've got Charlotte's new baby, Yancey. She's just six months old."

"Sylva, how do you take care of all those kids and still go to school?"

"I had to quit last year. Mama got sick before Thanksgiving, and I stayed home to help her. Echo and Charlotte both work away from the farm. Papa took a job a hundred miles away from here. I don't even know where he lives. He hardly ever shows up."

"So you missed most of the tenth grade? I'll help you, Sylva, every day, all month. I'll do whatever I can. It'll be fun. You'll see." Avery meant it.

Sylva had matured more than Avery during the year. Her responsibility with the children and even quitting school seemed to enlarge the gap between them. Adam's tampering had forced a wedge in their friendship.

"Why didn't Adam ever write to me? I kept thinkin' he would. I waited and waited. I needed him to care."

Avery hugged her friend.

"I hate him for hurting you," she said. "I wish I'd written to you more. I just didn't understand what you were going through."

"It's best to just forget about him, don't you think?"

"Yes, Sylva, I think so."

Avery spent her days with Sylva thinking the work was like playing house, playing grown-up, but the fun wore off fast. She spent evenings with Mars. Once in a while, they took the horses up to AMAS Falls. What they hadn't been ready for in the past seemed natural this summer. They held hands, kissed, and looked into each other's eyes. Avery loved being with him.

When Mars's band was playing, she went along and listened with the friends of the other musicians. He'd gotten a van to haul the instruments and amplifiers around in. Their music was so good, Avery thought he'd be a big star someday. When the audience cheered and howled for more, Avery was filled with pride.

Alone together in his van, their petting grew more and more intense. They weren't ready for the big event, at least Avery wasn't, but she allowed a lot. He respected her limitations. Avery watched herself become obsessed with him and understood more what Sylva had felt about Adam.

And then they were told the news: Mars and Sylva's mother was dead.

Avery remembered that their mother had looked stiff and skeletal a year ago, but never in a million years did she expect Kitty Marshall to die. Some hard days went by while Sylva and Mars tried to understand. Avery sat between them in the front row at the funeral, holding hands, linked forever. The Baldwins sent flowers and sat in the rear of the church. Neco-wee was there. All the Marshall family was there except Hunter. Avery couldn't imagine what would happen to them now.

Hunter arrived late. He stumbled down the center aisle of the church, steadying himself against every other pew. He went right up to the coffin while the preacher was talking, and patted it too hard. Sylva and Mars stared at him.

Even the preacher stopped to watch him.

The sound of the thump echoed through the silence. Hunter backed away, his hair not even combed, and sat hard on the first bench next to Mars. He twisted around to see who was there, offered a little wave to someone. Every eye in the church was on him. He rubbed his wiry red beard, turned to the preacher, and said, "Go on, then."

A spray of flowers quivered on top of the casket when they carried it to the cemetery out behind the church. Wildflowers swayed in the meadow beyond, bowed gently by a cool breeze. Avery couldn't imagine not having a mother. She feared the future for Sylva and Mars. Sylva suffered in silence and with dry eyes. No words could help them through this.

Hunter lurched up to the grave, swayed, and

regained his balance by leaning on the coffin. When the short service ended, Hunter turned, and without speaking to anyone, including his children, walked toward his truck. Avery watched him. He stopped to pee in the bushes. He never looked back.

Kitty Marshall was laid to rest between her father and her eldest son, Franklin, the one who'd been killed in the war.

Long shadows stretched over the Marshall farm by late afternoon. People crowded the downstairs, plates of food filled the table. Sylva went upstairs. Avery poured lemonade and took a glass up to her.

"Here, Sylva, I brought you this. Do you want any food? There's ham, fried chicken. You want a sandwich?"

Sylva held herself tight around the middle and sat rocking on the quilt her mama had made many years ago.

"She was living on borrowed time. I heard somebody say," Sylva whispered to Avery. "But I don't know what borrowed time means."

"Shhhh." Avery smoothed her long hair with easy strokes.

"She died of what they call a long illness. Avery, what are we gonna do without our mama?"

"Sylva, things have gone very bad for you. And now you have this to try and understand."

"Do I still have you for my friend, Avery?" she asked, still dry-eyed. "I couldn't live if I didn't."

"Of course, you do. I'll be your very best friend forever and you'll be mine forever." Avery gathered Sylva in her arms and hugged her. Then they curled up together, and Avery held Sylva until she fell asleep.

Mars was in bed when Avery crept into his room later. Soft music played on the radio. The lights were out. Avery slipped in under the sheet next to him, her front against his back. She put her arm over him, her hand against his chest. He covered it with his hand, stroking her fingers. She kissed his shoulder through his shirt.

"I'm so sorry, Mars," she whispered.

"I know."

"They have food downstairs. You want anything? I'll go get it for you."

He pulled his shirt up a little, and placed her hand against the smooth taut skin on his stomach.

"I just want you with me, Avery," he said.

"What will happen to everybody now?" she asked. She felt his breathing, his warmth. She moved her hand up and felt soft hair growing on his chest.

"We'll go on like always. Mama hasn't been here for us for a long time. Hunter's never here." Avery traced with her fingertips the long scars.

"Maybe he'll come home now."

"I doubt it," he said, and turned to her and touched her chest too, small breasts, nipples hard, tingling, surprising her. Between her legs new awareness felt urgent.

"I love you, Mars, and Sylva too, more than anyone on earth."

He kissed her, soft kisses on her lips. She tasted the sweet lemonade on his mouth.

"Mars, Sylva shouldn't have to take care of Echo's kid and Charlotte's new baby, and Shelby too." She put her hand on his face, felt tears on his cheeks and wiped them away.

"Shelby starts school in September."

"I know and so should Sylva." She ran her fingers through his long hair.

"You're right," Mars whispered, "I'll talk to Charlotte and Echo. They need to make other arrangements for their kids." He pulled her shirt up and kissed her again, tender little sucking kisses.

"Will you help Sylva?"

"What can I do?"

"Help her catch up at school, make sure she signs up again." Avery held him tight and wrapped her legs around him. "I feel terrible for you both."

"I know," he said.

He was touching her, moving his hand places he'd never gone before. She found herself responding, touching him, daring more also. Her heart was pounding, her breathing jagged. Nothing like this had happened between them.

Their petting took a turn toward urgency. She wanted to be with him, but was afraid. He moved forward in such a gentle way she didn't think to stop him. He hesitated. Then somehow things progressed to a reckless point. She wanted him in spite of her apprehension. Her body seemed to be making decisions her mind wasn't part of. But still she knew he would have stopped if she'd asked.

"I don't want to hurt you, Avery."

"It's okay, Mars. You won't hurt me. I love you with all my heart."

"I've always loved you too, ever since the first time I saw you when you were just a little girl."

"Don't talk," she said.

He pulled her into him, his hand pressed low on her back. A bulge in his front invaded, surprised her. She wanted to be close to him, closer than their clothes allowed. They took their shirts off and faced each other, naked skin touching for the first time, hands and mouths exploring, searching. Every inch of Avery was burning. The Patsy Cline song "Crazy" was playing on the radio.

She dared to touch him, and when she did he trembled.

They heard a soft rap at his door and a woman saying, "Mars?" They froze. Avery pulled her hand away.

"My aunt," he whispered. The door opened a crack. Avery shrank down under the covers and held her breath.

"Mars?" she asked again, "I came up to say good night. I'm leaving now. Let me know if you need anything."

"I'm sleeping," Mars said. "I'll see you soon. Thanks. Good night."

She closed the door.

"Lock it," Avery whispered.

"Doesn't have a lock." He turned away, reached for the drawer in his night stand. "I want to protect you. I'd never take chances with you. I hope this thing is still good. I've had it a long time. Are you okay with this?"

He gathered her in a complete embrace, both arms around her, their legs entwined.

"Are you?" he asked again.

"Are you?"

"Oh, yes, Avery."

He rolled onto her and pressed between her legs until she was able to receive him. Some unseen magnet joined them. Avery shivered with anticipation, but he was gentle, slow, pushed with small movements she met by lifting her hips to him. It didn't hurt as much as she'd thought it would. It felt right, complete somehow.

"God, Avery, this is amazing."

He moved deeper, hurt her. She tensed, tears rolled out of her eyes. He was aware at once, stopped, then she felt him tremble. He held her tight, breathing heavy.

"Sorry, oh God, I hope I didn't hurt you." His words were smothered in her neck. "I'll remember this night for the rest of my life."

Avery snuggled against him as he moved away, still holding her. He touched her in a new way. His fingertips explored the slippery silk of her passion. So complete, so perfect. She wrapped her arms and legs around him and loved him for being so tender, for guiding her into this with such care, for sharing this gamble with her.

They were quiet, still touching, a long time, digesting what they'd done. Thinking. Feeling. A full bronze moon rose above the silhouette of mountain, eclipsed through his window. Its lonesome crystal half-light fell across his face and turned his hair gold, his eyes to a miraculous aquamarine, a color only a baffled girl immersed in the blush of newborn sexual glow could ever see. Avery cried tears of tenderness, realizing the lasting impact of having chosen Mars.

"How'd you know how to do it?" she whispered into his neck.

"I don't know," he said, "I'd been afraid a long time and worried a lot."

"What were you afraid of?"

"Maybe of being too small or too big, maybe I would fumble or most of all, I might hurt you."

"Do you think we did it right?"

Mars chuckled and snuggled closer.

"I think we need to practice some more," he whispered.

Sylva came into his room and woke them when she crawled into bed. She curled next to Avery, put her head on Avery's shoulder. The three of them lay together without talking, finding comfort and security in each other. They slept, with Avery between them, like puppies in a basket, young, wounded, and vulnerable. Avery heard Sylva crying in the night.

They were alone at breakfast the next morning. Echo had Shelby and Bobby in the trailer. A light drizzle fell over the mountains and the meadow. Patchy fog drifted over the pond. The kitchen floor felt damp under bare feet. The muggy morning promised a hot day. Sylva went out on the porch and fed the dogs. Then she came in and sat down.

Their pain filled the house.

"You have a lot of responsibility now," Avery said. "Both of you."

"It's nothing new." Sylva dumped cereal into a bowl, then poured milk over it.

"Isn't there some way you can continue with school?" Avery asked.

"Of course there is," Mars said. "When Shelby starts first grade in the fall, Sylva will go to school. I'm going to see to it. You have my word."

"I've missed so much. I'll be so far behind."

"I'm going to help you, Sylva," Mars said. "And that's a promise. We've been waiting for years for some parental guidance. Well, we're not going to get it. So, now, we stop waiting and start taking charge of our own lives. You stayed home to help take care of Mama and Shelby. It was something you had to do. We'll go talk to the people at the school, tell them why you missed so much over the past two years. We can fix this. I won't let you give up. And Charlotte and Echo can take care of their own kids."

He put some bread in the toaster, rapped his fingers on the counter waiting for it. Avery saw in her mind the images of last night, felt filled with him still, connected in a new way.

"And you know what else?" he asked. "I'm going to college."

"Who do you think is going to pay for that?" Sylva asked.

"I'll pay for it myself with the money Wayne gave me before he left and the money I earn with the band. I'm going to spend the rest of the summer promoting the band." The toast popped up. "I can go around to all the bars, churches, even community centers, anywhere people want to hear music. Private parties at people's houses. Why not? I could put a little band-for-hire ad in the paper. Maybe charge more."

"You could paint the name of the band on the side of the van," Avery said. "Then whenever you drove around the sign could be seen by everybody. Put the name and the phone number."

"We need a name," he said. "We haven't been organized enough to even think up a name for ourselves."

"How about Mars?" Avery asked.

"Just Mars? The other guys might not like it."

"Ask them," Avery said. "I like it—it's simple. It's different and easy to remember. What are their names? Do they have better names?"

"Earl and Hoyt."

"Hoyt? Does that tell you anything?" she asked. "I rest my case."

Avery could see his wheels turning.

"How about Mars and the Little Green Men?" Sylva started to laugh.

"Somehow, I don't think the guys would think that was funny," Mars said, laughing too. "How about the Crowfoot Ridge Band? Should keep everyone happy."

They'd forgotten for a moment their mother had been buried the day before. The hopeful talk and the three of them together made everything seem okay. They had something to work toward, and they had school. Avery knew they both understood the importance of school. Sylva and Mars figured it out all by themselves. Avery watched them, clearing up the dishes. Things would be better now.

The vacation came to an end much too soon. Their last days together were spent mostly moping around. But Avery and Mars were alone the last night. Sylva spent the night at Charlotte's in Brevard to baby-sit Yancey.

"I love you so much, Mars, it fills me to bursting. I don't want to be away from you an hour let alone a whole year." Avery held him tight.

The promises they made with such good intentions were doomed, and they both knew it. They wouldn't write every day. He wouldn't wait for her without even looking at another girl all year. Even though Avery believed she could go the rest of her life without looking at anyone else, some little something inside told her that wouldn't happen either.

They snuggled close in his bed afterward, petting, wanting the memories of their touches to last. When Avery started crying and buried her face in his neck, he cried too. When her heart broke apart, she knew his did too. The pain burned through her like wildfire in a dry forest. And it ran through Mars. She believed he felt what she felt. She would never forget this boy with eyes the color of a lagoon, with hair soft as a baby's, with poetry and music filling his mind. Avery would never forget their first time or how tender he'd been.

She pulled him closer still and wept, her heart full of joy and sadness. He tried to kiss the tears away, but she thought they would flow like the water in their stream forever.

The next morning, they couldn't say good-bye. They held each other on the porch of his house.

"I'll walk over to the cabin with you," he said.

"No, Mars. I can't say good-bye to you in front of Mother and Daddy. I just can't."

Avery moved away, one step, his hand still on her arm, then on her hand, then fingertips touching.

"I'll never forget you, Avery. Remember I love you."

"I'll see you next summer, Mars. Write to me, okay?"

Avery turned and ran up the driveway. She stopped once and turned around. He was watching. He waved. She walked to MacKinsey's Farm and tried to stop crying before reaching the cabin, but it was useless. She would have to deal with her parents one way or the other. They wouldn't understand. The only way to make them understand would be to tell them things had gone beyond their wildest imagination. Something she could never admit.

She pulled herself together a little. Hardest thing she ever did in her whole life was leaving Mars that summer morning. Her parents noticed nothing.

Neco-wee came down to say good-bye as they packed the car. Avery stood talking to her while her father finished.

"Another beautiful summer on Crowfoot Ridge comes to an end," Avery said as she held Neco-wee's hand.

"This is the end of the beautiful time, Avery."

"Why do you say that, Neco-wee?"

"Because a dark sky will fall on the country."

"What country?"

"The United States country." Neco-wee always knew things. "Just like it did more than a hundred years ago."

"What happened then?"

"The people of the Cherokee Nation walked the Trail of Tears. Tens of thousands of my people were rounded up and forced to march from our lands in these mountains to a place called Oklahoma west of the Mississippi River."

"Why?"

"Because the white man wanted our land."

"Why didn't you kill them?"

"You see too many movies, child," she said. "We're not warriors. We're farmers and peace-loving people. We gave the white man food from our fields.

Still, they weren't satisfied, and they forced us to leave."

"When did your people return?" Avery asked.

"Some fled into the forest and were never caught. Others walked all the way back to reclaim our right to be here on our own land. Then the government gave what was not theirs to give, the land back to us. Now it's ours forever."

"What dark sky do you see?"

"Dark sky. Dark time. Same as Trail of Tears, same as the Cherokee Nation crying. Will I see you next summer, Avery?"

"Oh yes." Avery gave her a hug.

The car was loaded. The Baldwins acted like life was perfectly normal. Couldn't they see the change in their daughter? She felt like a neon sign blinked across her forehead.

What would happen if they ever found out the truth?

10

The nation walked a trail of tears when President Kennedy was killed in November, just as Neco-wee had predicted. Avery thought about Neco-wee every hour of every day. There was nowhere to hide. She expected the larger world to be normal, secure, and reasonable. She expected to be half-crazy as she celebrated her sixteenth birthday in December.

Kennedy's death changed the era of confidence. Stories about the tragic family lasted for months on the evening news, and in the programs Avery's current events teacher created to help them through their grief. He was the first president Avery's class had ever felt they knew. So, they watched the news on television, walked a little slower, talked a little softer. They felt shaken, like their innocence had been tarnished. The innocence of the country felt compromised.

Sylva's letters were filled with stories of Mars's band playing at school functions, and every detail she dared commit to paper about her new boyfriend, the wonderful Donald Thornsberry, whom she had met at one of Mars's gigs.

Mars's letters were full of poetry and words to songs and his love for Avery. Letters she read and reread, and cherished, and saved, tied with a ribbon, hid in a shoe box. At first his letters arrived once a week, then by Christmas they were coming twice a month, then by Easter they were coming once a month. The last letter arrived in late May.

Precious Avery,

I thought you should know the band got a job playing at the Fontana Village for two months this summer. We'll go right after graduation.

If you come to Crowfoot Ridge, I won't be here. I wanted to turn it down, believe me, but I need the money to start college with in the fall.

Try to talk your folks into going to Fontana instead. I think you could still get reservations. It's really a pretty place and there's lots of stuff to do. If that doesn't happen, let me know when you'll be here. I'll try to get time off to come home to see you.

I love you with all my heart,
Mars

Crowfoot Ridge, the particular roll of the hills, tasseled corn up and almost ready to pick, the forests, all seemed caught in suspended animation. Cabin 3 again. Down by the creek. As soon as the car was unpacked and they were settled, Avery's parents went up to join the other guests for drinks on the verandah. She ran the path to Sylva's.

They squealed and hugged and jumped for joy just as if they were still six years old. Then they settled down on the porch swing.

"We'll call Mars," Avery said, almost before hello. "Tell him I'm here. If he can't come, I'll force Daddy to drive to Fontana, and you'll go with us."

"He'll come. I know he will."

"So tell me everything about Donald."

Sylva raved about her new boyfriend and told Avery all the details she'd omitted in her letters.

Avery noticed the house was unusually quiet. "Where is everybody?"

"They all went off somewhere," Sylva said. "Donald is a cutie. He works at the bowling alley at night in Brevard. He has his own truck, bought it himself. I don't think he'll come over tonight, but I don't know for sure. Maybe tomorrow. He plays basketball on the school team. He's a senior in high school. I can't wait for you to meet him."

"And I can't wait to meet him."

"You know, Avery," Sylva said. "I can't believe how stupid I was when I had a crush on Adam. I almost lost you over it. You're my best friend, and I just wanted to tell you how sorry I am about it."

"It's okay, I understand. I was worried about you. Now the table has turned, and I'm in love with Mars."

"You shouldn't be," Sylva said, her head turned away.

"Why?"

"Because, he's going to college. He's away for the whole summer. He'll come see you, I'm certain he will, but he's busy. He's growing up."

"Does he see other girls?"

"You are the most special to him, I know. But Avery, don't put all your faith in Mars. Believe me, he's not perfect. He's been good to me, though, for a brother, I mean. He got me back into school after Mama died. He went over there with me, walked right into the principal's office, and told him the whole story. How Mama had been sick, how I had to stay home and help with Shelby. He spent every single night going over the books with me, trying to help me understand all the work I'd missed. I should have been put back two years. I couldn't hardly read. But because of Mars, they only put me back one year."

"I knew he'd help you. He always does what he says." Avery thought Sylva was lucky to have him for a brother.

They went inside and sat on the sofa; Avery wondered if they would ever take the ugly bear hide off the wall.

"When is everybody coming back?" Avery asked. "You're here alone?"

"Yep. First time ever. It's wonderful." She hugged herself. "Charlotte and her baby Yancey are in Brevard living with Wiley. I baby-sit Yancey on Sunday. Wayne and Echo took Bobby and Shelby to Fontana to hear Mars play, just for the weekend."

"So when did he get back?" Avery asked.

"Who? Wayne? He got discharged and came on home a while ago. Sure made Echo happy."

"I'll bet. You ever see Hunter since your mama's funeral?"

"Some, not much anymore. I don't know where he lives."

She lifted her hair and held it up off her neck a minute. "Hot tonight, and sticky."

They talked so much after dinner, Avery's voice was hoarse. She called Mars at Fontana, wound up having to leave a message, but he called back in less than an hour.

"We're playing tonight," he said. "The dance doesn't end until two in the morning, but I have tomorrow off. I'll drive over in the morning."

"How far is it? How long will it take you to get here?"

"A couple hours. I'll be there by noon."

"Okay. I can't wait. Mars, maybe next weekend

Daddy will take us up to Fontana. Maybe."

Sunday morning Charlotte maneuvered a fin-tailed boat of a car into the drive and honked. Sylva ran out, shouting back at Avery, "I'll be home by five or six."

Avery watched them leave. The clock marked nine o'clock. Three hours to wait, three long hours. Mars would come early, Avery convinced herself, at least an hour early. She showered, taking as much time as possible and dressed, taking extra care with her hair, adding a touch of makeup from Sylva's stash. She was all ready an hour later. Waiting was agony. Nothing on Sunday morning television except preachers.

By one-thirty in the afternoon, and every blade of grass lining the driveway had been burned into her mind, she had run the full scope of emotions. Lack of confidence assured her he wasn't coming, maybe he'd forgotten, maybe what she thought she heard him say yesterday was a misunderstanding. Maybe he was lost, or killed in an accident, or sick, or hurt, or what? The hours of waiting showed her the full extent of the power he had over her.

By two, Mars was only two hours late, but Avery had been waiting five hours, one year and five hours. His van pulled in and Mars got out. Avery hung back by the door, dying to run to him, angry he was late, relieved he'd come, insecure about what he felt. And the person walking up to the house was a man. A grown man with a beard. His blond hair had grown darker and longer. He had filled out and wasn't so stretched and gangly as before. He took the porch steps two at a time.

"Avery?" He stopped by the door, looking a little perplexed. "I'm sorry I'm late. I overslept, then the van overheated on the way. I didn't have the water jug full so I . . ." He had her in his arms, hugging her.

"You overslept?"

"Well, I got a later start than I figured. What's the matter?"

"I've been waiting so long."

"I'm only two hours late." He turned his arm over to check his watch. "I didn't expect this."

"I'm just being stupid," Avery said, smiled and hugged him. But the guarded beginning had cast a pause between them. They went inside and Mars made a beeline for the bathroom, came out, and stood in front of the refrigerator. He poured himself some lemonade and chucked ice cubes into the glass.

"Want some?" he asked after gulping half.

"I'm okay."

"Avery, we don't have much time. Has something happened, changed us? Something I should know about?" He settled on the sofa. Avery sat next to him. "Why so formal?"

"No, Mars. Everything is perfect." She pulled him close and kissed him. His lips were cold.

"That's better," he said playing with her locket. His arm brushed her breast. The next kiss was more intense.

"Can we walk around or something?" Avery pulled him up. "I feel a little, I don't know, strange."

They wandered around in the yard, catching up with their year of separation. They wound up in the barn, sitting in an old haystack. Barn smells and the familiar feel of the hay helped her relax. Mars was way more man than boy, Avery realized, and he moved a little faster than she'd expected. When he took his shirt off, she traced the scars from the bear attack and remembered he was still the object of her deepest passion. When he took her shirt off, he caressed her with his mouth, the beard tickled. She flinched when he circled her breast with his fingertips. He stopped.

"What?"

She took his hand to feel his callused fingers.

"Oh, playing every day, the guitar makes my fingers rough."

She touched his beard and said, "I never kissed a man with a beard before."

His urgency became apparent and she kissed him for the first time with her whole being. In moments, he ignited her flame and she grew desperate for him. The chemistry between them was still electric.

Panting, pulling him to her, she loved him just as

completely as she had all her life.

Later, they were both aware Sylva was due back. But then she called to say she was spending the night at Charlotte's. Avery and Mars made sandwiches and took them up to eat in his bed.

The next morning they stood by the van, lingering as long as possible before he had to leave.

"I can convince Daddy to bring me to Fontana next weekend," Avery said. "We might not get to be alone, but we'll see each other again. And if nothing else, you come back here next Sunday." Avery was confident.

"Go on then," she continued. "I'll see you in a couple days."

They kissed good-bye.

Avery waved as she watched him leave. She skipped back to MacKinsey's Farm and had lunch with her parents where she made the big pitch about going to Fontana. Got a maybe out of them, best she could do.

Sylva was due back around eight, so Avery walked over to the Marshall farm in the fading summer twilight. The Baldwins didn't know Sylva was at the house alone. What they didn't know wouldn't kill them.

Sylva spent an hour getting ready for her date with Donald. They talked while she fixed her hair, but Avery was falling asleep in the bed watching her friend.

"You look beautiful, Sylva, I've never seen you look so grown-up, so pretty."

"Thanks. I try. Is this skirt okay? I think it's dumpy-looking."

"No, Sylva, it's nice. I can't wait to meet Donald."

"Why don't you come to dinner with us? Then we'll come back here."

"I've eaten but I do want to meet him," Avery said. "I didn't sleep much last night so I'm fading. Wake me up when you get back. Promise?"

"And what kept you awake all night?" Sylva snickered at her.

"Wouldn't you like to know?"

The metallic thud of a car door slamming woke Avery. Sylva wasn't in the bed, wasn't expected to be. The clock glowed twelve-thirty. She heard the screen door squeak open and slap against the frame. She rubbed her eyes, smoothed out her T-shirt, and straightened the elastic waist of her shorts. She heard footsteps downstairs but no voices. Sylva and Donald were being quiet.

Avery started down the steps, called from midway, "Sylva? You back?"

Boots echoed on the hardwood floors. She heard a table bumped, and the lamp rattled in the quiet. The hall light shadowed the steps; otherwise the house was dark.

Avery touched the next-to-bottom step, barefoot silent, called again, "Sylva?"

Hunter spun around and surprised her. "Ah, what have we here?" he said. He staggered, lost his balance, laughed at himself.

"Sorry, I thought Sylva might have come home." Avery wanted no encounter with Sylva's father, so she turned to retreat back upstairs.

"Wait a minute there, girl. When did you get here?"

Avery halted. "Day before yesterday."

Hunter held the banister to steady himself. Avery turned again. She didn't like the idea of going to bed alone in the house with Hunter there. She shouldn't have come down.

"Wait now," he said, grabbing her arm. "I'm lookin' for Wayne. He ain't in the trailer."

"No," Avery said. "He and Echo took the kids to Fontana. Mars is playing." She realized her mistake. How could she be so stupid?

"You done went and growed up pretty."

Avery glared at him.

"S'a matter, girl, cat got your tongue?" His eyes were blood veined, coppery to match his beard.

"Sylva will be back any minute."

"Nah, she's off sluttin' with her beau, most like." He pulled her off the stairs. "Come down here in the light so's I can get a look at you. See what that boy o'mine sees." He shoved her under the hall light.

"Let go of me," Avery said dead serious. "You're hurting me."

"Ah, such a pretty little thing. Yep. Just ripe for the pickin'." His tone teased.

Avery kicked to free herself, pushed him away. He stumbled a bit but held tight.

"I said, you're hurting me." She pulled free and started for the stairs. He grabbed her again, and they both fell against the bookcase. The cups rattled. He spun her around. He was behind her, his arms around her chest.

"Get your hands off me." Avery's voice sounded high-pitched.

"Come on now, youngin'. I seen you eyeing me. I seen you looking at me."

"I never looked at you," she said, and pushed, shoved him away. But he gripped her arm hard. "Stop it. Don't touch me."

He twisted her arm. "How 'bout a little kiss?" He pulled her close. She turned her face away. The more she squirmed, the more determined he became. "Come on, girlie, give ol' Hunter a kiss."

Avery slammed her elbow into his stomach, put all her strength into the blow. He doubled and she got free.

He grabbed the back of her T-shirt, twisted her arm behind her back, shoved her toward the living room.

"You're breaking my arm. You're scaring me." She wiggled free again and he slapped her hard. Her face seared, and her ear chimed from the blow. She fell to the floor.

He picked her up like so much fluff and threw her down on the sofa.

Avery screamed. Her screaming enraged him. His rough hands groped to control her.

"Shut up," he shouted. "You ain't scared of me, girl. You been eyeing me for years. I seen you looking with those eyes of yourn. Comin' here with your highfalutin' ways, puttin' idears in my kids' heads."

"My daddy's on his way here right now." She writhed under his weight.

"Your old man ain't coming."

"Get off of me."

He held one hand over her mouth and nose, suffocating her and shutting her up at the same time. Avery tried to twist out of his grip, but he pinned her down with his weight.

"You like it, Missy, you like my boy to touch you plenty."

He had a death lock on her.

She could be quick. She could be clever. She could be lucky. Sylva would come home. Her daddy would come. She could always get free. Somehow.

Dirty denim rubbed her bare legs. He smelled of liquor and rot. His breath singed her hair. He let her arm go. It was numb, maybe broken.

He had her trapped under his weight and fumbled with his belt.

Avery tried to fight but couldn't move.

His right hand still covered her mouth, his left hand pressed against her back, trying to undo his pants. He lifted up, and Avery knew he had freed himself, felt him on her backside.

She whimpered.

"Guess my boy's had his share of this. What you be needin' is a real man."

Avery muffled screams into his foul-smelling hand, couldn't inhale.

He pulled her shorts down.

No, God, no. She tried to kick.

He pulled her up some, felt her chest with one big hand. She moaned into his wet palm, tried to bite and tasted grease. He put his hand on her stomach then and lifted her.

God, no. Please God, no.

He moved his hand away from her mouth, and she filled her lungs with air finally. He pulled her up to meet him, dog style.

She twisted beneath him, turned herself around, kicking and screaming.

Hunter had her trapped, pulled her legs apart with his other hand.

He positioned himself and shoved hard.

He would kill her.

He was tearing her apart.

She suffocated.

She beat on his head, grabbed his hair, pulled his head back with all her might hoping to break his neck.

He relaxed his grip for an instant.

She shoved him as hard as she could.

He didn't budge, just panted.

She twisted and got her legs free. She kicked with both feet and all her fear. Avery jumped across the arm of the sofa, pressed herself against the wall. She edged along toward the door, tripping on her shorts now caught at her ankles. Her head bumped the gun rack.

He was up, stumbling toward her again.

Her hand found the rifle and wrapped around it. She tried to lift it from the rack, but it was heavy. She turned and grabbed it down with both hands.

She could smash it over his head, knock him unconscious.

Headlights flooded the room with moving light, then stopped and focused like a spotlight on the bear hide across the room. Avery heard steps on the porch, the screen door squeaked open. The headlights moved again, flashed around the room for a second, then the room went dim, lit only by the hall fixture.

Sylva stood paralyzed just inside the door. Silent.

The gun swung around with an intention of its own. Hunter moved toward Avery, slow motion, bent forward, hand on the back of the sofa for balance as if he didn't see Sylva.

Avery's finger found the trigger.

She knew nothing about guns, only that the trigger made it work, only that things shot, like deer and bear, stopped.

He lunged at her. Sylva screamed, covered her face with her hands. Sylva flew at Avery, tried to shield her. She grabbed the gun and pulled it. As Sylva jerked the barrel, the gun went off. Hunter was right in front of them.

The kick knocked Avery and Sylva against the wall. They both held the gun. They were frozen. Avery began to collapse.

Hunter staggered back a step.

He fell backward, crashed into a table, and knocked the lamp across the hardwood. He lay face up on the floor, grabbed his chest, rolled side to side, and moaned.

Sylva screamed, "No, dear God, no." She was at his side in a second, kneeling, crying out, "Papa, no." She hovered over him, sobbing.

Avery gasped for air, her knees were weak, her feet tangled in the shorts. His slime seeped down between her legs.

His eyes stared at the ceiling.

A circle of blood stained his shirt.

Avery slid down the wall and sat on her heels using the barrel of the gun to prop herself up.

Hunter stopped moving.

Sylva shook his arm, held his hand. She looked over at Avery, then drew herself up and stood.

"Avery, oh God, what have I done?"

Sylva reached with a motion so slow Avery didn't see her hand take the gun. She helped Avery stand. She bent down and pulled Avery's shorts up. Avery realized what she was doing and slipped into them.

Gunpowder mixed with other scents in the room. Avery's legs couldn't hold her. She crumbled down the wall again. Other than the labored breathing of the two girls, the room was silent. Avery squatted against the wall, knees against her chest.

Sylva knelt, gathered her friend into her arms, and held her. Avery's eyes were locked on Hunter's. Blood pooled onto the floor.

"It's okay now," Sylva said. "It's okay. I never should have left you here alone. It's all my fault." She held Avery's head against her chest, trying to shield her.

But their eyes were riveted on him.

"I'm so sorry, Sylva. I think I killed him." Avery's voice was cracked, dry. Sylva lifted her up somehow, guided her into the kitchen.

"Tell me what happened."

They sat down on the bench by the table. Sylva got up and poured a glass of water. Avery took a sip. "I thought it was you. I came down. I'm so sorry."

"Go on."

"Oh, Sylva, God, he hasn't moved in so long." Avery's breathing was ragged. "He got hold of me, Sylva."

"I know."

"I think he's dead. I don't know how the gun went off. I didn't mean to shoot."

"Listen to me, Avery. We can't tell nobody what happened. I tried to pull the gun away. I think that's what made it go off. We're gonna say somebody else did this. A stranger or somebody."

"Who? We can't lie about it."

"I did it. I can say he abused me. God knows, it's his just due for what he done to Charlotte all those years. I'll get off easy. They got different rules in these mountains for different people."

"But I did it, I pointed the gun at him. I'm so sorry, Sylva." Avery realized what she'd said. "What do you mean 'just due'?"

"I thought I told you before. Hunter was the father of Charlotte's baby, the one who died. Least that's what everybody thinks."

"No, oh Jesus."

"We can't tell nobody about this. You hearing me?"

Avery sipped the water again, her hand shaking. "The police will know, will find out."

"It doesn't matter who pulled the trigger. The gun went off. We did it together. But you're from Florida. Your father is rich. I know these mountains. I can get away with it. You can't. They don't like some rich Florida people coming up here, killing folks. Listen, I know what I'm talking about. They won't even blink an eye if I say I did it. You understand? If we say you did it, your life will be over. You'll be put in jail here in North Carolina forever. Even your father couldn't get you out."

"My life is over anyway." Avery took another sip of water; her hand shook, the water spilled. "What you're saying is crazy. We've got a dead man in the living room, your father . . ." Her mouth was so dry, she couldn't talk.

"I don't have time to think about him right now. What I'm saying isn't crazy."

"What am I supposed to tell my folks? What are we supposed to do with his body?"

"Okay, let me think." Sylva looked down, her hair covered her face. Avery waited, tried to get some air into her lungs. Then Sylva said, "Okay, listen. We'll go over to the cabin and tell your father Hunter tried to attack you, but together we fought him off. He attacked me and I shot him. Your father will believe it and he'll call the police."

"And what was I supposed to be doing? Sitting around watching all this? He won't believe one word of it."

"He'll believe it on account of he'd rather believe I was raped than you. That's why he'll believe it. People believe what they want to hear. The police will come. They'll take care of Hunter. We won't tell nobody Hunter raped you, okay? If we tell them the truth they'll take you to a hospital. Then the doctor can see this wasn't your first time. And they'll know about you and Mars. Shoot, we can't say he raped me either, 'cause they'd be hauling me off to the hospital. We won't say nothing about any rape, okay?"

"No, Sylva, I don't want to go to the hospital." Avery was stunned, didn't understand Sylva's reasoning. She believed Sylva was right though, any story on earth would be better than telling her father she'd been raped and she'd killed a man and take the chance of his finding out she'd been sleeping with Mars.

She didn't know if Sylva's idea was best, but she wanted out of the house so much, she said, "Okay, Sylva, as long as nothing bad will happen to you."

Sylva helped Avery into the bathroom and washed her off. Avery was unsteady.

"Where are your shoes?"

"Upstairs."

"I'll run up and get them. Did you leave anything else up there?"

"Don't leave me alone."

Sylva guided Avery back into the kitchen, shielding her from seeing Hunter's body again. "Sit right here. I'll get your shoes."

The girls left by the back porch to avoid seeing the body. On the path, they were engulfed in a black tunnel, corn on one side, wild roadside daisies on the other. No passing cars to light the way. They held each other against the chill of fear, against the chill of the Appalachian night, all the way to MacKinsey's Farm. The moonless night cast no shadows. Nothing but gloom.

11

Something moved on a low branch as Avery and Sylva approached the dark cabin. Avery stopped, held her breath, looked up into the canopy of leaves, and locked her gaze on two luminous amber eyes leering from the shadows.

"What is it?" Sylva whispered.

The owl's eyes closed once on hinged lazy lids. A sudden extension of its wings expanded into a great flapping explosion, propelling the bird away and down the path.

"Come on, it's just a bird." Sylva pushed Avery toward the cabin. Mist collected above the creek, cruised the ground, formless and opaque. They waded through the fog and entered the safety of the cabin.

"Mrs. Baldwin, Mr. Baldwin," Sylva called out,

"something awful has happened." She kept her voice even.

The light snapped on in the bedroom and filtered into the living room. Avery ran to her mother when she came into the small room, still half-asleep, pulling on a robe. Avery's father was right behind her.

Sylva began to tell her story, and Avery's parents stood there listening.

"What? He attacked Avery?" Mr. Baldwin interrupted to ask. "Are you all right?"

Avery staggered to a chair and sat.

"He attacked you, Avery? Is this true?" her mother asked.

Avery nodded and looked at the floor.

Sylva assured them Avery was okay and went on with the story, still speaking in even tones.

"So, you're saying you fought with him?" Mrs. Baldwin asked. "Sylva? Are you hurt?"

"I'm okay," Sylva said. "Please let me finish."

Avery got up and stood next to her father. Mr. Baldwin wrapped his arm around his daughter, directed his questions to Sylva.

"Go on. What happened?" he asked.

Avery knew he was ready to kill, knew if she told everything he'd take her to the hospital, doctors would look at her, poke her some more, ask questions. She'd rather die. Sylva's story was best. Her arm wasn't broken, only sore. She was dead, but nothing was broken. Nothing had been penetrated that hadn't been penetrated before, but she didn't want them to know. A doctor could tell and would divulge the whole story, just like Sylva said. Sylva still hadn't gotten the worst part out.

She finally told the rest of it. The story knocked the breath out of Avery's parents, brought them to their knees.

"You mean he's dead, shot dead? Oh my God, I'll call the police," Mr. Baldwin said. "I'll call Mars at Fontana Village."

"What will happen?" Sylva asked through tears.

"The police will want to question both of you," he said.

"No! Avery wasn't there," Sylva said. "I forgot this part, see, while I was fighting him off, Avery ran out to go get you and then, well, I had the gun and somehow it went off. So, Avery heard the shot and stopped. She waited for me on the path."

Avery hadn't heard this part of the story before, but confirmed it by saying, "I was afraid Sylva was dead but I couldn't go back in the house."

"I'm going to call the police." Mr. Baldwin left to use the phone at the MacKinseys' house.

Sylva, Avery, and her mother went into the bedroom. Avery curled into a knot on the bed, shivering, and began to cry. She clung to her mother for a long time.

"No answer at Fontana Village. We'll call later," Mr.

Baldwin said when he came back. "I reached the police. I'm going over to the farm and meet them. Are you all right?"

"Daddy, don't go over there." Avery's cry was useless as he left anyway. All energy had left her. Every muscle in her body ached. Her mother put her in the shower, and then dried her off. She examined the red mark on Avery's shoulder where the gun had kicked her, and the bruises Hunter's hands had left. She wrapped her in a big terry cloth robe. Sylva took a shower too. Avery crawled into one of the twin beds. When Sylva was finished, she put on Avery's pajamas and climbed into bed with Avery.

The girls pretended to sleep and did sleep finally.

When Avery woke up, the sun was shining high through the window into her eyes. Sylva was still asleep.

"Wake up," Avery whispered.

Sylva seemed drugged. She stirred and rubbed her eyes as if trying to remember where she was, what had happened.

"We're not going to get away with this," Avery whispered.

"Why? What's happened?"

"Nothing, I don't know."

Mrs. Baldwin came to the door. "You're up. I brought a tray down from Neco-wee. It's on the porch if you want anything."

"Thanks, Mother," Avery said.

Avery and Sylva sat on the porch and ate a few bites of cold toast. Sylva peeled a banana, held it like a bouquet, took a bite, and gave it to Avery.

Mrs. Baldwin joined them.

"Mars and Wayne are on the way," she said, "and should be here by noon. Your father's still over at the farm."

Avery was an invalid. She could walk only with help. Fragile, hurting. They sat on the porch, waiting for Mars. Mr. Baldwin came back and paced by the creek.

When Wayne and Mars arrived, they stood talking to Mr. Baldwin a long time out by the van Mars drove. Mars looked over at Avery and Sylva with such pain in his eyes. Echo and Mrs. Baldwin stood with Bobby and Shelby.

Then Mars and Wayne left to go tell Charlotte.

A little later, a police car pulled up. Two officers walked up to the porch.

"We need to talk to Sylva Marshall." The officer looked apologetic. "We want to take her downtown and get a statement."

Sylva walked out to the car without a word and climbed into the backseat. Avery wanted to scream, "It's not true. Don't listen to this. I did it." But no sound emerged.

*   *   *

Arraignment. Lawyer. Judge. Trial. Autopsy. Funeral. Burial. Juvenile detention. Orphans. Police. Investigation. Coroner's report. Hearing. Bond. All these words peppered disjointed sentences and pieces of conversations. They floated in and out of Avery's consciousness over the next couple days.

A burial was arranged for Hunter. A memorial service was to be held at the cemetery.

Mrs. Baldwin insisted Avery go.

"No, I will not go. Never. Not in a million years."

"You have to, Avery," her mother said. "Funerals are for the living, not for the dead."

Avery stared at her, defiant. Couldn't believe her own mother would even suggest such a thing.

"You have to see a closure to this."

"I won't go. Don't even think it," Avery said.

"You have to see him buried."

"Why?"

"You have to be there for your friends, for Sylva, for Mars, and for yourself. You have to see it end."

"It's already ended," Avery said.

"You must go. It's the only way to begin the healing."

Avery stood between her parents at the funeral. Her father held his arm around her. Her mother held her hand.

Sylva, Mars, Wayne and Echo, Charlotte and Wiley, Shelby, Neco-wee, and some others Avery didn't know were there. An overcast day, humid and threatening, matched the mood.

The closed casket had a spray of gladiolus across the top.

Who would have bought flowers?

The preacher said words. Avery didn't listen. She looked at the ground with dry eyes. Then she looked across the field and saw wildflowers and the green of the woods beyond. The preacher's words were meaningless. He finished. Amen.

Mars walked up to his father's casket.

Avery's eyes were locked on him as he stood looking at those flowers. He lifted the arrangement with both hands, a calculated, slow movement. The flowers trembled with the motion. He turned and walked over to his mother's grave, knelt, and placed the flowers by the headstone. He stood, looking down, studying the flowers.

He squared his shoulders and walked back. Everyone watched him.

He stopped by a dark mound on the ground.

Mars stooped with his back straight, lifted it, and stood again, holding it like a flag in presentation. He looked like a grown man to Avery at that moment.

He shook the hideous thing out full and laid it over his father's coffin.

Adjusted it.

His movements were deliberate. He stood back a step as if to admire it. He nodded to the preacher.

Thunder rolled off in the distance. A light drizzle chilled Avery's skin, goosebumps rose on her arms.

Inch by inch, they lowered the coffin into the ground.

The bear hide rode it like a shroud.

After the burial, Mars came to the cabin. Avery met him on the porch. They sat on the steps.

"The juvenile protection people came and took Sylva away. She screamed until her voice was gone, but they took her anyway," he said.

They were alone for the first time, sitting on the little porch of the cabin by the creek. The day faded into a misty twilight.

"Why did they take Sylva away?"

"Well, seems they had several reasons. She killed Hunter, so she'll stand trial, I guess."

"She was protecting me and herself. It was self-defense."

"I know, but still, in the eyes of the law I don't think it's okay to kill somebody just because they're hurting you. I don't understand it any better than you do." His elbows were on his knees and he studied the ground before him.

"She can't go to jail. They wouldn't . . ." Avery couldn't even think the thought. How could she go on with the lie?

"Probably juvenile detention. She's underage and she's an orphan now."

"She's almost grown," Avery said. "She could live with Wayne and Echo."

"She's an orphan in the eyes of the state," he said. "They would have taken Shelby too, but Echo told them he was her boy. Quick thinking."

"Will they take you?"

"I'm working. Going to college in a month. Old enough to be on my own." He put his arm around her, drew her to him.

"Childhood is over for you," Avery said. She wanted to at least tell Mars the truth, but the thought paralyzed her.

"For all of us."

"I don't think we'll ever come back to Crowfoot Ridge. I might not ever see you again." Avery started crying. She had held it back as long as possible.

"I'll never forget you, Avery, not ever, not as long as I live. But you must leave and never come back. Go to school. Live normal," he said, holding her close.

They walked down to the creek arm in arm.

"I have to live without you too, Avery," he said. "We have to accept it. I'm going now. I'm driving back to Fontana tonight. You don't want this, my life, my family. Avery, I know you don't. Better things wait for you."

"No, Mars." Tears ran down her cheeks. "We'll write. We'll keep in touch. We'll see each other again."

"I can't," Mars said. "I won't write to you. I have to let you go. Don't you understand? I'd only hurt you more."

"No, you wouldn't ever hurt me." Avery couldn't believe her ears.

"Kiss me good-bye, Avery. And then forget me forever. I'm no good for you. I have bad blood flowing in my veins."

"I'll never forget you. I'll never stop loving you."

"It stops now. Hear me. It's over."

Her blood drained away, her heart stopped, no breath filled her lungs, no sound reached her ears, no birds sang, no breeze blew in the low branches, everything shut down. She couldn't fight for him, not with the weight of the lie so heavy.

One last kiss. Her tears streamed down her face and left her speechless.

He left Avery standing by the creek, trembling and limp. He climbed into the van. Avery was in shock. Couldn't breathe. She followed the van to the road and watched until it went around the bend, out of sight.

"I want to go home," Avery told her mother. "Why can't we just leave now?"

"Because the police asked your father to make a statement before he leaves. He's doing everything he can to protect you, so you won't have to go down there. We'll leave in the morning," Avery's mother said. "I'm taking Bobby and Shelby to see

Mary Poppins this afternoon. Echo is helping Wayne with something, and the boys can use the diversion. Go with us. It'll take your mind off things."

Her mind couldn't get itself around everything. Hate consumed her when she remembered what Hunter did. But she shouldn't have killed him and then lied about it. She never should have let Sylva take the blame. And then to lose Mars forever and her best friend all at once. Payment for murder? Payment for the lies?

His last words lingered and killed her even more. He didn't love her. Their passion had drowned anyway in the tragedy of these events. All hope and joy had gone out of her. He was thinking about his future. She didn't have one to think about.

He was right, and she knew it. But knowing didn't ease the hurt or hide her jagged breaths. Tears filled her eyes with no warning. How could she have ever faced him again in any case? How could she ever face Sylva again?

The silly movie made her want to scream. She shut it out so she could concentrate on her misery.

The next morning as they were packing the car to leave, Echo came over to MacKinsey's Farm to talk to Mr. Baldwin. Avery listened from the porch of the cabin.

"Mr. Baldwin, they've arrested Wayne," Echo said.

"For what? He had nothing to do with his father's

death. He was in Fontana. And Sylva confessed."

"No," Echo said. "When the police were at the farm, investigating Hunter's death, they saw the marijuana plants growing in the field and in the barn drying. It's against the law to grow it and to sell it. Now he's being charged with possession and dealing in a controlled substance."

"Jesus," Mr. Baldwin said. "I swear I can't believe this. Added to everything else. He'll do time, I feel sure. What was he doing with marijuana?"

"What should I do?" Echo asked. She paced beside the truck.

"I can't tell you. My heart goes out to you. See if Charlotte and her husband will move back to the farm."

Avery knew Charlotte and Wiley weren't married. She knew more than she could ever admit about a lot of things. Poor Wayne was in jail for growing some bushes, while she was getting away with murder.

"Yes, of course. I'm not thinking straight," Echo said. "Thank you, Mr. Baldwin. I'll go talk to them now."

She left in Wayne's truck.

"What does all this mean?" Avery asked when he returned to the porch.

"Did you know they were growing marijuana?"

"They were trying to survive," Avery said.

"You knew, then?"

"I didn't know it was against the law any more than growing tobacco is against the law," Avery lied, waiting to see if he believed it.

Then she asked, "What will happen to Sylva?"

"They won't know for months. The wheels of justice turn slowly."

Avery was learning to lie well. Surprising how easy it was.

But what would be the cost?

She stood alone looking toward the Marshall farm. She wanted to run down the path under a shimmering sun and find Sylva in the barn with Mars, maybe playing with puppies or telling ghost stories or cleaning the dried leaves. She wanted everything to be the same, for everyone to be eight years old again, for Mars to be a skinny boy, and Sylva to be a little girl. Avery knew she'd never run on the path again, never skip over the submerged boulder, never yell for Sylva from the road, never hold Mars in her arms or feel his warmth.

Daisies nodded along the road, corn grew in the field, but the path was empty. The void screamed in her ears. Avery wrapped her loneliness in a package of pain and buried it deep inside her soul.

What, indeed, would the cost be?

12

People were dying, children crying, bombs exploding all over the world on television as Adam was bringing his suitcases and boxes into the living room. His ride pulled up out front and honked. Avery switched the channel, as her parents helped Adam haul his stuff out to the car. A rocket blasted off into outer space from up the coast at Cape Canaveral, while Adam blasted off to the university. She changed the channel again and found a stupid movie. The movies playing in her head were better.

She paced by the mailbox for an hour every day letting anticipation build. Her heart pounded when the mail delivery jeep rounded the corner and made its way from one house to the next.

"Nothing for you today, Avery," the mail lady would say as she handed over the stack. Avery rifled through it anyway. Twenty-three hours of hope everyday reduced to an hour of debilitating disappointment.

At school, she slouched at her desk daydreaming or hovered over a notebook while fuzzy lectures played out around her. She wrote Mars Marshall, Mars and Avery Marshall, Mr. and Mrs. Mars Marshall, just to see how it looked, and covered the page with her arm. The kids talked about football games while she tried to focus on the happy times at AMAS Falls. She ran the path in her mind skipping over every root and stone, knowing every uphill slope, every downhill slant. Her grades dropped. No one noticed. She thanked God the swim team had accepted her once again even though her diminished skills confused the coach.

Alone in her room at night, she wrote letters to Sylva and Mars, labored over each word, but had no addresses, and wouldn't have mailed them anyway. She committed her growing fear to her journal and then never let it out of her sight.

The nightmares began with the bear hide riding the coffin into the ground and Hunter's hands on her, his breath mixed with the scent of gunpowder. She imagined Sylva in prison or some rat-infested asylum she'd seen in a movie. Her piercing screams brought her parents running into her room in the dead of night.

Avery sat on the bed one morning, legs crossed Indian-style, doubled over. She hugged her stomach and rocked.

"Come on, Avery, you'll miss the bus," her mother called from the kitchen. "Your breakfast is getting cold." Same phrase every morning. This morning Avery wouldn't dash down the hall, snatch a muffin, and hurry off to school. The thought of food turned her silence into a moan.

"I'm sick, Mother, I'm not going to school."

"You don't go to school, you don't go to the swim meet this afternoon." The voice approached, closer, from the hall.

Avery dreaded what she had to do. She held the locket dangling from her neck, stroked the heart, as she'd done a million times, for luck, for comfort, for courage.

Aproned, ironed, prim, tucked, starched, and familiar, her mother stood in the doorway to Avery's room.

Avery groaned. She cupped her grandmother's locket in her palm.

"What is it?" Her mother's face showed concern. "Your period? Cramps?"

Avery wanted to die. She couldn't say what had to be said.

Her mother waited with her arms crossed over her middle. "Well?" Slight irritation. "I don't want to drive you."

"Mother, I'm sick I said. I'm not going." Avery looked up into her mother's eyes, brushed her own hair away from her face. She jumped up and ran for the bathroom. Her mother followed and watched Avery retch up nothing from an empty stomach. She held a washcloth under the tap, mopped Avery's face with it.

"It's probably the flu, dear."

Avery coughed and took a sip of water.

"I'm sick as a cow."

Mrs. Baldwin's expression didn't change.

"Come on, Avery, tell me what's wrong."

"I haven't had my period since July, Mother, and my boobs are sore. I think I'm pregnant."

"That doesn't necessarily mean . . . I'll take you to the doctor. How could you possibly be? You can't be pregnant, child."

Avery went back to her bed, tucked her legs under the sheet. Her mother sat next to her, searching her daughter's eyes for something else. Avery knew there wouldn't be any hysterics, knew her mother would deal with this just like everything else. Deal with it, then sweep it under the rug, never to be mentioned again.

"I lied, Mother. Hunter Marshall raped me."

She gasped. "Why did you lie? Why couldn't you tell us? We would have taken you to the hospital if we'd known."

"Exactly. I knew you would. I didn't want anybody else poking at me. Looking at me." Avery told only part of the truth. "Everything was bad enough."

"My God, Avery." Mrs. Baldwin's voice faltered, winced. "You mean he actually . . . and what happened? Then Sylva killed him?" Her eyes reflected the awful realization and dawning ramifications.

She nodded with her face down, hidden in her hair.

"It was bad enough, him being dead and all," she said. "I just couldn't tell everything. I never thought this would happen." Avery had cried all her tears already, none were left. She covered her face with both hands in shame.

Her mother held her, rocked her. "Shhh . . . it'll be okay. It's not your fault. We have options. I'll talk to your father tonight."

"Please don't tell Daddy."

"Sleep a little while, dear." Mrs. Baldwin patted her daughter. "I'll call the school and tell them you're sick." She got up and went to the door.

"Call Coach, too. Tell him I'll never be back."

"I'll tell him you're sick, for now. We will take you to the doctor for a test."

Avery curled into the fetal position and hugged a pillow. Now this part of the truth was out. She'd miss the swim meet, all the swim meets, not just this afternoon. Swimming was the one thing she could do well. The one thing that made her a little okay. The ribbons she'd won were pinned up on the corkboard in her bedroom above her desk.

Her father would be home at six, ten hours to figure out how to face him. Three months' pregnant, a senior in high school, and her life was over. She thanked God Adam was away at the university. He'd have made some stink about this, humiliated her to death, no doubt. She pulled the covers up, an attempt to be invisible. The terror of the summer hadn't been enough, oh no, now she'd have to endure something more horrible than what had happened at Crowfoot Ridge. She shuddered. She wanted Sylva and Mars with her now. Oh God, Mars. What if . . . she couldn't even think it. She dismissed it. Mars used protection. Hunter didn't.

A soft rap at the door disturbed her thoughts.

"Avery, you want something to eat?" Her mother brought a tray in and put it on the bed. Her eyes were red and swollen. A bowl of mushroom soup steamed, surrounded by a grilled cheese sandwich cut into triangles.

Avery sat up. "What time is it?"

"Four."

"I must have slept awhile. Oh, God, two more hours."

"Eat, dear."

Avery picked up the spoon, the last meal of a criminal condemned to die at six o'clock. Maybe he'd be late. No, that would be worse.

"Mother?" Avery paused. "What's going to happen to me?"

"I think it's best if I tell your father alone. It'll be easier for both of you. We'll have to make some decisions, figure out what's best for you. He loves you, dear. He'll want to do what's best."

"I'll have to face him sooner or later."

"It'll be okay, we'll take care of you. I'm so sorry, but everything will work out." Mrs. Baldwin opened the curtains; the afternoon sunlight spilled into the room. Four o'clock, the hottest part of an October day in Florida, but the air-conditioned room defied the heat. Avery's mother stopped at the door, looked back, and said, "You've had some phone calls. I didn't think you wanted to talk to anyone." She went out.

Mother, the decision maker. Avery couldn't remember ever making a decision about anything in her life, except at Crowfoot Ridge, and those decisions weren't any good. The conspiracy she and Sylva conceived was terrible. Not telling the whole truth was the same as lying, and telling lies just made everything worse.

The front door complained when opened. Avery heard it and stiffened, felt the tension ride up her spine. She glanced at the clock: five after six. She tried to take a breath but couldn't. She heard her parents talking about what would be for dinner.

She got out of bed, went into the bathroom, and turned the shower on.

"Hello, Budlet," her father called through the bathroom door. "How's my girl?"

"Fine, Daddy."

Avery stood under the hot water willing it to wash away the guilt. At least she could delay what couldn't be delayed much longer. She lingered in the shower until the hot water was about gone. She didn't know what she'd face when she went into the kitchen.

Her mother was transferring rice from the pot to the serving plate. Her father was sitting in his usual place, sipping a highball.

"How was the meet?" he asked.

"I didn't go." Avery sat down. Her hair dripped on her shirt.

"Avery was sick today," her mother said.

"Poor little Budlet. Are you better now?"

"I'm fine, Daddy."

"Adam called my office today," he said. "Somebody at the school has set up a trip to take some of the kids sailing over Christmas break and he wants to go. It's expensive enough having him in college without extras."

"I think he should go," Avery's mother said.

"They want five hundred dollars."

"Doesn't matter. He should go."

"You surprise me, honey. I never thought you'd agree to it."

Somehow, in the midst of trivial dinner conversation, Avery managed to eat. She kept her eyes lowered.

"You're quiet tonight," her father said.

"May I be excused?"

"Go ahead," her mother said.

Avery went back to her room not knowing when her mother would tell the awful news. She figured she would have to quit school. She wondered how people kill themselves. She sneaked into the hall when she realized her parents had settled down in the living room. Her mother was going to tell him.

Her mother's words were careful, quiet, even. Avery hid behind the wall, listening. Avery was cold with humiliation. What utter shame.

"We'll have to arrange an abortion," her daddy said so softly Avery could hardly hear.

"No, I won't allow it. She's too far along anyway."

"Why? It's the only thing to do."

"They're not safe, Adam. She could be killed, or maimed."

"I know it's dangerous, and, not to mention, illegal," he said.

Her mother's voice again. "We'll keep her here."

"We can't. We'll have to send her to one of those unwed mother homes." His voice was filled with tears. "I can't believe she has to endure this, as if it wasn't enough to be attacked, have a man killed right in front of her. God, will she ever recover?

And now this. I thought he raped Sylva, not Avery."

"She lied about it."

"Why?"

"She just couldn't face any more. She didn't want to go to the hospital, didn't want an examination."

"At one of those unwed mother places, at least she'd have some companionship."

"I won't allow that either. We'll keep her here, Adam. Do you hear me?"

"How can we?"

"She's almost four months along already. We'll have labor induced when she's eight months, same as I did when she was born. Didn't hurt a thing. That way we only have four months to deal with."

"But Adam will be back at Christmas," he reminded her. "I don't want him to know about this."

"He can go on the sailing trip. What a gift from God. We'll say Avery's sick, has a heart murmur or angina. We'll take her out of school and keep her secluded." She paused a second. "Then it'll all be over when Adam comes home for spring break."

"All except we'll have a new baby to explain." Her father's voice sounded devastated.

"No, we'll have her give it up for adoption." Her mother's voice was calmer once some solutions were apparent. "She can't take care of a baby, and I certainly will not raise Hunter Marshall's child."

Avery sneaked back into her room, crawled into

bed, and cried. Her father came in later and kissed her good night. Avery pretended to be asleep. She'd have to face him someday. He closed the door with a gentle click.

She shook her head, rubbed her eyes, told herself to stop thinking. She ran the locket back and forth on the chain and focused on her grandmother, Thanksgiving dinners, birthday parties, happy times, before. As always, the main thing was to protect Adam from any of life's little tragedies, shield Adam at all costs.

Mrs. Baldwin arranged for Avery to have six months away from school. She told them her daughter had a heart murmur and couldn't leave the house. Avery tried to commit her terror to her journal, anything to get it out of her heart, so she could breathe again. Concrete blocks weighed on her. Her nightmares ranged from mild to devastating.

Avery stayed sequestered in her room most of the time. Her father bought her a television set of her very own. His eyes were filled with her tragedy.

Her mother was stoic, gracious, her decorum rigid. She picked up school assignments and delivered homework weekly. The confinement was not going to ruin her daughter's life, not if she had anything to do with it.

Avery watched television and worked a five-thousand-piece puzzle after she studied. She didn't feel imprisoned at all, just relieved she had no one to face except them.

And the movies played on in her mind. . . .

Adam came home for Thanksgiving. Avery was not showing too much under loose shirts. He wouldn't have noticed anyway. The phone rang as often as the air-conditioner kicked on. He dashed in and out, stopping only to change from tennis shorts to dress suits for the parties every night. He'd been told the same story they told everybody. Avery has a heart murmur and must be kept quiet. He cared for little beyond the upcoming Christmas sailing adventure.

Avery hoped he'd be blown away by a hurricane in the Bahamas or sucked up into the Bermuda Triangle.

A letter from Sylva arrived on the first of December after Adam had gone back to school. Avery ripped it open expecting a note, found a long typed letter. "Thank God, thank God," she repeated as she began to read the quivering pages.

My dear best friend Avery:
I'm living at the Blue Ridge School for Girls now. It's a wonderful place. You'll never know how happy I am. I live in a dormitory with seven other girls, all my same age. They are my friends. We eat in a dining hall. The place has pretty lawns and many activities. I've even been getting counseling with a nun named Sister Margarita. And as you can see I have learned to type. Finally found something I could do.

I hope you are happy and doing good. Getting sent to this place was the best thing ever happened to me. They said it was an accident and sent me here because I'm an orphan. I got to go home for Thanksgiving. I will stay here until I graduate from high school. Charlotte and Wiley are at the farm with Yancey and Shelby. Echo still lives in the trailer with Bobby.

Donald writes to me. I saw him when I went on leave. That's what they call it when I go home, like being in the army. He talks about us getting married when I leave here. Too early to make a decision. He's sure stuck by me through all this.

My best friend here is Sally but I'll never have another friend like you, Avery. I learned everything wasn't really my fault. I'm still dealing with all of it. I'm learning shorthand, typing, and all regular school classes.

I saw Mars at Thanksgiving, he came out to the farm just for the day. Then went right back to college. He's having a hard time. Books cost so much. He refuses to live at the farm and commute, although the distance isn't so much. Without Wayne's help, he struggles. He still plays music, but just doesn't earn enough to cover everything. It's good he got to go to college at all, even if he doesn't finish. He likes carpentry a lot, says he might quit school and become a carpenter.

Wayne was convicted to ten years in jail. Everybody says he'll only serve five. Mr. Mac died.

We study hard, decided to use this place to the best

*advantage possible, because it's the only advantage we
may ever get. We feel safe here.*

*I thought I'd die when they took me away. But now I
know it's best. I felt so bad for having left you alone that
night, Avery, it almost killed me. But Sister Margarita
helps me understand things. I'm still so sorry, Avery, I'll
never get over it.*

*I'm sorry it has taken me so long to write, but it was
hard to know what to say. It was all so horrible. I hope
you are okay now, forgetting all of it. I hope you are
having a great year in high school. Please write to me.*

*Love,
Sylva*

Avery couldn't write to Sylva, couldn't tell her
what had happened, couldn't ever contact Sylva
again. How had this happened? How had Avery let
Sylva take the blame for it? How? Thank God Sylva
was getting counseling, had friends to share her life
with. How had all those glorious summers ended in
such tragedy? What could she say to Sylva?

She read the letter time after time. She held the
pen above the paper and never wrote a single
word. Best to let it all go. Mars was in college and
he'd never written to her. Avery decided she could
love Mars forever, all the rest of her life, and never
tell a living soul, never hear his name spoken again,
never see his smile again, never touch his hair

again. Her love would be her secret treasure. She would never forget either of them. They would go on and have lives. They would marry and have children.

Avery's life was over. No man would ever want her, no college would ever accept her, no child would ever want her for a mother. Mars wouldn't want her anyway if he knew the truth.

Christmas was weird with Adam gone off on his big sailing adventure. The Baldwins invited no guests, had no parties, no family festivities. Avery's condition became more apparent and more embarrassing. On the bad days, she thought an evil seed, an alien thing was in her, made her skin crawl to think about it. Then she felt life, a tiny ripple, and knew it was her little tiny baby. She hummed lullaby tunes and let her fingers caress her stomach. What her parents had so conveniently forgotten was this baby was her child, too.

Lack of exercise and days spent indoors away from the sunshine caused her to look and feel like an invalid. But somehow days followed each other like elephants on parade, holding each other's tails. January, February, and March crept by. The doctor arranged for Avery's labor to be induced at a hospital in Fort Pierce just ten days before her due date. Avery carried the child all out front, hadn't seen her own knees in a month.

On April fifth, Mrs. Baldwin drove her silent

daughter up the coast to the hospital in Fort Pierce where they didn't know anyone. An adoption had been arranged.

"It's best if you don't see the child," Mrs. Baldwin told her daughter, keeping her eyes on the road.

Avery said nothing.

The baby had been active all day, twisting around and kicking. Avery thought of the child as a boy, didn't know why. It was as if he knew today he'd be let free. In a way, Avery would be free as well. She could return to her young life, according to her mother. But Avery didn't think there was anything left of her young life.

She remembered the bright lights. She remembered her legs tied up and out, everyone looking, a new kind of humiliation. The sound of screaming either from her own lungs or some other woman nearby. They had her all doped up. Time was a daze of sleep and wake, hard to distinguish between the two. The windows of her private room proved night had fallen, though dim lights from the hall shone in. She was alone. Her stomach was not flat, but the baby was gone. Avery let out a groan which became a wail from the deepest part of her. A nurse rushed in and tried to comfort her. When that failed, the nurse gave her another shot.

The next time Avery woke, a hint of dawn could be seen out the window. She slipped out of bed wearing the hospital gown and padded barefoot down the hall to the nursery. The babies were wrapped in either blue or pink blankets. All the tiny cribs had names printed on placards facing the window.

One baby, sleeping under a blue blanket, had no placard on the crib. She knew he was her son. She stood at the window watching him sleep until she felt wobbly and blood ran down her legs.

A nurse happened by and realized Avery was near collapse. She found a wheelchair, helped Avery into it, and took her back to her room.

But Avery had seen her son.

Mrs. Baldwin insisted Avery act as normal as possible when she miraculously recovered from her heart murmur. She returned to school to finish the last month of her senior year and graduate with her class. She had grown shy, distant, aloof, private. A neon sign blinked on her forehead. She didn't think anyone had been fooled.

"People will ask about your health, Avery. Just tell them you're feeling much better and thank them. That's all you ever have to say."

After what they had been through together, it seemed strange to Avery they didn't talk about it. They just swept it out the door like sand blown in by a storm. Mrs. Baldwin's proprieties were the only important thing.

Gary Gibbons, a basketball player, started following her around at school. At first, Avery ignored him, but when he asked her to go see *Doctor Zhivago* with him, she agreed. Everyone at school was talking about the beautiful movie. He picked her up in his own car but came inside first. He talked with her parents with pleasant manners. His father was a lawyer Mr. Baldwin knew from the country club.

When Zhivago told Lara he was leaving her, going to be with his wife and family, he asked if she believed him; Lara looked at him, shook her head. Of course she didn't believe him. Avery sobbed into Gary's shoulder.

Gary took Avery to the beach and to parties. Then he took her to the senior prom. She allowed a kiss now and then, but no heavy petting, and certainly no sex. She finally asked Gary why he put up with her.

"I have this feeling about you, Avery," he said. "Some funny feeling. You aren't ready. You seem fragile somehow, younger than the rest of us. I can't explain it. I love this frailty about you. I don't know what it is. I know you've been sick and think I have to treat you with great tenderness. I want to be patient." He paused, ran a finger along her jaw. "You remind me of a wounded rabbit. I wish I understood it. Do you know what I mean?"

"I guess." Avery thought she was a hundred years older than the rest of them.

She went to graduation with her parents, graduated without honors. What did she expect? When the ceremony was over, Gary's family and the Baldwin family stood around in the grass talking. The Baldwins loved him more than Avery did. She appreciated him. Her parents adored him. He was the boy they dreamed she'd marry someday.

Gary and Avery spent most of their time on his father's speed boat that summer, racing around the bay, getting tan, exploring some of the little islands. Quicksilver washboard waves reflected mirror images of the buttermilk sky. If they weren't in the boat, they were at the beach. When he played golf, Avery rode around in the little cart with him. If they weren't on the golf course, he was teaching her to drive. Before he left for college in Connecticut, he took her to get her driver's license. He left for school the day before she left for school in Gainesville.

Lissa Caldwell was assigned to share the dormitory room with Avery at the University of Florida. If her guardian angel had been on vacation the last few years of high school, she was back on the job and working overtime. They became instant friends, the first one Avery had had since Sylva. Lissa pulled Avery out of the doldrums, dragged her to every school function, every fraternity party, every sorority open house, every football game, and even to their classes.

She taught Avery how to play Scrabble and bridge. She taught Avery how to flirt with the boys after the letter came from Gary ending their relationship. She fixed Avery's hair and helped her update her clothes. She forced Avery to study so she wouldn't flunk out. She showed her how to use the library. They took a tennis class together and found out Avery had no hand-to-eye coordination whatsoever.

"It's a natural ability," Lissa said. "You're either born with it or you're not. There will be other things you can learn to do. Tennis isn't the only thing in the world, you know."

"I used to be a swimmer," Avery admitted.

Avery was filled with anxiety when Lissa started dating Jack. He was older than everybody, had been in the war, and was at school on G.I. money or something. The two of them had gotten serious real fast. Avery was afraid she'd be back on square one. Alone, shy, friendless. But Lissa included her and invited her with them on their dates until Jack got so fed up, he found a guy for Avery so they could double date.

"Avery, this is Ken Kessler," Lissa announced as if he were a gift. "Ken's a senior and Jack's fraternity brother."

Ken shook her hand and flashed an easy smile. "We're neighbors back home if you're from Stuart. I'm from Fort Pierce. You might have seen my dad's trucks around, Kessler Properties?"

"I have, I think," Avery said. "And signs at construction sites, too."

"No secret where I'll be working when I graduate." Ken brushed his sand-colored hair out of his eyes.

"Ken's a sailor, been sailing all his life." Jack offered this tidbit of information as if Avery needed encouragement to like this guy.

"I thought you meant in the Navy, at first. I've never been on a sailboat," Avery said.

"Nope, not the Navy. We'll take her out real soon. First chance we get."

And a year later, they were aboard his father's boat when Ken proposed. His eyes were as clear as the sky and Avery had come to know his nature as direct and uncomplicated. She never expected anyone to want her. His fun-loving, breezy attitude was easy to appreciate. His arrogance and self-confidence were easy to envy.

Her secrets could be kept, her past forgotten, the baggage left behind. No one had to know a single thing about Crowfoot Ridge.

Avery wore a spring green bridesmaid's dress when Adam married Tammy at a wedding fit for royalty. Five hundred guests. Tammy's gown of lace and satin had a mile-long train. Avery knew she didn't want any such hullabaloo at her wedding. Tammy's family gave them a honeymoon in Bermuda for a wedding present. Then Adam entered medical school.

Avery wore a sensible maid-of-honor suit when Lissa quit school to marry Jack. They went to the Bahamas on their honeymoon.

Avery wore an ankle-length dress of antique lace when she married Ken Kessler and became Avery Kessler in 1967. Avery Baldwin was finally dead and buried. Lissa was her matron of honor, her only attendant. The service Avery fought to hold to a minimum was a garden affair with forty guests, no bridal gown, no veil, no limousines. A single guitarist played soft classical music in the background.

Ken and Avery spent their honeymoon tooling around Florida on his father's forty-foot sloop.

Mrs. Baldwin had called what Avery felt for Mars so long ago puppy love. Avery's attraction to Ken developed out of kinship, mutual friends, similar backgrounds, shared goals, and most of all, gratitude. Whatever remained of her feeling for Mars burned in her heart like a trick candle, difficult to extinguish.

Maybe puppy love was a once-in-a-lifetime thing.

PART
THREE

13

Avery drove due north. Wind whistled through the open windows, blew her hair, competed with the music rocking from the radio. The turnoff to St. Augustine flew by. Traffic increased and a light rain caused delays in Jacksonville, where a peculiar paper-mill odor filled her lungs. Coastal flatlands vanished under her wheels before she stopped for a sandwich, a tankful of Georgia's cheap gas, and a quick dose of the cashier's southern drawl. Pecans were bargain priced in five- and ten-pound bags. A hundred miles beyond Savannah, she veered west on Interstate 26 under a cool South Carolina sky. The air turned drier and the temperature dropped.

As she climbed into the foothills of the Blue Ridge Mountains, hardwood forests simmered in the late afternoon light, beginning their display of autumn colors. Colors she'd never seen in real life.

And this was the beginning of real life.

The highway dropped into deeper valleys, and the car slowed to climb the steeper hills. Colors intensified. Clouds obscured the western sky tinged with faint sherbet shades of delicate peach and raspberry. She drove into the setting sun on a curving ribbon of highway, watching the colors stretch as far as her eyes could see. No small bands of color surviving only at the horizon, this sunset wrapped the world and reached from right to left and even behind her. The colors deepened gradually from pastels into the deep floral hues of dazzling roses and golds as the mountains came into view north of Spartanburg. The first glimpse of these mountains renewed an ancient knowledge of belonging that lived deep in Avery's soul.

She switched on the headlamps.

A sign said twenty-six miles to Hendersonville. Twilight raced toward night.

Her heart raced toward the urgency of the reunion. She didn't know how she could face them. She didn't know where she would find the courage. Ashes of fear had devoured her, left a shipwrecked shell of a life. She'd collapsed inward in the isolation. Each mile lifted the veil another microinch, each mile lightened the load. A moment closer to deliverance. Even the uncertainty vanished like a puff of smoke, replaced now with the anticipation of redemption, of freedom, or at the very least, an end to the immeasurable solitude.

Windows at a bed and breakfast in Hendersonville opened to a dry, chilled night. Avery had driven eleven hours and walked the neighborhood two more. The feather comforter wouldn't have been needed if she'd closed the windows. Instead, she snuggled under it, tired and content. She could picture Sylva at age seven, Mars at ten, Sylva at fifteen, Mars at seventeen, and envisioned the Marshall farm, every blessed detail, and MacKinsey's, the cabins, the creek, the barn, the blackberry vines, the distinctive angle and pitch of the ridge. How many times had she sneaked a peek into her toy box and wondered where she'd left her childhood?

Hard to imagine Sylva as the mother of three or Mars as a married man. What were the stages of their lives? What had they surrounded themselves with? What were their memories? What current events did they discuss? What television programs did they watch? How had twenty-one years of maturing changed them?

The long drive, the long walk, the cool mountain air, the comfort of the room, and safety of the feather blanket, were as effective as sleeping pills.

The next morning, fog, not yet burned off, shaded

coves and valleys in mist as Avery drove toward Crowfoot Ridge. Dew-spangled fields shimmered on the familiar roll of these hills. Oaks and poplars had turned topaz. Maples were tinged with cinnabar.

MacKinsey's Farm seemed smaller than she remembered when she drove by. The once big hickory out front had grown enormous. Always summer green in the past, its leaves were now red and gold. The columns on the covered veranda were still white. Was Neco-wee in the kitchen?

The Marshall farm came into view, bathed in a prism of light, part memory, part real. Squealing childhood voices filled her mind. Skinny legs ran with awkward sandals buckled on tanned feet. Daisies salted the edge of the meadow. Framed in autumn color, the setting was even more beautiful than she remembered.

She pulled into the driveway.

Mist still gathered over the pond longer than over the meadow. The daylilies of summer that grew around the pond were gone, waiting to bloom another season.

She stood by the car a moment, then walked toward the now sagging porch, the doorway to her childhood. A slow-motion scene of one night of horror flashed in her mind. This was a place of spinning stories, of lies, of secrets, and of conspiracy. She stopped in the yard, not able to take a step closer.

A woman came to the door. Avery thought she recognized Charlotte, only because she was standing in this particular doorway.

"I'm Avery Baldwin. Are you Charlotte? Do you remember me?" Avery's voice was tentative.

"Of course. Mercy me."

"I'm sorry to arrive unannounced and so early. I want to surprise Sylva, but I don't know how to find her house. I stopped here for directions."

"Easy as pie," she said, then gave Avery simple directions. "She'll faint when she sees you. You can be sure of it. She told me she'd written to you not too long ago."

"She did. First time in years. How are you, Charlotte?"

"Just the same as always, still married to my dear Wiley. He's put up with a lot, don't you know. Yancey's at the Blue Ridge Community College. Never thought a kid of mine would go to college. She married young, right out of high school, divorced, then she went back to school. She's learning all about computers. A mystery to me, but there you have it. Echo and Wayne got rid of their old trailer and built a cottage out back. Bobby's in the service. We're just getting by like always. Plant the garden every spring. Put up the excess end of every summer. Cut wood for the winter. Won't you come in, set a spell?"

Avery backed away a step, couldn't walk up to the porch, couldn't enter the living room of that farmhouse, couldn't see the Buck stove, couldn't see any pale wall beneath where the hide had been.

"Don't let me keep you," Charlotte said. "You'll make Sylva the happiest woman this side of Pisgah. I know you're anxious to see her, but come back to see me now, y'hear?"

"Thanks, Charlotte. I will stop by again. You can count on it."

Five miles down the road, then left, up the hill a piece, typical mountain directions. White cottage behind a hedge. Modest house, well kept. Avery pulled in, put the gear in park, cut the engine.

Sylva appeared at the door, behind the screen, caught in half-light like looking through gauze. Avery got out of the car and walked toward her.

"Sylva?"

Sylva flung the door back, slammed it against the wall, and ran into Avery arms, screaming, "It's you, Avery, I can't believe it. I can't believe you're here."

Avery began to weep and couldn't stop. They wrapped their arms around each other and rocked. Reflections of little girls danced in Avery's mind. Mosaics of their youth played out in fast-forward images, a dream catcher, a dappled horse, wildflowers gathered in small hands, a kaleidoscope of spinning visions, sounds, colors, textures. The shaggy bear skin, shooting stars, fireflies, and fizgig lightning in leaden clouds. Rough bread spread with sweet butter and fried green tomatoes. The sound of laughter.

They stood holding each other in front of Avery's car until they were dizzy with emotion. Why, oh, why had they let so many years pass? Avery held Sylva's face between her hands and kissed her eyes, her forehead. Tears flowed without shame and Avery wiped them from Sylva's cheek as they walked to the house.

Sylva served coffee at the breakfast table in the kitchen. They spoke at the same time, then were silent waiting for the other, holding hands. They started a dozen conversations but didn't get anywhere with any of them.

"Tell me about your children, Sylva, one at a time."

"There's Junior, he's the oldest, sixteen now. He works part-time at the bowling alley, just like his daddy did. All he talks about is going in the navy, sailing off into the sunset. Maybe he'll change his mind. Who knows?"

"Next?" Avery stirred sugar into her coffee.

"Next is Joey. He's fourteen, in his first year of high school in Brevard. Don't know what will become of him. He's a sensitive child, artistic, like

Mars." Her voice still reminded Avery of warm fudge melting on ice cream.

Mars . . . his name brought a pang to her heart.

"How's Mars doing?" Avery tried to sound nonchalant.

"He's married. I think I told you. His wife is great. Everybody loves her. They have a ten-year-old boy."

"And, your daughter?"

"Avery."

"You named your daughter Avery?"

"I never told you? I thought you knew."

"No, Sylva. What an honor." Sylva squeezed Avery's hand.

"She's a sweetie, thirteen now and doing well in school. They're all at home still, but I think Junior will leave next year."

"And Donald? How is he?"

"He's good. He went into insurance, works for a State Farm agency. What about you, Avery?"

"I married after my first year of college, quit school, and went to work selling houses. Ken's a developer. We've started divorce proceedings. I left the lawyers to work out the details. We never had any kids. Too busy, I guess, doing less important things."

"I'm sorry. What went wrong with your marriage?"

"Nothing."

"I don't understand." Sylva looked puzzled.

"Nothing. Everything was just as it was supposed

to be. Until one day, I decided I wasn't living my own life. I was living Mother's life or somebody else's life. Your letter . . . No, it wasn't your letter. I wanted to see autumn here. I've waited long enough, don't you think?"

"It's just starting. You'll have to wait until the middle of October to see the full color. Can you stay that long?"

"Just two weeks, I don't see why not. I might try to find a cottage to rent for a few months. I'd like to stay and see winter too. All that snow you told me about."

"You've never seen snow?"

"Nope. Spent my whole life in the Florida swamp, or out on Ken's sailboat. The leaves are already turning here." Avery looked out the window. "It's glorious."

"Just wait. The best is yet to be," Sylva said. "How did you find me?"

"I stopped by the farm and saw Charlotte."

"She's over forty now. Can you believe it?"

"She just had the one girl, is her name Yancey?"

"That's all. She wound up raising Shelby, of course. Echo only had one child. You remember Bobby? He's in the service. It's so hard to believe, all this time." She paused, thinking. "You had a sailboat?"

"Wasn't mine really, it was Ken's, his first love. Where's Shelby?"

"I've never been on a sailboat. Oh, Shelby, he's

fine, living in Atlanta. I'll bet it's wonderful, sailing, I mean."

"You know, we really should have traded places for a year back when we were children."

"Would have changed our lives, I'll just bet," she said. "Come see the house, Avery. We've lived here fifteen years."

The boys shared a room filled with posters of rock groups and motorcycles.

Avery's room had stuffed horses on her bed, pictures of horses on the wall, statues of horses on every horizontal surface, ribbons hanging from a corkboard.

"A horse lover, I see," Avery said. "I used to keep my swimming ribbons on a corkboard just like that."

"She's addicted to horses and she's an accomplished rider." Sylva's pride filled her words. "She wants to be a breeder, or trainer, or maybe a veterinarian. Talks about nothing else."

The master bedroom looked out over the wooded yard, leaves turning. They walked into the yard, holding hands still. Sylva showed Avery her herb garden and mums in full bloom.

"Where are you staying? You could stay here."

"No, I have a room in Hendersonville for the time being. I want to find a place to rent for a few months."

Avery kept thinking about Mars, felt funny asking too much but couldn't stand it any longer.

"And Mars? You said he has a son?"

"Yes, Frankie, and his wife is the sweetest woman. You must go see them."

How could she not see Mars?

How could she stand to meet the woman he married?

Today was not the day to tell Sylva the truth. Another day would be the right day, maybe, Avery thought. She should tell Mars first or tell them together. Just not today.

Sylva was saying, "Go see them. He has a cabinet shop in Crooked Creek on your way to Hendersonville. He does real well with it. You'll love his wife."

Avery doubted that very much. Jealousy whelmed in her. What stupidity.

"Don't tell him I'm here, okay? I'll surprise him," Avery said. "What am I interrupting in your busy day?"

"Not a thing. I would cancel a visit from the Prize Patrol to spend the day with you."

"Prize Patrol?"

"Publishers Clearing House. They said I won ten million dollars. Don't you get their letters? I'm just waiting for them to deliver the check." She laughed.

"I'll expect you to share it with me." Avery squeezed her in a little hug, couldn't keep her hands off Sylva. "You look wonderful, Sylva. I'm so glad everything turned out okay for you."

"That whole thing with Hunter . . ." Sylva paused.

"I never should have let you take the blame for it. What must I have been thinking? We were wrong to lie. You paid so dearly for what I did."

"For what we did. Our story held up and my life was not ruined because of it. Avery, don't tell me you've carried any guilt around all these years."

"Guilt and secrets, guilt and lies. Did you ever tell Mars the truth?"

"I've never told anybody. You and I are the only two people on earth who know what happened. The reasoning behind the lies are as valid today as they were then. Everything I said that night is still true. You were a rich Florida girl, Avery. They would have lynched you. As it turned out, I went to what was essentially a private school for three years. I got an education which I never would have gotten otherwise. I'd have done nothing but take care of Shelby and probably gotten stuck with Yancey and Bobby, too. Much as I love them, they weren't mine to raise. I even had counseling. Some of the girls from the school are still my closest friends. I admit I suffered at first, I missed you so much. We never even got to say good-bye."

"Still, it was wrong."

"Avery Baldwin . . . it was not wrong. Anyway, I

don't think we had many choices." Sylva used her index finger to emphasize her words.

"I don't think you'll ever convince me."

"Did you have trouble dealing with it after?" Sylva asked.

"Oh, God, you'll never know. Nightmares for a couple years. And other things too, the bear attack, things stuck in my mind. I was in love with Mars for a long time, took a long time to get over him. Longer to get over what happened with Hunter." Avery managed to sound sane, but her mind was gone. Even after this conversation, she came so close, Avery couldn't tell Sylva the whole truth.

"Like all the misery I felt thinking Adam would come back for me and marry me. Whatever happened to him?"

"He's an orthopedic surgeon, spent half his life in school. He married. They have two kids, little geniuses, both of them. Private schools. The whole nine yards."

"Boys?"

"One of each. Adam the third, no less, and Ashley. I don't see them much. They live in Miami. Everybody stays so busy. Their wedding was the event of the year in Stuart. Lord, that was a long time ago."

"Your folks?"

"They're fine. Still living in Stuart."

Avery spent the day with Sylva and held her thoughts in check. They went to lunch in Brevard, then back to the house, and sat around talking until the children came home from school. Avery couldn't leave without meeting them. When Avery looked at Sylva's daughter, she saw Sylva at thirteen. The boys must have resembled Donald's family, no trace of Marshall in them.

"Sylva, I have something for you." They were standing in the driveway by Avery's car. "I've had it for years, but now I want you to have it."

Avery held her grandmother's locket in her hand, let it tumble into Sylva's palm.

"It was my grandmother's. Do you remember it?"

"Of course I remember it." She looked at it, questioning. "I remember you running the locket back and forth on the chain every time you were scared or nervous. I can't take this."

Avery said, "Open it." Sylva clicked it open. "That's Adam at about ten, and me when I was six or so." Sylva began to cry and held it to her heart just as Avery had done when her mother gave it to her. Avery hugged her.

"You keep it, my darling Sylva," Avery said. "You'll never know what today has meant to me. I'll be here awhile. I'll see you again soon."

MacKinsey's Farm was booked solid.

"People make reservations a year in advance for the leaf season," the woman told Avery.

"Is Neco-wee still here?" Avery asked.

"No, I understand she retired some years ago. Eight or nine years ago."

"Is she still in the area?"

"Cherokee Village, I think."

"Thanks," Avery said. "You wouldn't mind if I looked around some?"

"Make yourself at home."

Avery walked up the double-track path to the barn, stood on the fence, looking up beyond the blackberry vines to Crowfoot Ridge. She remembered their shadowy forest and the waterfall.

Crooked Creek was nothing more than a crossroad with a nursery, hardware store, and a diner. Avery stopped for something to eat. A string of bells jingled on the door. Most of the tables were empty. Two couples were over by the wall in booths. The radio played country music. Avery took a seat and read the blackboard: baked chicken, meat loaf, country ribs, chicken fried steak, steak fingers—she thought it meant people fingers when she was a little girl; she smiled at herself—mashed potatoes, turnip greens, baked beans, squash.

"Just a salad," Avery told the young waitress. "Iced tea, I guess. Thanks."

One couple by the wall started laughing. The other couple lingered over coffee. Three guys came in wearing work clothes, took a table in the center, looked as if they'd had a hard day.

"Do you know where the Marshall cabinet shop

is?" Avery asked when the girl brought the order.

"Up on Turkey Gap Road, half mile back, then right," she said. "Mars just left. You just missed him."

Avery's hands quivered. Her heart raced.

"Oh, too bad. I'll catch up with him later." She kept her voice neutral.

If he'd been in that diner when she walked in, would she have recognized him? Would he remember her?

She drove by the shop after dinner. His shop, a converted depot. There were two trucks in front, one old, one new.

The sign said: MARS MARSHALL, WOODWRIGHT.

Her hands trembled on the steering wheel. Her breath caught in her throat. Twenty-one years since she'd seen him. She'd spent all those years looking for life, while Mars had gone on and lived it.

She wanted to stop, but couldn't. The day spent with Sylva was enough.

She would sleep. Prepare herself.

She fought for a balance between caution and harebrained recklessness.

She would see Mars tomorrow.

14

A trembling dream, gone without recall, caressed the first moments of the morning, fleeting like the lonely call of a whippoorwill, the scent of leather, the taste of marmalade, a glance, a certain smile, a sensual thrill; Avery had never been more alive. She showered, letting the hot water soothe her shoulders, flow down over her body. She dried herself with a thick towel, aware of its touch and texture. She stood naked before the mirror and brushed her hair until her scalp complained. Her eyes were more green than usual. She added blush to her cheeks, then wiped it off with a tissue. She put on a long skirt and a black turtleneck. Then she took off the skirt and pulled jeans on, tucking them into her boots. She carried her jacket and went downstairs.

A table had been set with coffee. Avery helped herself. No other guests were around. The owner came into the dining room with a tray.

"Morning, Mrs. Kessler. Looks like you're headed out early. Would you like breakfast? I have some blueberry muffins here, but I'd be happy to scramble some eggs." She put the tray down.

"Please call me Avery." "Kessler" sounded so alien, as if it had never been. "A muffin will be fine. Thanks."

"Did you sleep well?"

"The room is very comfortable. The trees outside the window are so beautiful, such a deep red color. I was lucky you had a room available."

"They're maples, my favorite in autumn. We had a two-night cancellation. This is our busiest season. You'll need to find something else tomorrow."

"I remember, I will find something, don't worry."

"Would you like some eggs?"

"No, the coffee is enough. Thanks."

The woman put a muffin on a plate, handed it to Avery with a napkin. Avery had forgotten she'd asked for it less than a minute before, didn't know what to do with it.

She didn't linger, timing was important; arrive too late, and he might be gone for the day. A disappointment she could not endure. Arrive too early and risk waiting, being there, idle, and nervous too long.

Finding another place to stay might not be easy, she thought as she drove, should spend the afternoon looking at least. The chain motels out on the highway might have vacancies, though the meager morning traffic didn't indicate any tremendous wave of tourism. What would she say to Mars? None of her ideas sounded right. The diner's parking lot was crowded.

The older truck was parked in front of the depot. Avery pulled in next to it. She took cautious steps from the car to the stairs.

There was no preparation for this, none possible. She felt queasy and eager at the same time.

How would he react?

How would she?

She gathered her courage, climbed up the steps to the platform, and went in. She surveyed work tables and cabinets being built. A man bent over his work, familiar, but not Mars.

Wood shavings turned the floor to sawdust. Saws and tools crowded every surface.

The man looked up.

"Oh, are you Hoyt?" Avery asked, recognizing Mars's band partner from high school. How did she remember him?

"Sure am. May I help you?"

"I'm Avery Baldwin. I used to visit Sylva and Mars years ago."

"You don't say." He reached to shake her hand. "I can't believe you remembered my name, but I sure do remember yours."

"Is Mars here?" She steadied her voice.

"He ran off somewheres. He'll be back in a minute," Hoyt said. "You're looking fine, woman. Mars will sure be surprised to see you."

"I'll wait. I don't want to interrupt your work. I'll sit in my car."

"We'll be having none of that. Let me get you some coffee. You can sit in the office if you want."

"No, I'll just watch you. Is that okay? How have you been, Hoyt? Still playing music?"

"Some. Mars is the one. He plays in Asheville and even Greenville now and then." He poured the coffee. "Cream, sugar?"

"A little of both, thanks. The old band broke up? What was it called, Crowfoot Ridge Bluegrass?"

"That's right. Wow. Long time ago." He handed her the cup. "Broke up years ago. We get together and jam now and again."

"Unusual cabinets you're working on," Avery said.

"Alls we do is custom work. Mars is a genius, you know. Perfectionist. Best carpenter in these parts."

Avery saw herself kneeling next to Mars, picking up a little piece of sandpaper, rubbing it on the coffin he made for the baby Janie, watching him, rubbing the wood just like he'd been doing so long ago.

"These cabinets are different than any I've seen before, really beautiful." She stymied a jagged breath.

Hoyt looked at her. Did he feel her anxiety?

"So, where you been all this time?" he asked.

"Florida. And you?"

"Right here, I never leave the mountains."

"Does Mars live around here?"

"Up the hill." He pointed toward the back of the building. "He built a house up there by the creek, bought the whole place here, must be twelve years ago, fixed up the depot for the shop, and then built the house. He's got himself ten acres here."

Avery tensed when she heard a truck pull up.

"Ah, here he is," Hoyt said.

Avery put the cup down on the worktable. She moved to the doorway and watched a tall man in jeans get out of the truck. His body was still lean and angular, his face hadn't changed.

Her mouth went dry.

Mars glanced up at her. Then, he recognized her, was caught off guard, almost staggered backward.

"Avery?"

He took the steps two at a time.

"Avery? My God, it is. Avery, I can't believe this."

She was in his arms clinging to him. She couldn't speak. He kissed her cheeks, her forehead. Avery felt as if she'd been holding her breath for twenty years, and now she could breathe. His hands were holding her face. He held her back, at arm's length, a minute.

"Let me look at you, I can't believe you're here. Jesus, Avery, you turned out beautiful."

Her joyous tears interfered with an answer but she smiled and shook her head, searching his eyes. She wrapped her arms around him, held him tight.

"Mars, it's been so long, look at you, look at your long hair. How are you?" She touched his ponytail held by a rubber band at his collar.

His eyes, though, oh God, those eyes were still electric.

And the smile . . . she'd never forgotten his smile.

She looked up at him determined she would not tell him she loved him, not tell him she always had, and never stopped. Never forgot.

"I love you," she whispered into his neck feeling his beard soft on her face.

"I've never forgotten you, Avery, never."

"You didn't forget me?"

"Not one day."

They parted, still holding hands.

"It's so good to see you, Mars. You'll never know how many times I've thought about you, how I've longed to see you."

"I'm overwhelmed," he said. "Flabbergasted. Avery, you are a beautiful woman, more beautiful than I remember."

"I'm not and you know it."

"Have you seen Sylva yet? She'll go crazy when she finds out you're here."

"I saw her yesterday."

"Why didn't she tell me?"

"I asked her not to. I wanted to surprise you."

"Well, you accomplished that in spades. Might have given me a heart attack."

He collected himself and went inside. He spoke a moment with Hoyt, then ushered Avery back down the steps. They walked to the diner she'd been to the day before, selected a table, separate from the others, and ordered coffee. He held her hands over the table.

"I roost in this place," he said as he waved to a man across the room. When the waitress brought the coffee, Mars ordered two breakfast specials.

They talked the morning away, remembering everything, every word ever spoken between them. All of it. Not one childhood memory forgotten. Mars told her about his wife and son as he buttered an oversized biscuit. She told him about Ken, their marriage, the impending divorce, while struggling to slice the thick salty ham.

"Don't you need to get back to work?" she asked when she realized lunch customers were coming in.

"Not on your life, I want to be with you. What do you want to do? We can't sit here all day."

"Let's drive somewhere."

They walked back to the depot arm in arm. He wanted to drive her BMW, so they headed up into Pisgah National Forest. They sat by Looking Glass Falls and remembered AMAS Falls. They hugged and talked and held hands. They drove up to Sliding Rock Falls, found themselves there alone. Autumn was exploding all around, more so at the higher elevations.

At last they went to the Blue Ridge Parkway and drove along it for a while. Stopped for a late lunch at the Pisgah Inn, took a table by the window, and looked out over the mountains.

The day was cool, breezy, dry, tinseled with sunshine.

"Where are you staying?" he asked as he waited to pay the bill.

"A bed-and-breakfast in Hendersonville."

"How long can you stay?"

"I want to see autumn. Winter too. I've still never seen snow."

He finished with the cashier. They walked back to the car.

"Doesn't snow every year. But it will this year."

"How do you know?"

"Because the woolly worms are furry and black."

"Wearing fur coats?" she asked, laughing. "I thought I'd look for a place to rent. I stopped by MacKinsey's yesterday to see if they had a cabin available, but they didn't. It wouldn't have been good to stay there anyway."

He pulled off the road and they walked along a ridge, admiring a panoramic view of the mountains.

"Everything's full because it's leaf season. You won't find a thing, but I have an apartment you can use."

"You do? Where?"

"It's in the shop. It's noisy during the day, but quiet at night. I lived there before I got married, while I was building the house. It's not much, just a bachelor pad."

"I couldn't impose." She thought it was the worst idea she'd ever heard.

"It's not an imposition. It's empty and it's free."

"You don't want me right under your nose."

"Avery, that's exactly where I want you." His arm was around her shoulder. He squeezed her, held her. Almost by accident their lips met, and the kiss reached into her soul, deep into the past, igniting a passion she had not forgotten.

She pulled away and said, "Mars, no. What about your wife? We can't do this. I can't move into your apartment. Are you insane? Your wife wouldn't be too happy to have me there, either. Can't you see how volatile this is?" The kiss had left Avery feeling weak.

"I'm sorry. I didn't mean to do that. I couldn't help myself. I want you near me, for a while, anyway. I want to get to know you again. We can control it. No, Beverly won't mind. I can't wait for you to meet her. And Frankie too."

"I don't know, Mars. You might be able to control it, I'm not so sure about me. I'm not here to ruin your marriage or interfere in your life. I had to see you and Sylva again."

She didn't want to be meeting any wife. She was already jealous. Frankie, yes. Wife, no. Would Frankie look like the child Avery had seen only once? She decided she would never tell Mars about her baby. Never tell Sylva either. Why ruin their happy lives?

"I'll have to think about it," she said.

"You'll come home with me," he said, inspired. "Yes, meet Beverly and Frankie. Why wait? She'll talk you into staying in the apartment. I'm sure of it. You'll have dinner with us."

"I think your wife will think of a hundred reasons not to have me in the apartment."

Mars drove back to the shop, pulled in, and went up a steep driveway, almost hidden, to a house in the woods. Twilight shadowed everything already, due to the shortened days of autumn. The house blended into the woods, all the colors in harmony, sepia. Avery didn't want to meet his wife. She trembled at the thought. He parked, opened the door, took her hand, and led her up to the deck and into the house.

"I'm home," he called. "Got a surprise for you."

I'll bet, Avery thought. A bird squawked.

"I can use a surprise today." His wife sat in a

wheelchair, tucked in with a quilt over her legs. She was a beautiful woman. Her face glowed in the curtain of somber light. Mars switched on a lamp and the room sprang to life. Wood against wood was mellow in warm milky ambiance. He kissed his wife's forehead. Her hair was obscured under a cotton bandanna, tied at the nape of her neck.

"Look who's here," Mars said as the bird squawked again. "Quiet, Pecker."

"Come closer." The woman held her hand out. Avery moved toward her. "Sit by me."

Avery took the straight-backed chair next to her. She grasped Avery's hand.

"It's Avery Baldwin," Mars said as if she would recognize the name. "Avery, this is Beverly."

"Avery, are you the childhood friend?" She squeezed Avery's hand and looked into her face. "How nice to meet you."

"It's nice to meet you too," Avery said, faltering. Avery wondered about her illness. Mars hadn't said anything.

The bird squawked. "Kiss Pecker," it said clear as could be. Avery still didn't see any bird.

"Your quilt is lovely," Avery said. "Is it very old?"

"Very. It's a churn dasher. My grandmother made it for her wedding bed, hundred years ago near about." Beverly smiled. Avery couldn't detect an ounce of anything other than true delight in her expression.

Squawk. "Kiss Pecker." The bird again.

"We'll have to say hello to Pecker or he'll never shut up," Mars said. "Okay, Pecker. Come." The bird flapped down from somewhere high in the rafters, landed on Mars's arm. Mars made little smacking kisses at the bird's beak. The bird was silvery gray with snow white circles around its eyes and long red tail feathers.

"Kiss Pecker," the bird said. *Squawk*.

"He's an African gray parrot, not too pretty, but very affectionate."

"His name is Pecker?"

"What else?" Mars held the bird, lifted his arm, the bird flew back to the rafters. "He can't stand not to be introduced when someone comes. He'll settle down now. He's twelve years old. Can you imagine? I'll open a bottle of wine."

"Your house is wonderful," Avery said, and stood, wanting to explore it.

"Show Avery the house, Mars," Beverly said. "He built it himself, did he tell you?" She smiled with luminous pride.

Mars served each of them a glass of wine. First sip strangled Avery, her mouth was so dry. Beverly held the glass with both hands, struggled to take a sip.

He guided Avery into the other parts of the house. Every inch of it—floor, walls, ceilings, furniture, cabinets, every surface—was wood. Ashes were cold in the stacked stone fireplace. Mars pointed to a special old cabinet he'd restored, and a bookcase. She followed him up narrow stairs.

"Frankie's room is up here," he said. "Frankie. Prepare yourself. Got a strange woman here."

The boy turned to them from the bluish glow of his computer. Mars at age ten, except for the copper hair. Hunter's hair. How genes do squirm through the generations. Avery wondered again if her baby had red hair.

"Hello," the boy said.

"Hello," Avery replied. "You look like your dad when he was your age."

"Everybody says that. You've known Dad a long time then?"

"You could say," Avery said. "Computers confuse me."

"Not Frankie," Mars said. "He's a computer junkie. This is Avery. She's the woman Aunt Sylva named your cousin for."

"Oh, I know who you are. I've heard a lot about you from my dad and my aunt." Frankie stood then, came to her, and shook her hand.

"I've received a warm welcome here tonight and yesterday I spent with Sylva. If I'd known all this, I'd have come sooner."

"Dad? You cookin'?"

"Oh yes. I'd better get something started. We won't eat until midnight if I don't."

They went back downstairs and into the kitchen.

"May I help?" Avery asked.

"You don't have to. Go talk to Beverly. She hates television; she'd much rather talk to you."

Avery went and sat next to Beverly again, poured each of them another glass of wine.

"I met Frankie. He's a sport," Avery said.

"Everybody says he looks just like Mars when he was a boy. I don't know, of course, except from pictures."

Avery wanted to ask her what was wrong with her. She didn't, but Beverly read Avery's mind.

"Chemo got my hair. Such a shame, I used to have pretty hair. They say it might grow back, but it's been a long time now. I think it would have started if it was ever going to."

"Beverly, I'm sorry." Avery was sorry her thought had been so transparent.

"And what have you been doing all these years? Are you married? Do you have children?"

Mars joined them, and said, "Avery is thinking about staying a few months. I suggested the apartment. She won't find anything to rent this time of year."

"The apartment?" Beverly questioned. "It's been closed a long time. It would be a mess."

"No, of course not," Avery said. "I wouldn't dream of it. I'll be able to find something."

"You won't find anything, and anyway I insist," Mars said. "Bev, I could clean it up in half an hour."

"I don't think so," Avery said. "I'll have to think about it."

"Mars is right. Nothing else is available this time of year," Beverly added.

Mars went back into the kitchen. "Dinner will be ready in a minute."

"Now, Avery, tell me about your family."

Avery told the short version, not that any long version existed. To change the subject, she complimented their house, raved about it. Avery thought Mars and Beverly must have an extraordinary marriage.

Mars announced dinner. Frankie pushed his mother's chair to the table.

Frankie monopolized the conversation, talking nonstop about school and friends. He had his father's eyes. Avery watched his animation, his eyes laughing, expressive, warm. He was bright and sensitive, just like Mars had been.

"Pork and beans?" Mars asked. "Doctored them with molasses and some onion." Avery took the bowl from him, served herself. Then spooned some coleslaw on her plate. Beverly's meal had been mashed to the consistency of junior food. Avery thought it was just beans and applesauce. The reality of her illness began to sink in.

"Mars never forgot you, you know." Beverly's comment stunned Avery. "Did he tell you? Oh, yes, he told me about you before we were married. He told me about a very special girl from his past."

Avery was speechless. Was there a little trickery in her smile?

"Beverly, you don't need to be telling Avery such things. Do you want some more wine?" Mars offered.

"He's honest," Beverly continued, ignoring him. "He told me the truth, let me make my own choice. You're special to both of us, Avery, because what you and Mars had was unique. First love can be harmful, even destructive sometimes. But you two, you were lucky. I married him knowing the truth, and that's more than most wives can say."

Avery was embarrassed, wanted to crawl in a hole, and she didn't think she and Mars had been lucky. She wondered what else his wife knew. Mars refilled her glass with the delicate wine. Beverly took a sip, her hands were shaking, and the glass fell. Frankie and Mars jumped to help her.

After dinner, Mars took Beverly into their bedroom. He was gone a long time. Avery helped Frankie in the kitchen.

"Frankie, your mother's illness?" Avery hesitated. "Has she been sick long?"

He washed the dishes; she was drying them.

"We've known about two years," he said. "She has leukemia. They gave her all sorts of treatments, chemo and everything. I don't know what all, but nothing much helped."

"I'm sorry. It must be very hard."

"How's it going?" Mars asked, coming into the room. "Can I help?"

"We're about done." Frankie shut off the faucet.

"I should be going," Avery said. "Thank you for dinner. It was wonderful."

Mars walked Avery to the car and held her. All day she had wanted him more than anything on earth. In his arms, she knew he wanted her.

"Don't," she said, pulling away.

"I know."

"We have to get a handle on this," Avery said, her hand on his precious face.

"I know. . . . We will. Avery, please take the apartment. Come by tomorrow and look at it, at least."

"There's no way. I can't live here right in your laps. I'll find something. I should have looked today."

"But Avery . . ." His voice pleaded.

"I know. We can handle it. I will handle it. I want you here. I won't betray Beverly."

Avery felt crippled with emotional exhaustion. She needed to sleep. To think.

She left Mars and drove back to her room at the bed-and-breakfast.

She curled up under the big feather comforter with all the windows open. Visions of the day swirled around her.

*   *   *

The owner of the bed-and-breakfast confirmed the situation the next morning over coffee.

"The chain motels will have rooms," she told Avery, "but I doubt you'll find a small house to rent unless you want a year's lease. Then maybe. But the bed-and-breakfasts will be full."

If she wanted to stay—and she did—then she had no choice.

Mars accepted a hundred dollars a month rent, though with reluctance. Real trepidation filled Avery about moving into his apartment.

"It's not much," he said. "I'm sure it needs some cleaning." He unlocked the door and handed her the key.

Dust swirled in the sun-washed room when he pushed the door open. Everything was wood, more rustic than the house, but the same handmade style.

"Oh my, it's worse than I thought," he said.

"I can fix this. No problem," Avery said. "Help me open the windows. Are there linens?"

"In the cupboard." He pointed. "They might need to be washed. Take them up to the house. Beverly will show you where the washer is."

"Mars, go on to work. I can take care of myself. It's just as cute as it can be. I'll be very comfortable here. Thank you, I'll take care of it. Go on now." She pushed him out the door.

She spent the morning cleaning the little place.

A place he'd built. A place where he had once lived. She collected sheets, towels, the curtains, and went up to the house to wash them.

Beverly was in the living room in her wheelchair. The fire had almost burned out.

"Beverly? You aren't here alone, are you?" Avery asked, almost shouting over Pecker's squawking.

"Mars comes up every hour or two," Beverly said. "Pecker, hush. He'll settle down in a minute."

"I decided to take the apartment. I hope you don't mind."

"No point worrying about it now, is there?"

"Mars said I could wash these things. I'm sorry, Beverly, this must look awful. I'll take them to a laundromat. Shall I put a log on the fire?"

"Don't be silly. There's a washer and dryer through there, beyond the kitchen. You'll find soap and whatever you need on a shelf."

"I should leave." Avery backed away. "You shouldn't be here alone. Isn't there someone who could stay with you?"

"Start the washer. Then we'll talk. That is, if Pecker will let us."

Avery went through the kitchen and took care of the business at hand, feeling intrusive and awkward. She went back into the other room, put a log on the fire, stoked it some by poking it. The coals were hot, so the log caught right away.

"Add another, please," Beverly said pulling her

wool robe tight around herself. The quilt was over her lap.

When a nice roar was established, Avery sat down.

"My family doesn't live around here. Mars comes home often, and Frankie is here after school. We've decided to manage this way as long as possible, without outsiders."

The last word stung Avery like a wasp.

Beverly's eyes were charcoal black, stark, without lashes and only a hint of eyebrow.

"I'll help if I can, please just ask. Don't consider me an outsider."

"Why are you here, Avery? Why now?" A slight lift to her bald eyebrow seemed to accent the question.

The directness of the question caught Avery off guard. She struggled to assess the implication, if there was one.

"My circumstances in Florida deteriorated. I should say my marriage broke up."

"Yes, please be straight with me."

"In the last months, it became more and more apparent the events here, at Crowfoot Ridge, I mean, old long-ago things happened here. I don't know how much you know, but Sylva, Mars, and I were close." Avery hadn't even made a complete sentence, she didn't think. She was still rattled by Beverly's direct gaze. Her narrow face was smooth, perfect like a doll's face. She seemed intensely cold. Avery stood to poke the fire again, adjust the quilt a little higher on Beverly's chest.

"Thanks." Beverly tried to fix the bandanna, couldn't manage it. She turned her head to look at the fire.

"Are you cold?" Avery asked.

"I'm aware you and Mars were lovers."

Avery caught her breath. The realization burned. Of course Beverly resented her.

"Yes, well," Avery stuttered. "The fact is this. We had two summers, not even whole summers. We were together for a couple weeks the summer of my junior year in high school, and one weekend the summer before my senior year. Then I never heard from him or wrote to him, or saw him until now. That was twenty years ago. Twenty-one to be exact. Things were left unresolved way beyond whatever teenage romance there might have been." Avery swallowed hard, mouth dry as dust bunnies, hands sweating, the fire burning her cheeks.

"You mean you were only together two weeks? Seems you both have suffered for such a short relationship." Beverly's voice had weakened. She stifled a yawn.

"We'd known each other, been friends, since we were children. My friend in Florida said it all escalated out of proportion because of our youth, the distance between all of us in time and miles, and then it all ended in such an abrupt way." Avery stood. "Is there anything to drink? You want some tea?"

"Okay, thanks."

Avery moved the wash to the dryer and made tea in the kitchen, grateful for a moment to collect her thoughts. She took the tea out on a tray with a plate of cookies, a pitcher of milk, the cups, the sugar bowl.

"I didn't see any lemon."

Beverly couldn't pick the cup up. Avery realized and handed it to her. Beverly clutched it with both hands. It wobbled until she took a sip. "Everything's a damn trick now," she said.

Avery let a laugh escape, was instantly sorry.

"You can laugh. God, if we couldn't laugh, it would be a tragedy."

"I'm still sorry. I didn't mean to laugh. Do you want milk in your tea?"

"I can't eat those cookies."

"Why not?"

"They're too hard to chew. I'm weak as a worm and bald as an eggplant."

Avery could not hide a grin at least. "What if I dip it in the hot tea?"

"Okay, try it."

When a tiny nibble of the cookie seemed to be finished, Avery sat back, her mind swirling around the reality of this woman's condition.

"Are you in love with my husband?"

Avery froze, repeated the words in her mind. Her punishment for having loved Mars all her life was now concentrated in Beverly's eyes. The pause was agonizing.

"Yes, Beverly, I am." This may well have been the first straightforward honest answer Avery had ever uttered. "I've always loved him. But I didn't come here to upset you or your lives. I came here to try to find a part of me that was lost a long time ago. I don't know what else to say. I don't want to add to your burden or cause any trouble. I hope you believe me."

A loud buzzer sounded. Avery jumped, spilled the tea she was holding.

"It's the dryer." Beverly nodded toward the kitchen.

Avery went to turn off the awful thing. She stayed and folded the linens.

"The house is remarkable, I've never seen anything like it," Avery said when she returned.

"It's a work of art, a work in progress. You know, space influences the lives within. There's good space and bad space. Space can give serenity or take it away. I want to die in this house. Die as I have lived, in peace." She turned toward the fire again.

Avery noticed Beverly's exquisitely delicate profile. A pang of profound appreciation came over her for Beverly's courage and honesty.

"I hope we can be friends, Beverly," Avery said as she heard a truck pull up on the gravel drive. She took the cup from Beverly and clasped her hand.

Beverly didn't respond.

Avery took the stack of linens and walked out. She passed Mars on the steps.

"Hi," he said. "You okay?"

She nodded and hurried down the stairs. She felt him watching as she ran down the driveway, but she didn't look back.

15

October's spectacle of color turned more vivid every day. Avery drove through Pisgah National Forest dangerously unaware of the curving road and other traffic, her eyes on the scenery. When she wasn't with Sylva shopping for winter clothes, Mars drove with her to the parkway a few times. And once they took Beverly so she could enjoy the colors. For both women, the situation was awkward.

When Avery began cooking the evening meal for them, Beverly warmed to her a little. Cooking hadn't been a favorite pastime for either of them. They planned the meals together and laughed about not especially liking the one thing all women were supposed to love. But for Avery, preparing meals for a family gave her new enthusiasm. Beverly shared favorite recipes with her and even helped when she could.

So many things needed attention. Gradually, Avery took over the laundry and some cleaning. She wanted to be with them, to be part of the aesthetics of their lives, and to get to know Frankie. But every visit to the house was fragile. The mood had to be judged and respected. At first, Avery worked in silence, jumping if she rattled the dishes. She drifted around like a ghost.

Her heart bled for what they were facing. Beverly had told Avery she wouldn't live to see another autumn.

One day, Mars lifted Beverly into the BMW, and Avery drove up to the parkway.

"I'm grateful for what you are doing, Avery. I wanted you to know," Beverly said. "I don't quite understand your motivations. But when you cook for us, do the laundry, and just everything you do helps us so much."

"My motivation? I'm not certain I understand it either, if I even have one. It's no problem, not like I have anything else to do. I want to be with you, to get to know you all."

Avery knew she was stalling and in no hurry to do what still had to be done.

"What attraction do I need beyond this?" Avery

gestured wide across the windshield to include a panoramic view of the mountains at the peak of autumn color. "This is the first time I've ever seen this. You probably take it for granted. But for me, it's astonishing. We don't have anything like this in Florida."

"I don't take anything for granted. I cherish every day I have with these mountains, the house, and most of all with Mars and Frankie."

"So tell me, Beverly," Avery asked, "how did you meet Mars? You said you weren't from around here?"

"I was visiting a friend in Asheville. We went to hear Mars play. Later, he came to sit with us. My friend knew him from college. For me it was love at first sight, I guess. But not for Mars. We exchanged addresses, wrote letters, planned visits, got together when we could. I was in school in Greensboro, so it wasn't easy. He was busy building the house at the time. When he took me to see it finally, I fell in love with the house, as well."

Beverly seemed to be flagging.

"Are you tired? Do you want me to turn back?" Avery asked.

"Yes, I am a little. We should start back." Beverly yawned and rubbed her eyes. "Sorry, but I get so sleepy." She paused, then she said, "Mars told me once you influenced his decision to become a carpenter."

"Me? I don't know what I did." Avery glanced at her. "I do remember he was amazed by the Biltmore House. My folks took us there one summer. Sylva, Mars, and I, even my brother went along."

"What was it like? What happened?"

"The house is beautiful really. It sits in the middle of some forty acres of gardens, like a palace. We couldn't believe it. Sylva thought they must have fifty children to need a house so big. We went inside and looked into the different rooms. They have velvet ropes across the doorways, but you can see in. You can go all over the house, upstairs where the bedrooms are, down in the basement where the kitchen is, should say kitchens, because there are two. There's an indoor swimming pool, didn't have any water in it, but you can imagine how astonishing it was for us to see such things.

"Adam, who was always doing something mean, told us he'd seen a skeleton in the closet in one of the dressing rooms."

"Adam is your brother?"

"Yes. Anyway, we all went to look at the skeleton. Mars opened the door and it fell off its hinges. Of course he nearly died thinking he'd broken it. But my father found a carpenter who fixed it with no problem. I think Mars was pretty embarrassed and Adam razzed him about it. But Mars was thrilled to meet a real carpenter in such a fancy place."

Avery pulled into a parking area and turned the car around.

"So, we went all around the house, every room more amazing than the last. We went to the winery. Daddy drove us all around the grounds. We had lunch in some fancy restaurant. But afterwards, every day, Mars drew pictures of the things we'd seen. His sketchbook was just full of drawings, all absolutely exact. Rows of wine barrels we'd seen at the winery, the swimming pool in the basement, different cabinets and whole walls of bookshelves, canopy beds, the pantry, the big wide curving stairs. Just everything. He was definitely fascinated."

"I can see such a place would leave a lasting impression on a boy. How old was he?"

"I don't remember, maybe eleven or twelve."

"He told me about a waterfall you used to go to. Where is it?"

"I don't know if I could find it again, it's been so long. We rode horses to get to it, must have been up on Crowfoot Ridge."

"Mars needs you here, Avery," Beverly said, suddenly quite serious. "He needs your friendship now. He'll need your support later. There are no coincidences, and I don't think it's any coincidence that you turned up now. I've lived the most wonderful life with Frankie and Mars. They're more than I ever deserved."

Avery was stopped cold, again, by Beverly's directness. She didn't know what to say. She turned onto Route 276 and headed back. Finally, she said, "They love you very much."

"I had pretty hair, used to wear it longer than yours. It was thicker than yours is and much darker. I miss it."

Avery knew Beverly was living with terrible pain. Time after time, she was confronted with the reality of it all. She never knew what to say.

Beverly yawned again and said, "I'm tired now. I loved doing this. Thank you, Avery."

"No problem, I enjoyed it too."

Mars had been asked to play at a coffee house in Asheville and invited Avery to go with him. The coffeehouse was dusky, candles flickering on the tables, a fire roaring in a big stone fireplace. Recorded folk music played in the background. Most of the tables were occupied. Everyone had long hair and wore hippie clothes, leftovers from the seventies, Avery guessed. Abstract paintings crowded the walls. It was a mole hole—close, natural, mellow. Laughter washed over the music. Hushed conversations rose and fell. Avery sat alone at a table for four but not for long.

"No tables left. May we join you?" a couple asked. College students perhaps. Avery motioned for them to sit. "Can't ever get a table when Mars plays," the girl said. "We were lucky you had this one. Thanks for sharing."

"No problem. I'll save this one seat here. He's that popular?"

"Oh, everybody loves him. Haven't you heard him before?"

"A long time ago," Avery said. "He was in high school last time I heard him play."

"Oh, wow," she said. "He's a treat. I've had a crush on him my whole life and always thought he'd make it big, but he didn't pursue it. Guess he's not looking for fame. I have every cassette he ever made."

"I didn't know he made cassettes. I've been out of the state for a number of years."

"He's made four. They're great. I never listen to anything else."

"That's not true," her friend said.

"Well, right. Still. Oh, there he is."

Mars sat on a barstool with the spotlight on him. He strummed the old Martin guitar. The tone of it felt familiar to Avery. He leaned into the microphone and said, "Hello, everybody." His hair was loose around his face and shoulders, not tied back in the usual ponytail. A bandanna tied around his forehead looked foxy.

The crowd exploded in applause, hoots, and cheers.

"Where's Pecker?" someone yelled from the back.

"Oh, Pecker, he couldn't make it tonight. Had an engagement. It's a little too cold for him to be out this time of year," Mars said into the microphone in a soft tone. He strummed the guitar, looked at the ceiling, thinking. He strummed a chord or two. The crowd cheered, knew where he was headed.

His voice was casual and as friendly as his stage presence. They loved him, knew his music, sang along. The girl at Avery's table cast loving glances at her friend and at Mars.

"He writes most of it," she said. "He's so talented."

"I can see," Avery said, bursting with pride.

He played fifteen minutes, voice full of suffering, songs full of unrequited love, loss, pain. Everyone identified. Then he joined Avery, sat in the chair she'd saved for him. The girl almost died right then and there.

"Get a grip," her boyfriend said. "You'll embarrass the poor man to death."

"I rather like the adulation." Mars smiled at the young woman.

"Oh, Mars. I love you so much. Please, please sign my book."

He took her pen, signed her spiral school notebook.

"Well, aren't you the star," Avery said.

"Right. About one night four or five times a year."

"You're good."

"Thanks." He ordered a coffee.

"I want a copy of those cassettes I never knew about."

"No problem."

He played two more sets of sweet melodies. Avery loved being there, listening to his poetry and music. How much she'd missed, all those years. She could have been with him. She could have fought for him. Fought for what was right, for both of them. She should have come back years ago.

There are no coincidences, Beverly's melancholy voice said in Avery's memory. Can't have joy without pain. The pain of their twenty-year separation gave all this new inspiration. Enthusiasm. Energy. She might have taken it for granted, might not have been conscious of his disarming truth, his completeness.

Still, Avery held her secret. She'd found new strength with which to drive her life. Not Mars, not just using his energy. She felt as if she'd been asleep for twenty years, woken up refreshed, alert, and ready to live her own life. Mars's part in it was a miracle, not a miracle so much as just preordained.

Snowflakes splattered on the windscreen when they were driving back. A half-moon was shining bright, making the snow glitter like falling stars.

"I thought snow was supposed to pile up and cover everything," Avery said. "This is just making a mess on the windshield."

"These are flurries. It's not even Thanksgiving yet, still too early, but I promise you one good snowfall this winter," Mars said.

"I'd forgotten about Thanksgiving."

"We go to Charlotte's. They always do Thanksgiving, and we do Christmas. You'll go with us."

"To your old house?" An alarm of fear went off in her mind. She didn't know if she could go inside the farmhouse. Didn't know if she wanted to go.

"You won't mind going, Avery." He was quick to understand her thoughts. "They've done a lot to the house, painted, put carpet down, changed the furniture. We'll be with you." He paused. "You know what we ought to do before it gets too cold . . . we ought to rent horses and go up to AMAS Falls. I haven't ever been back, have you?"

"No, of course not." Avery thought it was a dangerous idea.

But he kept on about it for days until she finally gave in. They rented two horses at MacKinsey's Farm. While they were there, they walked around the barn, climbed up into the loft, and then rode up on Crowfoot Ridge. The hills were blazing in full color. The blackberries were finished.

"Do you remember the story I told about Jennifer getting buried alive?" Mars asked.

"No."

"Remember? We were up in the loft, it was raining. Adam and Sylva were there. Don't you remember? You were scared to death."

"I don't remember it."

"She rode up on the ridge and got knocked unconscious. Then they went and buried her alive. She haunted the cabins at Mac's place."

"Oh, I do remember. You said the madman of Crowfoot Ridge had gotten her or something. God, you were just as mean as Adam. I couldn't have been more than eight years old then."

"Remember when the bear got me?"

"Oh yes, that's one thing I'll never forget." She pointed. "Look at the valley, like an artist's palette." Avery reined in the horse, stopped to stare. "I lived my whole adult life in black and white," she said. "Now, I'm living in Technicolor. It's like I wasn't plugged in before."

"Why didn't you ever come to the mountains in the autumn?" Mars kick-started his horse again, and they moved on toward the falls.

"I don't know. Every time we had vacation, Ken wanted to sail. Sailing is his passion, his first love, so we sailed."

"You like to sail?"

"Of course. Although I never really did the sailing. I made the sandwiches, stocked the cooler with beer, and cleaned the boat afterwards. We anchored out and swam. I liked that part."

"You know, it's all perspective. People travel from all over the world to visit Florida. The pictures I see make it look like a paradise."

"I know. I love Florida too. But now it's almost paved solid. Either paved with asphalt or with sod, rolled out, manicured, clipped. There's no wilderness left, precious little, anyway. The developers have ruined it."

They tied the horses to the crippled branches of the laurel bushes and climbed down to the waterfall in total seclusion. They sat on the rock they'd sat on before, so long ago, and watched the water tumble. Butterflies fluttered yellow everywhere.

"Did you finish college?" he asked pulling a bottle of wine from his pack along with two plastic cups.

She traced her fingers along the AMAS Falls sign he'd carved into the boulder. Adam, Mars, Avery, Sylva. July 1962. "You carved this twenty-three years ago," she said. "I quit school to marry Ken. A lot of people got a lot of useless degrees. I got a degree of uselessness."

Mars laughed and handed her a cup.

"I didn't graduate either. Ran out of money after Wayne was arrested. Thought I'd study architecture but decided on carpentry, which I didn't need a degree for. First, I went to work framing up houses and then worked for a master woodwright in Asheville for years. Mr. Olsen—do you remember him?—we met him at the Biltmore House. He taught me everything I know, sorta the father I never had."

"You would have been a good architect." Avery was pulling the petals off a wild daisy, listening.

A long silence followed. Mars seemed to be thinking about something. Avery waited sipping her wine.

"Avery, can I ask you something? How did you ever get over what happened the night Sylva killed Hunter?"

She shrugged. "Not sure I did." This was the time, if there ever was one, to tell Mars the truth. So easy not to.

"I guess not. Something so horrible . . . you don't get over things like that," he said. His voice seemed far away.

"When you put the bear skin on his coffin, that image stuck with me. I can see it now. Most dramatic thing I've ever seen in my life." She turned into him and hugged him around the neck.

He kissed her.

Red flags. They backed off.

They sat watching the water drift down over the rocks, fall away. Avery wanted to go swimming, but it was way too cold, way too dangerous.

"Beverly is wonderful," she said as she refilled the cup.

"I know."

"Her attitude is incredible. She accepts her fate."

"She faces everything head-on," Mars said. "I

admire her completely. We've always been honest with each other. I never hid how I felt about you. Did you tell Ken?"

"I wasn't honest. I never told Ken anything, which was probably the reason there was never any real bond between us. I don't think anything is possible without the honesty. He deserved better. I filed for divorce before I left Florida."

"What you meant to me seemed too important to keep secret from Beverly," Mars said.

"To me, you seemed so important, I thought I had to keep it secret. Mars, how are you going to cope?"

"With what? Us?"

"No, when it happens."

"When Beverly dies?"

"Yes."

"You can say it. We know what the situation is. We've known for two years. We're thankful we've had so much time together."

"Can't they do something more for her?"

"She's refused any more treatment. They've done enough damage already."

Mars looked serious. "I was going to come for you. After she dies. I wasn't going to kidnap you or anything. But I was going to go to Florida and find you, somehow. I was going to see you. I'd made up my mind about it."

"You were? What did you expect to find?"

"Some peace maybe," he said, "forgiveness. I needed to know if you were all right."

"My heart was broken, Mars, but I survived. You made a good life here. Beverly is extraordinary."

"I know." Mars looked into her eyes. "Extraordinary, just like you."

He pulled her into a gentle hug. She lifted her face to see his eyes. He gave her a deep lonely kiss. He held her face, traced her neck, and moved his hand to her chest, touching her. He pushed her back against the rock, pulled her jacket open, and pulled her shirt up, kissing her everywhere. She kissed his neck, his chin, his face, his eyes, his hands. Longing exploded into lust without containment, and passion consumed them.

How could they stop? Too much time. Too long to wait.

Something rustled in the bushes. They stopped short and looked up. A deer moved toward the stream—so beautiful.

They regained their senses.

Avery pushed Mars away so hard he almost fell in the creek. She jumped up, scaring the deer away, and hopped across the rocks. "Bet you can't catch me."

He followed, catching up. She spun around, knelt to splash water on him. "Man, that water's cold."

Her fingers were red just from one touch. She scampered across the rocks, laughing. He chased, threw a handful of pebbles at her. They plunked into the creek. He caught her and tried to kiss her, but she twisted away and ran again.

"You can't hang on to me. I'm slippery as a trout," she called.

"If I catch you, I'll eat you for dinner then."

"You'd have to scale me first."

He started laughing and couldn't go on. "Come on, let's finish the wine and go back. It'll be getting colder soon."

"And dark. I don't want to be stuck out here in the dark with the madman of Crowfoot Ridge."

All of a sudden, Avery felt terribly selfish. The play had transformed them into children for a few minutes. Allowed them to forget the unbearable sadness. They went back to the rock and found it was no longer in the sun. The pool at the bottom of AMAS Falls was in shadow. They finished the wine, a little breathless, and without much conversation.

"Why did you leave Florida? Did something happen, other than the divorce?"

"Something did happen, I guess. I ran my car off the road in a rainstorm about five months ago. I swerved to miss a deer. You know, I'm not even sure it was real, I might have imagined it. Anyway, I was knocked unconscious. Afterwards the dreams started, not just at night but all the time, dreams and memories. Vivid images, like movies playing in my head. Maybe I'm crazy."

"Why crazy?" he asked.

"I feel foolish now," she said.

"Why?"

"Because I was reckless. Everything started moving in slow motion. Slow enough for me to focus. I felt an incredible sense of direction, a force to reclaim myself. I needed to see myself from the beginning, identify what I'd lost."

Avery took his hand.

A look of raw hopelessness came over him, and he whispered, "You'll never know how much having you here now means to me, Avery. I don't think I could have faced another month alone." He melted into her, pulled her to him, buried his face in her chest, and began to weep.

All the pent-up pain seemed to gush from the deepest part of his soul.

Avery held him.

16

The house Mars had built for himself seemed to have a unity of mind and spirit. After spending a lot of time in the rooms, Avery began to recognize a harmony and connectedness about the place. Fire crackling in the stone fireplace cast light around blending materials and textures like batik. Rustic though it was, she saw a sophistication in its simplicity. A refinement. He'd salvaged many materials, reused them in different ways, ingenious ways. Everything was handmade, hand hewn from the forest. Limbs, twisted as they had grown with bark left in place, formed the stair and balcony rails.

Every visit was one of discovering a new spontaneity or something whimsical about the house. Plumbing pipes had been left exposed in the kitchen, the counter tiled with a mismatched collection of tiles. A remnant box? The reused brick floor was set in an abstract pattern. A square pane of black glass had been installed as a diamond by the front door, a reclaimed stained-glass window installed lopsided in the bathroom. The ceiling was wood decking, vaulted, made from planks recovered from a cattle box car, Mars said. They were mottled, variegated, a spectrum of colors. A mother-of-pearl light played against the walls, always cheerful light.

Even Pecker's perches were built-in, three or four of them, made to be a part of something else. Upholstery fabric, table linens, and the few curtains were homespun fabrics, natural and undyed. No plastic laminate existed anywhere, no plastic at all. And the lighting was so hidden, so offhand, obscure, like dancing firelight, candles in a gentle breeze.

Filled with love, the house was, filled with humanity, giving off a complexion of trust, grace, and honesty. It was cultivated with conscious charm. It must have taken years to build and seemed to have been expanded many times. Exterior materials, angles, architectural complications showed signs of growth or maybe just Mars rethinking things.

Mars carried in a shadow box and placed it on the floor.

"What's that for?" Avery asked.

"Oh, just something I've been wanting to do a long time. I made it to put those carvings in." He pointed to a shelf where his grandfather's wood sculptures were displayed. He hammered two nails in the wall and hung the shadow box. Each opening had been measured to receive a particular carving. She helped him arrange them.

The house Avery left in Florida was a poor excuse of a house compared to this. Her Florida house was an example of her lack of spirituality, her settling for any old thing, her lack of judgment. The house Mars built shouted at the world that the builder cared and the builder was a craftsman. The builder loved what he was building. The houses Ken built said nothing more than this will do, prepackaged boxes for prepackaged people.

Avery sensed the same purity of design in the apartment too. Mars showed her how to light the Franklin stove, supplied small logs and pieces of scrap wood from the shop. It warmed the one room apartment well. The apartment was compact, convenient, and everything had a place. Cabinets and shelves were built into the walls. The kitchen seemed to belong right out in the open. The bed doubled as a sofa, all built-in. A reading light had been tucked just in the right spot. The skylight opened to an ever-changing sky. Windows looked out to woods at the back of the shop.

Avery thought the house defined the spirit within, just as Beverly had said.

Autumn faded into the edge of winter, leaving

branches bare and exposing the land as the under-brush died away. Sylva and Avery drove into the mountains to the Cherokee home where Neco-wee lived. Apart from the Christmas lights, the early decorations were natural things collected from the forest—pinecones, dried vines decorated with pine needles and holly berries, handmade bowls filled with nuts or polished apples.

Neco-wee was sitting at a craft table weaving a basket when Sylva and Avery found her. Her gnarled fingers moved slowly over the work. Her salt-and-pepper braid hung almost to her waist.

"Remember us?" Sylva asked. "Sylva Marshall, Avery Baldwin?" Each of them held little gifts they'd brought.

"My girls." Neco-wee's voice was wrinkled too. "How in the world did you find me here?"

"Echo gave us the directions. We came to see you."

"I'm glad you did."

"We brought you something." Sylva put her gift on the table. Avery gave Neco-wee a hug and put the gift in her hand.

She began fumbling with the ribbon, her hands unsteady. She opened it and found herself with a box of herbal teas.

"Thank you for bringing me something I can share with my friends here. It's best to have something to share."

She opened Sylva's gift, a box of candy. Sylva and Avery exchanged glances, smiled.

"You're both happy now?" Neco-wee asked.

"I am," Sylva said. "I have my husband and three children. But I don't know about Avery."

"Avery? You aren't happy? You should be."

"Neco-wee, the truth is, I've never been happier in my life."

"Now that's what I wanted to hear," Neco-wee said, satisfied. "Just don't expect me to make your picnic lunches anymore." She laughed.

"They were the best. Show me the basket you're making," Avery said.

She turned it around in her hands.

"Come back in about a year, and I'll give it to you," she said, "Take me that long to finish it." She laughed. "My mind races, but my hands can't keep up."

"Next time, I'll bring my kids," Sylva promised.

"Good girl. Tell Echo to come see me sometime soon too." Neco-wee smiled a sweet smile and went back to work on her basket.

Arrangements were all made. No choice seemed apparent to Avery. Thanksgiving was a blustery bitter cold day. She needed more winter clothes: gloves, boots, wool scarves.

She dreaded the celebration at the Marshall farm, but dressed and walked up to Mars's house. The cold hurt her to breathe.

Beverly was in the wheelchair waiting by the door.

"Avery," she said. "Before we go, could you help tie my scarf, maybe wrap it around so it's more like a turban." Avery knew Beverly was trapped in constant pain, fighting to keep her mind clear. She complained the pills caused dry mouth and fuzzy brain.

"Of course, and you could use some makeup too." Avery turned the chair around and pushed her into the bedroom.

"Mars manages to get clothes on me, but he doesn't do the little things."

"Men. What do they know?" Avery positioned the chair in front of the mirror and untied the scarf Beverly was wearing. Her baldness embarrassed both women for a moment. "Look here, I think your hair is starting to grow back." Avery ran her hand over the scalp. "I feel some very soft baby hair here."

"Peach fuzz, nothing more. Just fix the scarf and stop imagining things," Beverly said.

Avery wrapped the scarf around and tied it just right. She rummaged around on the dresser and found some makeup.

Mars called from the door, "You guys ready yet?"

"Not quite. We'll be out in a minute," Avery said as she pulled a chair up to the wheelchair and applied some blush to Beverly's cheeks, added eye shadow, and lipstick. "Your skin is so beautiful, Beverly, just needs a touch of color. There, see what a difference this makes."

Beverly looked in the mirror and smiled.

"I'm nervous about going, are you?" Avery asked.

"A little, I guess. Why would you be?"

"My last visit there was . . . I mean, it's been a long time. I'm silly, I guess, but I feel some reservation about going." Avery felt more apprehension than reservation, and the admitted nervousness was really anxiety.

"Come on." Mars sounded impatient. "Can we get a move on?"

Avery wheeled the chair around as she said, "Hold your horses, we're coming."

"How beautiful you look, Bev." Mars grinned and kissed her. Beverly blushed. Mars took Beverly in the truck. Avery followed with Frankie in the BMW. When they arrived at the Marshall farm, they parked and Frankie jumped out to get the wheelchair from the back of the truck. Mars carried Beverly up the steps to the porch, and helped her get settled.

Everyone kissed and hugged.

Sylva, Donald, and their kids were already there; everyone saying Happy Thanksgiving. Avery trembled when she went in, but the room was different, just as Mars had said it would be. Warm and crowded with people, the memories didn't catch hold.

She realized her roots were buried deep in their soil.

"So much to be thankful for on this day," Beverly said.

"It's a blessing to have Avery here too," Sylva said, hugging her old friend.

Sylva introduced Donald to Avery.

"I feel like I've known you for years," she said.

Junior and Joey, Sylva's boys, were dressed up, hair combed for the occasion. Her daughter, Avery, was a beautiful girl. Frankie was younger, but they charged him with deciding what music to play. Yancey was there as well, looking very grown-up in her early twenties.

The house smelled of turkey baking. The Buck stove was roaring, and they warmed their hands by it. The benches at the table had been replaced with straight-back chairs. High-low sculptured gold carpet covered the hardwood floors. An art deco lamp stood by the sofa. Charlotte served warm cider with a little rum, nutmeg, and allspice.

Charlotte and Echo had cooked for days, it seemed. The table was laden.

When Wayne entered, he recognized Avery at once, shook her hand, and said, "Well, well, the years haven't treated you so bad."

"Thanks, Wayne. It has been a long time. It's nice to see you again."

Shelby—Avery never would have known him—had grown into a pleasant and refreshing man. He sat with her telling her about his work and his life.

Avery felt soul-stirring love surrounding her. From such difficult beginnings, a family had formed, a true family, and she was part of it. The Marshalls had done better than she had, until now.

"Sylva and I went to see your mother," Avery told Echo from the kitchen door. "She wants you to visit more often."

"I do drive up there, but I can't go every day. She's never satisfied," Echo said. "The Cherokee Nation supports their old folks. She's cared for by the tribe. Her friends are there and they talk the whole day long, talk about the past. She's in a good place." Echo's great beauty had faded.

Wiley carried in an armload of split wood for the stove. The room was in shadow. The light faded fast at the end of November.

They gathered around the table with everyone holding hands.

Charlotte said, "Lord, we thank thee for this day, for the food we will share, for our family, our health, and for our good friend who joins us on this special day. Amen."

Still holding hands, everyone said one thing they were thankful for.

When it was Avery's turn, she said, "I'm grateful to have shared my childhood with you all."

While Wiley carved the turkey, platters were passed from hand to hand.

After dinner, thunder and lightning threatened a

downpour. Mars thought it was best to go ahead and take Beverly home, but they both insisted Frankie and Avery stay.

Three weeks after Thanksgiving, Mars put up the Christmas tree.

"How lovely," Avery said as she removed a cookie sheet from the oven. "Is it for my birthday?"

Mars grinned. "I'll bet you say that every year. We can celebrate your birthday tonight when we decorate it. Okay?"

Beverly decorated the bottom part of the tree, as much as she could reach. Frankie climbed the ladder and did the top part. The decorations were all handmade—carved ornaments, knitted or crocheted, things found in the woods and spray-painted gold or red. When they tested the lights, instead of singing a Christmas song, they sang "Happy Birthday" to Avery.

Sprigs of mistletoe were hung above every door. Candleholders were dragged out and filled with new red candles. Avery had made candy earlier in the week and, finally, the Christmas cookies. Every day another present found its way under the tree. And Beverly taught Avery how to make the famous pineapple upside-down cake, which was their Christmas tradition.

On Christmas Eve, the Marshall family gathered at Mars and Beverly's house. Charlotte and Sylva were sitting by the fire, balancing their plates on their knees. Charlotte's wire-rim glasses caught a glint of firelight and sparkled.

Pecker had started singing "You Are My Sunshine," keeping everyone in stitches.

"Why didn't you teach him a Christmas song, Mars?" Sylva asked.

"I tried to. 'Jingle Bells.' Pecker ... here ... sing 'Jingle bells, jingle bells, jingle all the way ...' If he had learned it, he'd just sing it all year. This way he's only wrong once."

Not a peep. Then, *squawk*. "You are my sunshine."

Everyone laughed.

"Mars taught him that song." Beverly's sentences were reduced to few words.

"Pecker has more personality than most people," Avery said.

They roasted marshmallows in the fireplace and sat around talking. Beverly was tired and asked Mars to take her to her room. Another downpour greeted them when Sylva and Donald were ready to leave, so they drove Avery down the hill to the apartment.

Christmas morning, it was just Mars, Beverly, Frankie, and Avery. Mars made coffee and served the cake they'd made the day before. He stoked up the fire. Beverly seemed very weak but joined them. Her wheelchair was pushed up close to the fireplace. Mars, Frankie, and Avery sat on the floor around the Christmas tree.

"Mars?" Beverly pointed to the package for Avery.

Avery opened the big box. Under the lid and under the tissue, she found the churn dasher quilt Beverly's grandmother had made.

"You can't give me this, Beverly."

"I want you to have it." Beverly's voice was dry, and she constantly moistened her lips. Frankie helped her take some hot tea.

"Thank you," Avery said, touched, trying not to cry.

Avery gave Frankie the leather slippers she'd gotten him. She gave Beverly a batiked silk scarf, long enough to make a good turban. She gave Mars a handmade metal bell, like a big cow bell, for the front door.

"I couldn't wrap your present, Mom." Frankie ran to his room and came back with a bowl of Narcissus already blooming. "I forced them, didn't think they'd bloom in time, but they did. Do you like them?"

Beverly hugged him tight.

Mars pulled a flat package from behind the tree and handed it to Avery. She tore the paper away to find a framed and matted drawing of the mountains, the sky, the clouds, the familiar undulating hills.

"Crowfoot Ridge," he said.

Avery couldn't speak. She hugged him around the neck, held him just a second too long, she realized too late.

Beverly sat with them for an hour before asking to go back to her room. Frankie took her.

The day wasn't so cold that they really needed the fire. They opened the French doors to the deck to let some cool air in, and listened to the creek alive with recent rain.

Hoyt and his family stopped by in the afternoon. Mars served eggnog.

Avery was worried about Beverly, as she seemed less alive each week.

On a rare warm, sunny day in late January, Beverly and Avery were able to sit on the deck awhile, listen to the creek, and enjoy the winter-bare surroundings. Avery was reading aloud.

"Time for a nurse now," Beverly said.

"I think so too. Someone who can really help you."

"My body humiliates me. I can't let Mars continue to care for me."

"He'll find someone to come in or even live in. I know he wants the best for you."

"We need help."

"Yes, Beverly, I agree. We'll get some help."

"Everything will be all right now. You know, Avery,

I've envied your friendship with Sylva. I allowed my life to revolve around Mars and Frankie. Not having a close female friend left a terrible void."

Avery watched Beverly's eyes, saying nothing.

"I realized this the first time when you helped with my scarf before the Thanksgiving dinner."

"Such a little thing and no trouble."

"I don't think you came here with any malice in your heart. Maybe you were looking for something in your past, a lost treasure, I don't know. But what you found here is a family, a home, and Avery, you have my friendship too. I'm lucky to have made a friend so late in my life."

"I'm the lucky one, but I don't see how you can accept me." Avery feared this conversation, its direction. She knew Beverly well enough to know something was coming.

"What do death and acceptance have in common?" Beverly asked.

Avery shook her head slowly, and said, "Don't, please, Bev. I know you are about to say something I don't want to hear."

Beverly laughed, and then she asked Avery, "What is it about the truth which causes you such apprehension?"

"It isn't the truth, it's just that you are so direct."

"So what do death and acceptance have in common?" Beverly asked again. "Both bring an end to fear."

Though weakened by the conversation, she continued, "And I accept you because I don't need to fear you."

"I'm glad as you have no reason to fear me."

And then Beverly asked to be taken inside. Avery rolled the chair in, realizing her knees were weak and her heart was breaking.

Over the next few weeks a nurse—Joyce—took over Beverly's care. Mars and Avery both felt relief, but also a sort of uselessness. A sense of death infected the house. The barren trees, stark winter landscapes, dormant and dead, waited under February's confused sky. And it was bitter cold. One messy weather system followed the other, marching in from the west, bringing either rain, sleet, or snow. Avery began to understand every great joy had a counterbalance in pain. For these mountains the joy of autumn was paid for with the gray mists of deep winter. For her, years of stoic denial, a particular kind of unhappiness, nagging like a toothache, were balanced by stolen moments with Mars. Her reason for being in North Carolina pushed to a back burner by the urgency of their current overwhelming reality. No thought of leaving ever crossed her mind.

Avery found herself alone with Beverly for the first time in a while. She'd made soup for lunch and took a tray to the fireplace, positioned the wheelchair. The nurse was out running errands.

"Joyce is a big help," Avery said as she placed a napkin on Beverly's lap.

"Yes, we needed her."

"She's very efficient, don't you think?" Avery asked.

"And kind, just as you are. You make Mars and Frankie happy. I don't want to think about Mars alone. I don't want either of them to be alone."

"They won't be, they have each other." Avery tried not to look at Beverly, concentrated on stirring the soup to cool it.

"Try to understand, I've struggled with your being here. I was jealous, then threatened. I was wishing you hadn't come and at the same time, so very grateful to you." Her breathing was labored and she struggled to finish. "Please, Avery, stay with Mars and Frankie. Help them for me."

"Beverly, don't. Please, I can't listen."

"I don't have time to be anything but sincere, Avery. I'm sorry my blunt comments offend you."

"No, I'm not offended. Your honesty is frightening."

"I see the love in your heart. Please, I must say this, you and Mars have my blessing. I've already told him."

She searched Beverly's eyes, shocked again by such directness. "What?" She couldn't hide her tears and managed to say, "Oh God, you're giving us your . . ." Avery wept.

"Don't cry for me." Beverly's voice was so sweet. Her eyes were such a dark chocolate and stark without eyelashes.

"I'm alone with this now," Beverly said.

"No, you aren't, you have Mars and Frankie."

"I am utterly alone."

"I'm so afraid for you," Avery said, not even trying to hide her sobbing. She hated herself for loving Mars, but she loved Beverly too. Both of them.

"Don't be." Beverly reached out with icy fingers to touch Avery's hand. "Don't think I'll see the daffodils this spring. I've planted them by the driveway. I love them so much."

"They'll be up soon. It's been a warm winter, everyone says unusually warm."

Avery felt sick and sat staring into Beverly's face, into her eyes, holding her hands. She couldn't say a word. She felt so filled with guilt, she couldn't move. So filled with the pain of everything.

"You'll see the daffodils. I think you will," Avery said as she stood. "I'll get us some ice cream."

Vanilla ice cream brought a smile to Beverly's lips, but she never finished even the smallest serving.

When Joyce returned she took Beverly into the bedroom to rest. Avery put a roast in the oven.

When Mars came in that evening, Avery sat him down. "You know we've hurt Beverly. She sees the looks, the loving little glances, the touches, all of it. I didn't want to hurt her." Mars was looking at Avery with a question in his eyes.

"Don't even look at me with those eyes of yours."

"I can't not look at you," he said, confused.

"Just look at me like a normal person, then. Mars, it breaks my heart. How can you stand this? Having me here like this."

"It's what Beverly wants as well," he said. "She told me she was glad you are here. That's the truth, Avery."

"Well, the truth is, don't look at me. Anymore." Avery got up and went to check on the pot roast. He tried to hug her, but she pulled away. "You aren't listening to one word of this." Tears streaming down her face, again.

"There's no way to hide what we feel," he said.

"We must find a way. Both of us. We have to. Now, don't look at me," she said. "And find us some daffodils. Some florist has them, maybe forced in a greenhouse in California or somewhere. I want fresh daffodils in this house."

"Daffodils?"

"Yes. Beverly loves them."

"Okay, we'll have daffodils."

Frankie interrupted and began setting the table.

Pecker started to sing from the rafters.

"Shut up, Pecker," Avery said.

Mars and Frankie laughed at her.

She didn't know how they had lived with this so long. How could they still laugh? How could any of them face her death?

And then Avery realized no spirit as strong as Beverly's would ever die.

17

How many funerals had Mars and Avery attended together, stood side by side listening to the words? Charlotte's baby Janie, Kitty, Hunter. The day was arctic cold for the first week of March. The frigid wind went right through them. They shivered. The sky was chalk. Snowflakes swirled in the air. The trees were bare without a hint of pale green on the tips of the branches yet. Must have been a hundred people there all bundled in dark coats, scarves, holding themselves against the biting chill.

No wildflowers. Not yet.

Most eyes were dry.

February had been warm. Avery thought they'd have an early spring. She was ready for the spring. March was already colder than January or February had been. Not what she expected. Then what did she know about North Carolina winters?

An ashen day.

Tree branches were black with moisture, stark, naked, curved, knotted shapes against the raw sky. Grief gnawed at her.

Her heart scalded her chest, wounded by the injustice of it all. Mars put his arm around Frankie. Sylva came to Avery, put her arm around her. Avery felt as if people were staring at her. What was she doing there? Ready to step in and take Beverly's place with Mars and Frankie? A place she knew could never be filled. Not by her, or anyone. Did they think she was his girlfriend? Long lost lover, diving in for the . . . Mars and Frankie joined them. The four of them held each other, pulling Avery into their circle.

Mars had gotten so many daffodils for the coffin, they covered it completely. Hundreds, all bright yellow, prismatic.

The words, spoken on the visible breath of the minister, separated, floated off into the mist with no continuity. They broke into fragments, a disengaged trance of words.

In her mind, Avery saw the deer family enter the meadow, drinking at the pond, nibbling sweet clover, heard the blast of the rifle again, saw the buck fall, and felt the guilt again. Mars telling her, with his eyes, not to speak. She heard Sylva's tears, remembered her pain. Heard Mars playing the guitar, memories screamed into her reality. Long-ago memories and recent ones, Beverly's dark eyes filled with so much love.

A blue jay landed on an inky branch—the first sign of spring.

The daffodils lining the driveway were about two inches tall, poking their little green heads up by the middle of March. There were clusters of them by the door to the apartment. The ground was squishy from weeks of cold rain. Hadn't seen the sun in a month, it seemed. Avery was tired of the damp weather, but the daffodils loved it. A faint hue of tender green, just a whisper of a blush of green, washed the forests.

Mars and Frankie needed space and time to recover from Beverly's death. Avery stayed in the apartment, reading one book after another, but couldn't remember the titles, the authors, or the stories. She went up to the house and cooked for them. Always went back to the apartment early. They talked about the weather a lot.

A knock at her door late one afternoon startled Avery. She expected no one. She opened the door.

Adam, the last person on earth she expected to see, stood there smiling.

"Adam! What in the name of God are you doing here?"

"Surprised you, didn't I?"

"I should say." She hugged him and ushered him into the tiny apartment.

"How in the world did you find me here?"

"You said your apartment was in Mars's cabinet shop, which wasn't hard to find."

"No, I guess not. I'm positively astonished to see you." Avery pulled a chair away from the table for him and stood staring at him, especially the silver dusting in his dark hair. "Do you want some tea or coffee?"

"I brought a bottle of wine," he said, checking his watch. "Oh, yes, it's time for some wine. It's in the car." He dashed out and returned with the bottle.

"I can't believe you're traveling without Tammy and the kids."

"Do you have a corkscrew?" They looked in the drawer, found one. He opened the bottle and filled the two glasses. They sat at the table.

"Adam, I'm just dumbfounded. Mother? Daddy? Are they okay?"

"Yes, fine. They came down to Miami for Christmas. We had a nice time."

"What in the world are you doing here?"

"Well, sometimes there's just nobody to talk to quite like your very own sister."

"Is something wrong?"

"Can't I visit my sister without something being wrong?"

"No, I don't buy it. I know you too well. And you're way too busy."

"I took some time off, just had to get away. The drive up provided some good thinking time. I needed to do it and I needed to see you." He swirled the wine in the glass. "Cute place you have here." He glanced around the room. "Unusual. I've never seen anything quite like it. Did Mars build it?"

"Yes, he did. You should see the house he built. It's up the hill behind here." She motioned and then tasted the wine. "He's a carpenter. Oh, I guess you knew. This is a nice wine. So, you'd have me believe you drove seven hundred miles to share a glass of wine with your sister?"

"It's more than seven hundred miles."

"Adam?" Avery managed to repeat a drawn-out tone of voice she'd used with him since they were kids.

"I guess there's no point beating around the bush." He took a swallow. "There is a problem."

"Is someone sick?"

"It's not that. Tammy's having an affair."

"That's hard to believe. She's always been crazy about you. I thought you had a good marriage. Are you sure?"

"Oh yes, I'm certain."

"What are you going to do?"

"Unfortunately I'm well aware she's been neglected for a long time." He sipped the wine again. "I've thought about asking her for a divorce, but Tammy's father and I are linked together in inexplicable ways. The hospital, the practice, and some major investments. He was instrumental in shaping my career. I can't divorce Tammy without throwing a wrench in everything. Of course, she might divorce me."

Avery was surprised. "I'm sorry, Adam."

"I'm trapped." Adam looked sad, older. The silver in his dark hair gave him a distinguished look.

"Maybe you could separate for a while, see how it goes."

"I could get a condo. Already know one I can buy. I can't leave Miami, of course. Certainly, can't leave the practice."

"I hate it when I hear doctors say they are practicing medicine. Seems like you ought to perform without any more practice."

"We do practice. It's such a gamble. We never know enough."

"Adam. Why did you come here?"

"I wanted to see you. I really needed to talk to you, get to know you again. Maybe drive around and see some of our childhood haunts. Talk about Tammy, maybe see if you have any ideas. Is your divorce final yet?"

"So now I'm the expert. It was clean and neat. I get half the house money, but as far as I know, it hasn't been sold yet. I've driven around the old haunts a lot. We even saw Neco-wee just before Thanksgiving. Sylva and I went."

"How is Sylva?"

"Fine. Great. She married Donald, you know. Oh, you never met him. They have three children, can you imagine? The whole Marshall family seem to be very well adjusted. Charlotte's still with Wiley. Echo and Wayne are still together, hard as that is to believe. They all made good marriages. They did better than either of us."

"Neco-wee! I haven't thought about her in a long time. I'm surprised she's still alive." Adam stood, paced around a minute, refilled the glasses.

"You didn't ask Ken for alimony?" he asked.

"What for? Ken doesn't owe me for the rest of my life."

"If Tammy and I divorce, I won't be so lucky," Adam said. "How's Mars?"

"His wife died two weeks ago. She'd been sick a long time. It's been pretty rough, but we're coping."

"Do you plan to stay with him?"

"If he'll have me." She sipped the wine.

"Is he around?"

Avery got up, looked out the window for the truck. It wasn't there.

"I don't know. He's gone, I think. I cook for them, Mars and his son, Frankie. You'll join us for dinner?"

"Let's go out. There's no need for you to cook, Avery. Where does Sylva live?"

"They have a little house in Brevard. I see her often. Coming here is the best thing I ever did for myself. I don't know why I waited so long."

"Every time I talk to you on the phone, I hear a happier voice."

"It's true," Avery said. "We've had an intense six months with Beverly's illness, but you know what? I felt needed, really needed, maybe for the first time in my life. I'm sorry about Tammy. Do you know who it is . . . how long it's been going on?"

"A long time, and yes, I know him. The whole thing makes me sick. I'm never around. I've been a terrible husband and a worse father. God knows, I don't blame Tammy. The worst part of it is, I really don't even give a damn."

He was quiet then. Avery waited.

"Oh, Avery, I almost forgot to tell you, some guy called my office looking for you. I have his name and phone number here." He fished around in his jacket pocket. "A lawyer. He said he wanted to talk to you about some property in Florida. Seems you have an interest in it."

Adam found the piece of paper and gave it to her.

"Funny he should want to talk to me." She put the slip of paper down under the vase. "I'll call him."

Going out to dinner that evening provided a diversion Avery, Mars, and Frankie all needed more than any of them realized. Adam and Mars talked their heads off like old buddies. Of course, they hadn't seen each other in over twenty years. Adam was interested more in the music Mars played than his carpentry business. Even seemed a bit envious. Adam admitted he'd always wanted to learn to play the guitar. Naturally, Mars told him it was never too late.

The restaurant was crowded and lively. They'd somehow forgotten life went on outside their isolated little corner of the world.

They went back to Mars's house for coffee later, and Adam investigated every corner of the house, very impressed. They listened to the cassettes Mars had recorded at appearances, audience in the background. His voice was simply wonderful, in Avery's opinion.

Adam spent the night in the guest room Mars had fixed up for Beverly's nurse, as there wasn't room at the apartment.

The next day Adam and Avery drove up to MacKinsey's Farm, walked around, relived shared memories. The dogwoods were forming buds up on Crowfoot Ridge. They walked up the double-track lane to the blackberry vines. Avery told Adam about Mr. Mac's exposing himself to her, how she'd felt when she went back to the barn. They talked about it some, about the other girls Mr. Mac had molested and how he'd died in jail. First time Avery had ever mentioned any of it out loud to anyone. She'd felt such guilt all those years and said so.

"Why did you feel guilty about it, Avery?" he asked "You hadn't done anything wrong."

"It was wrong not to tell." She looked into his eyes. "Not telling is the same as lying."

"Sometimes, though, not in a case like that." Adam looked up to the ridge. "I remember that day. You wanted me to help get Moonshine's saddle off. I thought you were a crybaby."

"I know. You thought I was always a crybaby. If I'd told someone at the time, they'd have put him in jail, and he wouldn't have bothered any other girls."

"Mr. Mac and Daddy were pretty good friends. You might not have been believed."

"No, probably not."

They drove back to Mars's house, spent another evening together. The next morning Adam was getting ready to leave.

"This has been good for me," Avery said. "I'm glad you came. It was good to see you. We didn't even talk about your problem very much, though."

"I had to talk to someone, and I trust you."

She hadn't thought about trust in a long time, realized she didn't trust him. Once trust was compromised, she wondered, was it lost forever? Avery didn't think there would be any divorce, figured they would work something out even if it was a business arrangement.

Avery walked Adam to his car when he was ready

to leave. The morning still dark, foggy. Adam hugged her.

"I love you, Adam. Just wanted you to know."

"I love you too, little sister. Don't think we've ever said it before. I always thought you hated me."

"What?" Avery couldn't have been more surprised. "I always thought you hated me."

"I thought you hated me because I took Sylva away from you that summer."

"Well, I did. And it took a long time to forget about it. The fact is you didn't take her away from me. She's still the best friend I have in the world."

"Have you forgiven me?"

"No." She managed a mischievous smile.

Avery waited as he pulled out, watched the red taillights until he turned onto the highway and was gone.

Sylva and Avery had been planning a trip to Asheville for ages. After they'd fought the blustering wind all day wandering in and out of the shops and boutiques, they settled at a table by the fireplace in a coffeehouse, both freezing.

"We couldn't have picked a colder day to do this. I thought it'd be warm by now."

"March is always cold. So, Avery, tell me about Adam's visit. Weren't you surprised to see him?"

"*Surprised* is hardly the right word. He never

drove three hours to come see me in Stuart all the years I lived there."

"He's still in Miami?"

"Yes. But, we all know doctors never have any time for themselves."

The waitress came and they ordered. Avery rubbed her hands together trying to get some blood circulating.

"Will you ever get used to this cold weather?" Sylva asked.

"Truth is, I absolutely love it. I spent my whole life in subtropical heat, remember?"

"So, how is he?"

"His marriage is in trouble. I guess it's why he came up here. You interested?" Avery laughed at Sylva.

"Are you kidding? Donald isn't perfect, but he's kind and good all the way through to his bones."

"I was just kidding. You know, it's funny, Sylva. Someone told me once or maybe I read it somewhere: if the first half of your life is filled with strife, then the second half will be filled with joy. Maybe it works the other way as well. Adam's early life was as near perfect as you get. He had it all. Somehow, now I think he's in for some hard times."

"Are your hard times behind you now?" Sylva asked.

"No, I'm sorry to say, it's not finished. When I

came up here I had a mission. I wanted to tell the whole truth about everything. I haven't had the courage to face anything, to say anything to you or to Mars."

The waitress brought the cream of chicken soup they'd ordered.

Avery said, "Thanks." She picked up her spoon and stirred the soup. Steam rose.

"What exactly do you want Mars to know?"

"I want your permission, not permission, but approval. He's your brother. We've kept this secret too long. I believe not telling is the same as lying. I don't know what Donald knows, and I don't care if you want to tell him or not. But Mars must know. Things are happening between us. He expects honesty from me and from everyone in his life, including you. It's not fair for him to go on thinking you killed Hunter. I want to tell him and I want to do it soon. I've already been here for months, and haven't had the courage. We've had Beverly's illness and death. Frankie's hurting. They're both grieving. Then Adam showed up out of a clear blue sky. I can find an excuse regardless. I can't tell him if the sun is shining. I can't tell him if it's raining. But I have to face this. I think we all have to face it."

"I told Donald." Sylva looked up from her plate into Avery's eyes. "Just recently. I told him we were both holding the gun. I can still feel that cold steel barrel in my hands." She shuddered. "Are you sure you want to do this?"

"I need to put an end to it. Now."

For a minute or two they concentrated on lunch. Sylva cut a piece of French bread. Avery added pepper to the soup. A barrier had been reached, but not quite crossed.

"I'll tell Mars alone. The truth will be harder for us because of what is between us and because he should have been told when it happened. It's not going to be easy for me to admit all this to him."

"I think he'll understand, Avery. I even think he'll understand why we lied about it."

"Well, Sylva . . ." Avery reached across the table and placed her hand on Sylva's arm. "There's more. Stuff you don't know."

"What? Avery, darling, you can tell me anything after all we've been through together."

"I became pregnant." Avery's face burned either from the fire or from the words.

"What?"

"My folks talked about abortion, but by the time I told them it was too late."

"What? Avery . . . when?" Her expression was both shock and concern.

"Right after. When we went back to Florida. I knew by late summer, but I didn't say anything until, I don't know, October? By then an abortion would have been too dangerous. I had the baby, Sylva. My folks arranged to have it given up for adoption."

"Oh, Avery, I'm so sorry. Oh my God, Avery . . ."

"The child was a boy. I wasn't supposed to know, but when I was in the hospital I went down to the nursery, looked at all the babies. Each little crib had a placard with the family name and either a blue or pink blanket. There was one with no name. I knew he was my child."

"How terrible for you."

"So the thing is. Oh God, Sylva, I hate this, but I gave birth to your brother, stepbrother? And gave him away."

"But you had no choice."

"I had no strength. And I can't sit here and say I wanted to take care of a baby, even if I thought I could raise a child. But lots of teenagers take responsibility for their children. I know it now. I didn't know it then. Well, my folks, they never even let it be an option."

"I'm so sorry. I wish I'd known." Sylva's eyes were a comfort. "I can see how you'd have trouble telling Mars, but I think you're right. Yes, Avery, he should know the truth."

"Like the one thing wasn't bad enough."

"He'll be understanding. God, I wish you'd told me."

"Sylva, I didn't even know where you were. And by the time I got the letter from you, I just couldn't."

"Why didn't you ever write to me?"

"I couldn't. Maybe if I could have seen you or even talked on the phone, but Sylva, I couldn't write it in a letter. And then, when I came here in

October, I was going to tell Mars first. But when I realized how sick Beverly was and everything, it was just too hard. Now I feel better because you know and you approve of the secrets coming out. So, now I'll just do it. I've only been worried about this for over twenty years."

Sylva's support helped.

Nothing could save Avery from the terror she still faced.

18

Frankie ran to Avery's apartment, banged on the door, and shouted his breathless warning, "A storm's coming, a bad one. Dad says for you to get your stuff and come to the house. TV says to expect ten inches of snow."

"I thought winter was over. Spring's almost here. The dogwood is blooming, didn't you see it?"

"There's a blizzard coming anyway." Frankie sounded like it was the best news he'd heard all month. "Can I carry anything?"

"Why do I have to go up there?"

"We don't know how bad it will be. Wind. Snow. You might not be safe here or warm enough. Anyway, Dad said. If it's real bad the power will go out."

Avery threw a few things in a tote bag. "Okay, whatever."

She followed him up the hill. Icy wind was already whipping through the trees; the sky was white, clouds flying by, snow swirling.

"Bad storm coming," Mars said when Avery and Frankie entered the house.

"I heard." Avery shook snow off her coat. "It's freezing out there."

"These spring storms, you never know about them. We need to fill the buckets. Frankie, get the other buckets."

"Why?" Avery asked.

"If we lose electricity, we lose the water. The pump's electric."

They filled the buckets with the hose, lined them up on the deck at first. Then later brought them all inside so they wouldn't freeze.

"It's supposed to go down to zero tonight," Mars said, carrying in another load of firewood. "We'll be okay. We have plenty of wood."

"Zero?" Avery asked. "Like in zero degrees?"

They listened to the wind howl during dinner and to the weather reporters preempting the programs on television after dinner. The message was clearly to be prepared for the worst. Branches scraped the siding and the windows. The power went out about ten o'clock. Avery lit candles and an oil lamp. Mars stoked up the fire. Frankie made popcorn in a wire basket held over the flames.

"The temperature will drop fast now," Mars said. "We should all sleep together in the downstairs bedroom because it's closest to the fire. If it goes down below zero like they're saying, it might be in the teens or twenties in here."

"Can't we keep the fire going all night?" Avery asked.

"We will, but it won't heat the whole house, no way without the central heat on, not in this wind."

The snow was blowing white outside. The driveway wasn't even visible from the front windows.

"Gonna be a howler," Frankie said. "I'm sleeping out here by the fire. My down bag is supposed to keep me warm at thirty below." He put pillows on the floor.

"Won't be that cold," Mars said as he put a big log on the fire and placed the screen to guard against flying embers. "In wind like this we might get a back draft. Could blow embers all the way to the kitchen."

Avery didn't want to sleep with Mars so soon after Beverly's death, especially with Frankie right outside the bedroom door, but there didn't seem to be a reasonable alternative. She doubted the storm would be as bad as predicted. How many times had they prepared for hurricanes in Florida that veered off and went somewhere else or fizzled out at sea?

The wind raged outside, rattled the windows, howled through the trees, and kept her awake. Branches slapped against the walls of the house. When a tree fell, the whole house shook.

"Those damn white pines don't have any roots," Mars mumbled, snuggling down under the comforter. "Good thing it didn't hit the house."

Avery fell asleep in his arms thinking the worst had to be over.

Mars awakened her in the dead of night. The room was pitch black except for the tiny glow from the fireplace through the open door.

"I'm cold," he whispered, cuddling against her.

Avery turned to face him, snuggled against him, and rubbed her hand on his back. He ran his hand under her sweatshirt, up to her breasts. His cold hand gave her goosebumps. He was touching her stomach, caressing her, then moved his hand down to a warmer place. She didn't want to move, aware Frankie was asleep in the next room. She held still and let Mars touch her. He played with her until it was too late to turn back. Unbearable anticipation ignited under his teasing touches until an intense release rendered ecstasy incomplete. Their agonizing restraint paralyzed them like a wave racing for the shore, then exploding against a seawall, aborted, the force rerouted. She tried to be still and quiet. They reached their crescendo without either of them barely moving or making a sound.

Blizzard wind buffeted the house all night and whistled through the branches. Another tree fell. The fire spit and crackled in the living room. Their breathing returned to normal, but it took awhile.

Thirty inches of snow, not ten, had fallen during the night. Avery stood at the window in the morning rejoicing over the most beautiful sight she had ever seen. The deck was buried almost to the top of the railing. They made coffee, grateful for the gas stove. Mars tramped around outside to see which trees had fallen.

"Both pines," he reported when he came back with another armload of logs. "One along the back of the house was a huge one, a forty footer. Another fell along the west wall. Either one of them would have wrecked the house if they'd fallen a foot or so closer."

The trees were laden with snow, branches drooping to the ground under the weight. The thermometer showed the temperature at seven above outside; inside it was twenty-six degrees. Glass blue icicles hung from the eaves.

"I promised you some snow," Mars said. "And I keep my promises."

"And I appreciate every little thing you do for me."

Mars stoked up the fire while Avery made a big breakfast. Afterward, they went out to stomp around in the snow and explore the winter won-

derland. They fell down a lot, returned all cold and
wet, laughing. When Frankie made his way down
the hill crashing through the deep snow to visit a
friend, Mars and Avery were alone for the first
time in days. They went back to the house.

"What was that all about last night?" Avery asked
clearing the dishes away.

"Couldn't help myself." His innocent smile didn't
fool her. She'd always loved his smile. He brought a
bucket of water, poured some in a pot to heat on
the stove.

"Well, we are going to get this under control. Do
you hear me?"

"Why?"

"Because you need time to recover. To mourn. We
both do," she said. "And with Frankie sleeping right
in the next room, what were you thinking?"

"You didn't stop me."

"Well, I'm human too, you know. But, we need
time."

"I want you to move in here," he said.

"Mars, it's too soon. Don't even think such a thing."

"Look, Avery, I've mourned for two years. I've
been mourning for Beverly since the day we heard
the diagnosis."

"Well, I haven't."

"I need you with me."

"And what would Frankie think? Have you
thought about him?"

"He knows we'll be together. I'll talk to him." Mars washed the dishes in the warm water. Avery rinsed them in cold water and dried them.

"It isn't right, Mars. I'm surprised at you. Can't we show a little discretion?"

He pulled her into his embrace. "But Avery, I love you," he said, "with all my heart and all my soul. I've loved you all my life. I don't want to wait anymore."

"And I love you too, Mars. You know that, but we must wait. I'll go back to the apartment tonight."

"No. Frankie can sleep upstairs. It won't be as cold tonight, I don't think. Please stay with me. Avery, don't let our first fight be about making love."

"You'll talk to Frankie, today?"

"I will."

"Well, we'll see how he reacts."

The electricity was still off the next night. Frankie went to sleep upstairs in his room. Mars and Avery went to bed together as if they had gone to bed together every night of their lives.

"You talked to Frankie?" Avery asked.

"I did, and he understands, he's fine. He misses his mother terribly, of course. But he accepts you, Avery. Having you here, helping, and becoming friends with Beverly helped a lot. I think he expected you to stay."

Soon a serenade of kisses, tasting, lingering, savoring, aroused to the razzle of cymbals connecting. Avery absorbed him, such a long-awaited union, dreamed of, fantasized, wanted. Satisfied finally, satiated for the moment, she drifted on a timeless, tideless dream of echoes of their first time together, harmony, a song, a poem, a ray of light, bodies entwined, fingers threaded into one hand. One heart. One life. She had cried long ago and she cried again listening to the even rhythm of his breathing.

In the chilled obscure morning quiet, they made love again, savoring every touch, every movement. Adults now, with miles of history to share, they were aware of the beauty and of the commitment.

Snowbound for five days, they baked cookies and muffins, cooked and ate everything in the freezer. They carried buckets of water to flush the toilet, use for bathing and washing dishes. They melted snow by the fireplace, on the stove, or hauled it up from the creek. They played Scrabble and talked. Frankie was antsy without his computer. They held in-depth conversations with Pecker. They made soup and bread and marveled at how many things they found to do without work, school, television, radio, or cassettes playing.

Snowplows came and plowed, but they still couldn't get Avery's car or the truck out of the driveway. Way too much to shovel. A bright sun came out and cast glints of spangled light over the snow. A royal blue sky was cloudless. The snow melted fast then, dripped off the roof, off the pine

branches, and by the time it was gone all the daffodils bloomed along the driveway.

All through the woods, dogwoods and redbuds
were blooming like pink and white fairies dancing.
Tulips were up everywhere nodding bright colors.
The mountains shed winter the way everyone shed
their coats on the first warm days of spring. The
blizzard had blown winter to the edges of hell. If
Avery thought autumn was something special,
spring sent her into ecstasy.

They began planning a trip to Florida during
Frankie's spring break from school, so Avery could
empty her storage unit and have her things
shipped to North Carolina.

"We'll go to Disney World. We'll go fishing. We'll
go sailing. We'll go out on a boat. We'll swim in the
ocean." Frankie couldn't wait.

"We'll do all those things and more," Avery said.

Mars was just as excited as Frankie.

"I want to see where you lived," he said. "I want
to see your folks after all these years. I want to see
Adam again and even meet Ken. That way, everything will be complete. The circle will close."

"You're crazy, Mars. You know that, don't you?"

"What about Pecker?" Frankie asked. "We can't
leave him alone."

"I'll just bet Hoyt would take care of him. We
could leave him in the shop. Pecker, come down
here," Mars commanded. The bird flew from his

perch, landed on his outstretched arm.

"Pecker, if we go to Florida, you can stay in the shop with Hoyt, okay?"

Squawk.

Frankie went to bed early. Mars was in the living room. Avery finished up in the kitchen and carried two cups of coffee out to the living room. She gave Mars one and sat next to him with the other one.

"Mars . . ." She hesitated. "There's something I want to ask you, talk to you about. Something has bothered me for a long time."

He looked at her. Waited.

"Remember after your father's funeral, you came over to the cabin and we said good-bye. You were driving back to Fontana. You said you didn't love me, didn't want me. You put an end to it, remember?"

"I never said I didn't love you."

"You put an end to it with a certainty that hurt me very much. I never understood why you wanted such an absolute end to everything."

"I didn't want to, but I had no choice."

"We did have choices. We could have kept in touch, written letters, seen each other again. We were almost adults."

"I didn't want to hurt you anymore."

"You didn't. It wasn't you, Mars."

"Hunter's blood runs in my veins. My father attacked you. How could I continue? How could I ever face you again?" His eyes filled with guilt. "Hadn't we imposed on your life enough? Hadn't we done enough damage? My blood was bad, Avery, don't you see? My blood was tainted. I was forever flawed by his brutality. The guilt ate me up and forced me to abandon any hope about us."

"Mars, no."

"I wanted you, thought about you for years, but I had no choice."

"Mars, we made love together in agreement. You never forced me to do anything."

"You were so young, Avery."

"But I came to you, remember? I climbed into your bed."

"To comfort me, not to be molested. You were a virgin, a child."

"So were you," Avery said.

"We wasted all these years. I wish we could change things, but we can't."

"Mars, there's something I have to tell you. Should have told you twenty years ago or at least last fall. Your father raped me."

"No. No. He attacked you and Sylva, that was all. He was probably drunk. But he wouldn't . . ."

"We lied about it because we didn't want anybody to know the truth. Sylva and I made up a whole elaborate story. Then, when I went back to Florida, I, well, the worst happened. I realized I was pregnant." He tried to interrupt. "Please Mars, let me finish. I've needed to tell you this for so long. I had the baby and my parents arranged to have him given up for adoption."

"No, this isn't possible, you couldn't have." The shock in his eyes killed her. "You couldn't have had his child."

"I did, Mars, I had a baby. It was a boy."

"But, it's not possible," he managed to mutter. His voice quivered. "Hunter had a vasectomy after Shelby was born. He didn't want any more children. Wayne went with him to some clinic in Asheville. Wayne told me about it. Hunter was embarrassed, thought it emasculated him somehow. But Mama was sick, she'd had six kids, and Hunter couldn't seem to put an end to it. That's why he got the operation. I don't think he ever even told Mama. Wayne was the only one who knew."

"No. A vasectomy? Hunter?" Avery's mind couldn't see the truth staring her in the face. Mars had always used condoms, they had been careful every single time. "Not possible . . . then . . . it must have been . . ."

They realized the truth at the same instant.

"God, Avery. You had my child." His eyes were full of the dawning perception, then insight as he grasped the wonder of what they were discovering. He held her in his arms.

"I thought it was Hunter's." Her voice sounded

weak, far away. "You had always protected me, Hunter didn't. I carried the child to term and delivered a baby boy. My father arranged the adoption. All those years, I never guessed he might have been your child. I never let myself think the possibility existed. Mars, honest, I never knew."

"Of course not, you couldn't have known." His look was strangled. "It must have been awful for you. If Wayne hadn't told me about Hunter's operation, we would never have known the truth."

"There's something else. Please let me get all of this out. You have to know the whole truth."

He sat in shocked silence for a minute and then said, "We had a child together? A son? You and me?"

"And I gave him away." She buried her face in her hands. "This has killed me all my life, but now knowing he was your child makes it worse."

Mars lifted her face, wiped away tears running down her cheeks.

"I'm sorry I didn't know, Avery, I would have done something. I had to leave you. I didn't think there was another choice. I had no idea you were pregnant. I thought life had something better waiting for you." He looked bewildered, and in a minute he said, "It must have been awful for you."

"There was nothing you could have done, darling. We were too young. The distance was too great. We didn't know the truth about anything. Nothing better was ever waiting for me."

She took a sip of coffee, now ice cold, and frowned. She put the cup down.

"Please let me finish, Mars. Please listen, I have to tell you what happened. Hunter came home and found me in the house alone. He was drunk and he slapped me around and then he attacked me. I got away from him finally. I was against the wall, headed for the door, but I bumped into the gun rack. Then he came at me again. I grabbed the gun down, I remember it was so heavy. I was going to hit him with it, and somehow, oh God, Mars. Then Sylva came home and tried to get the gun away from me. It just went off. I didn't mean to shoot. I didn't mean to kill him. But then he was dead."

Mars held Avery in his arms trying to comfort her.

"I know you won't understand any of this. We couldn't believe what had happened. We didn't even know how it happened. But Sylva, she was afraid I'd be put in jail forever. She thought she'd get off easy if we said she did it. We said I wasn't even there. Neither one of us ever told the whole truth about any of this."

"My darling Avery, what hell you went through, both you and Sylva. I'm so sorry."

"No, it wasn't your fault. No one is to blame." She pressed her face into his neck. "We just coped with the hell we were dealt."

"How can you ever forgive me?" Mars asked, looking into her eyes.

"You? I was about to ask you the same thing."

"There is nothing to forgive. I'd never blame you for protecting yourself. Please tell me about the child. When he was born, where, tell me everything."

"I gave birth on April fifth, in sixty-five, at a hospital where nobody would know us. As far as I know, adoption records are sealed in Florida. I don't know any more. And, like with everything in my family, we didn't mention it again."

"Were you alone?"

"No, Mother went with me. They had me drugged up so I don't remember much. But Mars, I saw him. I wasn't supposed to, but I went to the nursery and I saw him sleeping. He was so tiny, so beautiful."

"Avery, my poor darling . . ."

"We have to have the strength to face the past," Avery whispered as she wiped tears from his cheek.

"No Avery, we have to have the strength to face the future."

19

The truth had roots like the forest and a roof like the sky. Anchored at the bottom of their adolescence, it was tethered and indelible. Instead of lifting the screen of secrecy, instead of liberation, it pervaded the present, infiltrated their souls, covered everything like a mist. The new reality had to be threaded into the existing fiber of their lives and digested.

Words floated between Avery and Mars like vibrations from a tuning fork. The scars were visible. Ordinary conversation collapsed under the weight of the discovery. What if Mars had known? What if Avery had known? How would they have changed things?

And mixed with the questions, the aching sorrow of Beverly's death began to surface as grief and mourning. Avery wanted to help, to share the pain, but her presence seemed to be an intrusion on their intensely personal loss, and on her own need for privacy. As Beverly had been utterly alone with her pain at the end, so too were Mars and Frankie alone with the consequence. They went to visit her grave without Avery. When Avery went, she went alone or with Sylva.

Beverly's death had been followed immediately by a time of comparative normality. Maybe they'd been distracted by Adam's visit, or the blizzard, or by the energy of spring bubbling up and blooming in such riotous color everywhere. Maybe none of them knew how to grieve.

Talk about a vacation subsided when Frankie came down with the flu and stayed home from school for a week. Avery took soup up to his room and left the tray by his bed. He'd stopped talking almost all together, often slept or pretended to sleep.

Avery spent more and more of her time in the apartment, alone. She sat at the breakfast table, staring into cold coffee, twisting the vase of dried flowers around in a circle. She saw the note Adam had given her and looked at the name and the number, wondering what property. She called the lawyer, but couldn't imagine what he wanted with her.

"You're not the easiest person to track down," he

said once he understood who she was and why she was calling.

"I've been spending time in North Carolina. How can I help you?"

"You've inherited a piece of property."

"I have?"

"Yes. I'm sorry it's taken so long to unravel. But we were given a handwritten will some months ago now, and it took time to establish its legality."

"Whose will?"

"Do you know someone named Osceola Oscipee?"

"Of course I do. We called him Skeeter. He was my gardener."

"He left you a piece of property."

"He did? Where?"

"Well, it's complicated. The property seems to be in an undeveloped area out west of Palm City. The records are a bit sketchy. It's in the middle of an area Kessler Properties wants to develop. Their lawyers have been trying to clear the title. Then they discovered you own the center section. My records indicate you're recently divorced from Ken Kessler, vice president of Kessler Properties. Is that correct?"

"Yes."

"Well, to further complicate the issue here, you were awarded one quarter of the Kessler tract of land in your divorce settlement. Apparently, Mr.

Kessler had half of the site deeded to the corpora-
tion, Kessler Properties, that is, and half was held in
your names as a married couple. Then, in the
divorce settlement your lawyer had your half or
one quarter of the property awarded to you."

"Has any development begun?" Avery asked.

"No, Kessler Properties wants to purchase the
land you and your husband once owned jointly, and
also buy the land you inherited from Mr. Oscipee. I
understand a very generous offer is being prepared."

"I'll never sell it."

"I'm afraid they'll fight for this property," he said.

"Let them. Do you represent them?" Avery asked.

"No. I represent Mr. Oscipee's estate." He sounded
calm. "As I said, it has taken time to establish the
legality of his will."

"And who hired you exactly?"

"Mr. Oscipee's brother."

"Do I own enough of the land to stop Kessler
from developing it?"

"Of course they can only develop the part they
own," he said.

"Are there infringements? Right of way restrictions?"

"You'll have to have it surveyed to find out. You
should return to Florida and take care of this. The
Kesslers aren't going to back off without a fight."

"Yes, I understand. I appreciate your efforts in

tracking me down. I'll take care of it. Thank you."

The property haunted her. She'd been so sure she would stay with Mars, she'd never considered anything else. Yet saving Skeeter's land seemed a sacred responsibility to her. And everything nagged her about trying to replace Beverly. She didn't say anything to Mars. Once again not telling was the same as lying.

She called the lawyer again a few days later, talked it through in more detail and asked some questions.

At the end of a long call, she asked, "What can I do to protect that property? Skeeter, Mr. Oscipee, was my gardener, but he was also my best friend for many years."

"I think you'll have to be here, Mrs. Kessler."

"Please call me Avery, Avery Baldwin. I had my name changed back legally. Will you represent me in this or do you see it as some conflict of interest?"

"Not at all. I'd be happy to represent you."

"I'll call you when I get to Florida and set up an appointment then. Thank you."

Would this be the same as running away? Was Avery afraid to stay with Mars and Frankie? If she stayed, would she have to give up something of herself? She felt as if she stood on the edge of a cliff, didn't know whether she would fall or fly.

She called Ken. He was surprised to hear from her.

"I understand you have an interest in buying some land from me," Avery said.

"What's this going to be, another stickup? Our lawyers say you have refused to cooperate."

"I haven't gotten anything so far."

"The land out there isn't yours, Avery." His voice was bitter. "It wound up in your name by sheer accident."

"A happy accident," she said.

"What do you want for it?"

"It's not for sale. That's not why I called. Have you sold the house yet?"

"No."

"I want it," Avery said. "I'll buy your share somehow."

"You want to come back to Florida?"

"I want my garden. I'll buy you out. I don't know how but I'll find a way."

"Avery, I don't know how to tell you this," Ken hesitated.

"What?"

"I had the garden plowed under. I sodded the area to help sell the house. I never thought you'd want the house or any part of it."

"Nor did I." Avery suppressed anger, felt betrayed again, hollow.

"Are you coming back?"

"I'm coming back to try to save one tiny speck of Florida."

"I didn't expect this."

"Forget the house, sell it. Whatever. You won't like what I'm going to do. I don't care whether you like it or not. I'm going to make a difference. One tiny difference. And I'm going to do it in Skeeter's name."

"We'll fight you for the land, Avery. You have no right to it."

"Fight. See if I care. I'll contact you when I get back to Florida, Ken. I'm sorry about all this."

"You're not sorry. We'll talk again. Good-bye."

The hard part would be telling Mars. She stayed to herself for days thinking about what to say, began to think she'd lost her mind entirely. Always thought she would, so it was no surprise. She had belonged with Mars all along, and now the path was open for them. Mars kept asking what had gotten into her. She had to tell him.

Frankie recovered from the flu, his spirit improved as well, and he returned to school.

One morning after Frankie left, Avery put the tea kettle on to heat water for coffee.

"Sit down, Mars. You have to hear this." She took his hand and led him to the sofa. "Please try to understand."

"What? Don't even tell me you have another bomb to drop."

"No, darling. Something has come up, an unexpected thing. I told you about my garden. Skeeter and I had worked on it for years. We were very close. I respected him and considered him a cherished friend. Anyway, it appears as if he left me some land. When Adam was here he gave me a message from an attorney. I'd actually forgotten about it, but I called and found out Kessler Properties wants this land. Now I have a chance to protect it. I have to go back to Florida and have it surveyed. I need to know exactly where it is."

Mars looked as if he'd been slapped in the face.

"For Ken?"

"No, Jesus, of course not. For me. Our time together over these months has been the best time of my life." She tried to choose the right words, "Mars, we had to be together. Both of us did. We had to see each other again. I had to be here for you, and for Beverly. After all those years, the time had come for the truth to come out. We had to go through this together."

"You're not leaving," he said. "I won't let you."

"I'm going back to Florida on a mission. This is your home, Beverly's home. Not mine."

"I want it to be yours."

"I know you do. I love you with all my heart. But this isn't my life, not yet anyway. I have to live my life before I can share yours."

"What are you going to do?"

She explained it in as much detail as she could; even she didn't know much. She told him everything about Skeeter, his wisdom, their friendship, shared interests, the garden, about how it had been her salvation all those years.

"It was a thing of my own making." She explained about Ken's housing developments, and how he and all the other developers leveled everything. And now, a piece of property in which the natural environment might be saved was hers to protect.

"But I thought you hated Florida."

"I inherited Mother's hatred. She hates Florida, the heat, the bugs, the tourists. But I can't let her hatred, her denial of everything, influence me anymore. There's a part of Florida I love. Part of it is my birthright."

"But what we have together, Avery, we've waited a lifetime. I know we've been under this awful strain lately. I've had a delayed reaction or something. We will get past this. I miss Beverly so much, it comes over me in waves, not all the time. When it hits though, God, I can't explain it."

Tears filled her eyes. She held him.

The kettle whistled. Avery went into the kitchen and made the coffee. She brought two cups back to the sofa.

"I was thinking we could start a search to find our son," he said.

Nothing would have given her more joy.

"No, we can't. He has his own life. He may not even know he was adopted. We can't chance throwing a wrench in his life or his relationship with his adoptive parents. We have to let it go. He'd be twenty now. I'd love to see him, love to know him. But no, it's impossible. We mustn't even try."

"Don't leave me." She heard his jagged breath.

"I'm not leaving you. I have to go take care of things. I have to do this. We won't even say good-bye, we'll see what happens."

"I can't believe you're leaving." His voice was filled with disbelief.

"I know, leaving now, even for a few months will be the hardest thing I ever did," she said. "I'm not leaving, I'm going to take care of something important to me. And at the same time, give us a little time to heal. Frankie needs your undivided attention right now. My being here distracts you. Mars, please let me go with love in your heart."

"Not the way I left you all those years ago?" He took a sip of coffee. "Why isn't this enough for you?"

"This is more than enough. And Beverly expected me to stay. I'm not leaving you. I owe something, a debt has to be paid. I can't take Beverly's place with you or with Frankie. I can't live her life, Mars. In time, yes, things will be different. But now we need time apart. When we start over together, it will be new and fresh. And I have to take this opportunity to right at least one wrong. The truth has given me freedom and I have to respect it."

"How can you say good-bye to me, Avery?"

"No good-byes. I guess spring break is out now, but summer is better anyway. We'll just run back and forth for a little while. Plan to bring Frankie to Florida in the summer, you both need a vacation."

"Do you mean the door isn't closed for us?"

"Of course not, I don't want to do anything to destroy what we have."

"So the door isn't closed." Mars looked at her with those eyes of his and her heart crumbled.

"Of course not, I love you. I've loved you all my life, but loving you will never make me whole. I have to be whole before I can share my life with you." Avery hugged him. "We are Band-Aids for each other, not cures. My being here keeps you from grieving. And you keep me from healing. Whether it's divorce or death, we both need time to recover. We distract each other. Please try to understand. We can't build the rest of our lives on a foundation of distraction, joyous though it is." Her tears now ran free. "Plus we have a whole lot of truth to digest."

Avery wasn't certain about any of this. She knew she couldn't stay and step into Beverly's shoes and never look at her other responsibilities. She had to leave Mars to see herself and let him see himself. He'd consumed her since she was six years old. He'd infiltrated her marriage, doomed with or without him. He'd controlled her mind all of her adult life. She took him into her arms and rocked him, held on tight.

"All my life, I've lived out of focus, Mars. I've never lived in the present. None of us knew the truth about anything. I've played and replayed movies in my mind, movies of our childhood. These are your mountains, this is your landscape." She sat back, watching his face and continued, "Mine is a different landscape. Now my mind is quiet. The movies are finished. I never grew up, just kept reliving the past over and over again." She lifted the cup, drank some coffee, and looked at him.

His eyes were full of understanding.

"Anyway," she said, "as hard as it will be to leave you, my dear, it's going to be downright tragic to leave that dogwood tree out by the deck. I've never seen anything so beautiful."

"I moved the house back so the tree wouldn't be disturbed. It's very old and I thought it was pretty special." He held her hand caressing her fingers.

"You saved it. You felt a responsibility toward it. Mars, I know you understand why I have to go."

"I may understand, but I don't want you to go. I want you to stay with me, live here, make this your home."

"We'll be together in our hearts, Mars. You won't be out of my mind or my heart for one minute."

"But it wasn't my heart I was thinking about."

She laughed at him, and he flashed that miraculous smile of his.

Avery had always loved his smile.

20

A sea breeze ruffled the palms and whirled a bit of trash into a mini-tornado. Stopped at a traffic light on the simmering fast-food alley, a sedan with tinted windows waited next to a dune buggy. Avery laughed at the image—the wasp and the doodle-bug. In the dune buggy, the kids in their Ron Jon shorts rocked to beach music.

April, just a year ago, she had attended her last company meeting. Ken would put up a fight about the land, tease her with big money, maybe even sue. An H & R Block sign reminded her that taxes were due. Ken would not be doing her taxes this year. Still, the IRS would expect her to file. And Kessler Properties wouldn't be renewing her car tag, either.

The timing was right for Avery's return. Frankie

deserved to have Mars alone now. She knew the details of her current and former life needed attention. But she didn't know how her mother had talked her into staying with them.

She pulled into their driveway, stopped, and let the feeling of defeat bunch in her shoulders. Why had she agreed to this? Twenty years since she'd spent the night in her old childhood room. Her mother would have been offended if she'd gone to a motel. Hadn't there been enough rancor in the family to last a lifetime? She grabbed an overnight bag from the backseat.

Her mother met her at the door.

"I'm so glad to see you, we've missed you, dear."

The bag prevented much of a hug.

"How are you and Daddy?"

"Oh, we're just fine. I didn't expect you to come back, but I'm glad you did. Here, let me take your bag, just the one, won't you need more?"

"I'll just be here a few days." She followed her mother down the hall.

"How was the trip? Did you get your fill of the mountains?"

Stacks of files covered the bed in the redecorated den, once Avery's childhood prison.

"Taxes, what a mess," her mother said as she cleared them away. "What can I get you? Iced tea? A snack? Dinner won't be ready until your father comes home and that's not for a little while yet."

"I'll take some tea, thanks. Ken always did our taxes. Guess I'll have to do them myself this year."

"You don't have much time left. You'll have to hire an accountant. I could give you the name of the one we use."

"I know, Mother. I have a lot of things to deal with right now."

When they were settled by the screened-in pool with tall slender glasses of iced tea, the conversation came to a halt. Pleasantries complete.

"Tell me," her mother began again, "how did you feel seeing your friends after all this time?"

"Autumn in the mountains is spectacular. It's a shame we always went in the summer."

"You and Adam had school. We couldn't leave in the autumn."

"Wouldn't have hurt to miss a couple weeks one year, just to see it."

Another long silence seemed to make her mother nervous. She plucked a few dead leaves from a potted plant.

"I don't know you at all anymore, Avery. We don't have anything to talk about. You look at me with such a judgmental expression."

"Sorry, I don't mean to."

"What was it like for you returning to Crowfoot Ridge after all these years?"

"Like going home, like I belonged there."

"See, you just make small talk. You avoid answering questions. I care about you and want to know what you're doing, and what you're thinking."

Avery realized tears were forming in her mother's eyes.

"I'd hoped you'd be happy to be home, happy to see me, show some joy or something."

"I'm sorry, Mother, what did I say wrong?"

"It's always what you don't say. You're so cold, so hard to talk to. I wanted to know if you saw Sylva and Mars." Her mother dabbed her eyes with a tissue.

"Of course, I went up there to see them. They're fine."

"That's it? Fine? You've been gone seven months, you've been through a divorce, you've seen people from your childhood, and all you can say is it's fine?"

"You? You want to talk? What about when I wanted to talk to you? What about when I needed to talk to you? What about when you shut me in my room for five damned months? And I was scared to death." Tears boiled in her eyes, a weakness she didn't want to show.

"But Av—"

"You gave me a damned television set so you wouldn't have to talk to me. You never asked me how I felt back then. You never asked what I wanted or what I could handle."

"You couldn't ra—"

"Now, you want to know how I feel? I'll tell you. I

feel betrayed. I feel filled with rage. Rage I've suppressed and held back. I can't talk because I can't be sure I won't say the wrong things. Say what I really think. But you are—"

"Avery! How can you say such things?"

"You're the one who's distant, Mother, not me." Avery fought for control. "You're the one who avoids the issues. I never know how to get past it. I never know what to say to you. It's like walking on glass, watching every word. Anyway, the whole thing with Mars and Sylva is complicated. They told me their truth, I told them mine. Then, Beverly died. We had a lot to deal with, a lot to digest." Her tears spilled out at the mention of Beverly's name and the rage turned into a sadness.

"Beverly?"

"The woman Mars married." These words, she whispered.

"I'm sorry about everything, Avery. I'm not perfect, but I do love you." Her mother covered her face with trembling hands when she began to cry.

"Please don't cry, I didn't mean to hurt you." Avery reached out and took her hand. She looked at the aging woman, saw the gray in her hair and wrinkles around her eyes, maybe for the first time.

The front door opened. Her mother stiffened, stared at Avery as if expecting an instant mood change.

"Budlet, you're back. How was your vacation?"

Avery got up slowly. She wiped her face on her

sleeve. She held back, but her father swept her into a hug.

"Could you possibly call me Avery? I'm not a little girl anymore." Immediately, she regretted snapping at him.

He let her go as if he held something dangerous.

"I'm sorry, Daddy, honest. It's a cute nickname, really, I don't mind."

Vacation? She wondered where he'd gotten the idea she'd been on a vacation. She stifled it.

"What's the matter, honey?" he asked his wife. She got up and brushed passed him without answering.

The awkward moment dissipated as he followed his wife into the kitchen, fixed himself a drink, sniffed the pots on the stove, fiddled with the ice cubes.

"This will be ready in about ten minutes. Here, Avery, put these things on the table."

She set the table and followed her parents out to the pool again. They waited, searching for words to begin a conversation. The pool sparkled, gurgled its continuous self-cleaning.

"Did you know your ancestors are from those mountains?" her father asked. "My family was from Asheville and Weaverville, I don't even know where all, dating back into the early eighteen hundreds."

"No, I didn't know, Daddy. You never mentioned this before."

"We knew some of it, but just a month ago we received a document with the full history. One of my distant cousins took genealogy up as a hobby, I guess. He researched the dickens out of it and sent us a copy."

"I'd like to see it." Avery took a sip of her tea. "Your parents and grandparents were from North Carolina?"

"Born there, but my folks came to Florida during the twenties, started out in Miami, Coconut Grove, and then moved to this area. But you could probably find the graves of your great grandparents up there. He sent a list of the cemeteries with their locations."

A perception of probability dawned on Avery, like seeing the shape of a puzzle piece and the corresponding void.

"Funny," she said, "I always felt like I belonged in those mountains, and then to learn our roots are there. I'm glad you told me. I'd love to see everything he sent you."

"You belong right here in Florida," her mother said as she retreated to the kitchen.

Dinner was served, finally. Avery was too tired to eat but she managed to be pleasant through most of the meal. The conversation centered on passing the barbecued chicken or the potato salad, a few words about the weather, her father's golf game, and then a long silence.

"Mars is the father of the child I gave away," Avery heard her own voice blurt out.

Her mother's mouth dropped open.

Her father looked as if he'd been kicked by a mule.

"He wanted to start a search to find his son, our son," Avery continued in order to fill the awful gap, "but I think it's best to leave things alone. After all, the child might not know about the adoption. I don't believe it's our right to destroy another family because of this."

Her parents stared at her as if she'd put a snake on the table.

"Regardless of who the father was, he was still my son and your grandson," Avery said in a matter-of-fact tone. "I guess everybody forgot about that."

"We did what we thought was best, Avery." Her father's voice shook with pain. "You were sleeping with Mars? You were so young." Pain turned into shock as he realized this.

Avery had finished picking at her food, pushed the plate aside. "Yes, too young."

"We didn't want to see your life ruined." She heard her mother's words but thought she meant they didn't want their lives ruined.

"I didn't mean to upset you," Avery said. "I just thought you should know the truth. There's nothing more to discuss."

"There is more," her father said. "Did Hunter Marshall rape you or not?"

"He did."

"Then you didn't know who the father was?"

"I thought it was Hunter's. I found out it wasn't and it breaks my heart. I don't know if anything would have been different."

"We wanted you to forget it, move on with your life."

"I did move on, Mother, but I never forgot it." Avery stood, positioned the chair back at the table. "Would you have forgotten Adam or me if one of us had been taken from you? I'm sorry, I shouldn't have mentioned any of this. Please forgive me. It's been a long day, ten hours driving, I'm dead tired. You won't mind if I go to bed early."

She left them speechless and stunned, and retired to the den. After a shower, she tossed for hours dreaming fragmented dreams, reliving more than she cared to remember.

The next morning, Avery apologized first thing.

"I hadn't meant to hurt you. There just wasn't any good way to tell you the truth."

"We understand, dear."

"Do either of you remember the old Victorian house being renovated down by the river? Maybe they have rooms to rent."

"You know you're welcome here," her mother said.

"Of course, thanks, but I want my own place. I've never actually had an apartment before."

"They did a fine job there, turned it into a boardinghouse," Mr. Baldwin said from behind the newspaper.

Late morning, Avery went to see about renting a room. The owners mentioned they had renovated a cottage out back, which Avery hadn't known about.

The shingle cottage had two bedrooms and was all gingerbread and vine roses. They agreed on a month-to-month lease. Avery moved into the place, delighted to have found it. She retrieved her things from storage, forced by the need to find her papers and satisfy the ticking clock of the tax deadline.

During the first month after returning to Florida, she met with the lawyer and hired a surveyor to define the boundaries of the property she inherited from Skeeter, including the adjoining land she'd received in the divorce. The single tract sat right smack in the middle of a huge Kessler site.

She went to work reclaiming Skeeter's shack, putting in the essential pathways, cutting back six months of growth, chasing off the snakes, and beginning to identify the native plants. Every television station and newspaper within a fifty-mile radius showed up when the sign was installed.

Skeeter's Garden would be open to the public seven days a week. Schools were encouraged to bring children on field trips to visit the garden, have refreshments, and come in contact with the many varieties of plants native to Florida.

"And there will never be an entrance fee," she told the reporters. "Skeeter's Garden is open to all and free to all."

"Where did the name come from? Skeeter's Garden? Do you mean mosquitoes?"

She laughed. "No, Skeeter was a Seminole Indian who lived here. He died not quite a year ago. He was a very special man and he was my dear friend. This garden is a small attempt to honor him. Skeeter was his nickname, his real name was Osceola Oscipee." She spelled it for them. "I'm having a bronze plaque made that will say 'In Memory of Osceola Oscipee' and will be installed at the entrance." Avery showed them where she wanted it placed.

"You let us know when you're ready to install it and we'll be back," one of the reporters said. "This is a fine thing you're doing. Somebody should have done it years ago."

"Do you need any volunteers? Workers? Any financial help?" Another reporter asked.

"I can use all the help I can get. Young or old. Anyone who wants to become involved, who wants to learn about these plants, or who just wants to bring a jug of lemonade will be more than welcome. We are going to need to enlarge the parking area and I think the more footpaths we have, the better. All paving will be natural materials, either shell or mulch. Trucking it here is expensive." She smiled into the cameras. "When a truck is needed, a truck seems to show up. It's been rather amazing."

"The word is out now and I think you can count on some help with this," the reporter said.

The articles hit an otherwise uneventful weekend, making the Sunday magazines. She hadn't expected so much interest. Reactions following the interviews were overwhelming.

She hadn't expected to see Ken parking his sleek company truck in front of her cottage either.

"I didn't even know you were in town," he said, "had to read it in the newspaper. And I certainly didn't expect you back now."

"I meant to call you, Ken, I just haven't had time." He looked the same, foxy as ever in casual clothes, designer sunglasses. His sandy-colored hair was shaggy around his ears.

"You've obviously been busy. We had hoped you would sell us the land. You knew we had plans for it." He stood on the path by the cottage. She stood at the door.

"Well, I have plans for it too, my own plans. I had to follow my heart about this. And selling it to you just wasn't in the cards."

"Avery, how in the world do you expect to support a public garden out in the middle of nowhere? Do you have any idea what it will take? Have you thought about insurance? Advertising? Parking areas built to code? What if somebody gets bitten by a snake? Do you realize what your liability is?"

"I hadn't thought about those things."

"I didn't think so." He pushed past her, went inside. "Why are you living here? You could have taken the house, you know. You didn't even ask about it."

"I don't want to live there. Why don't you lower the price a little? Put your realtors on it so it will sell."

"Avery, I'll tell you what. I'll trade you my half of the proceeds on the house for the land." He sat on the edge of a chair. "Now, this is a generous offer. Would bring you a hundred thousand in cash."

"I don't want the house. I want my share of the money when it sells."

"But you could move into it."

"I told you, I don't want to live there."

"Shit, Avery. You can't run a public garden." His voice filled with anger, his neck turned red.

"Don't tell me what I can't do."

"And it's right in the middle of a fine development site. Why are you doing this to me? Just to spite me? Just to make me miserable?" The muscles in his jaw contracted.

"You? Believe it or not, this isn't about you, Ken. It's about what Skeeter would have wanted. Just forget it. Do what you have to do." Avery opened the door. "I don't think we have anything to discuss. You have no idea what I'm doing or why I want to do it."

"I'll never understand you." He started through the door. "Our lawyers will be in touch."

"Go ahead, but you don't have a case. You can't develop land you don't own."

He stopped and turned around. "You got that land by sheer accident. The parcel awarded in the divorce was an oversight. I should have had it transferred back to the company before the divorce. You had no right to it."

"Well, we pay for our little mistakes, now don't we?"

"Don't be flip with me. Jesus, Avery, don't you feel anything for our past, our history together?"

"Just leave, Ken."

He shook his head as he climbed into the truck. He backed out slowly.

Avery hadn't wanted a nasty confrontation with him. She'd even thought about inviting him to lunch, maybe trying to smooth over the animosity, and to find out how he was doing.

No chance.

Her hands trembled when she searched the Yellow Pages for a detective's advertisement. One ad claimed twenty-five years' experience, a former district attorney's investigator, licensed, bonded, insured, specializing in missing persons, divorce, custody, surveillance. Her hands shook when she tried to dial the number. Her breath became short and jagged. She replaced the receiver before anyone answered. She sat back in the chair, tried to collect herself, and took a deep breath. Was she really going to do this? She dialed again.

"Patterson Investigations, Pat Patterson speaking."

"I want to talk to someone, uh, my name is Avery Baldwin. About finding someone. I'm interested in, well, it's quite old. The records might not be current." She realized she was blathering, hadn't made one complete sentence.

"How much information do you have?" Mr. Patterson asked in a professional voice, somewhat comforting.

"I have no idea where to begin. Not much. I'm sorry. I don't know how to proceed. I don't know what to say."

"Who are you looking for?"

Okay, here it was, right out in the open, up front and in her face.

"I gave a child up for adoption twenty years ago." Avery's voice was as steady as a stone, surprised her. There it was. Out finally. She'd told Mars a search for their son was wrong, but then, after all, there was nothing left to hide, no reason not to try.

"We have very specific policies regarding searches for adopted children and biological parents, as well. You will have to come in, discuss this in person. When would you be available?"

"Anytime, I guess."

"I have an opening on Thursday. Ten in the morning okay?"

"Yes, fine, thank you." Avery was glad the conversation had ended, sorry she'd agreed to a meeting. She tried to put it out of her mind while waiting for Thursday.

When the time came, she sat in the reception room listening to the girl clicking away on the computer. She flipped through a magazine and then put it down, got up and started to leave. Mr. Patterson opened his office door. She turned back.

"Please come in." He held the door for her, closed it behind her. "I know how difficult this is. When we dredge up things from the past, well, it's always hard. Please have a seat."

His maturity was a comfort, seemed grandfatherly. He fingered a pack of cigarettes. The ashtray overflowed with butts. He didn't light one. His family stared at her from his credenza, big smiles.

"In your case, since you are the biological mother, I'll outline exactly how we work," he said in a professional voice. "Avery, was it? Yes, Avery, first you should know adoption records are sealed in the state of

Florida, and because of this we are not always successful. Assuming you agree to our terms, we take the information you have and begin our usual search. You will be billed monthly. You may receive a report regarding our progress if you wish. Some people don't want the ongoing reports. We understand this is a very emotional process. In any case, if we find your child, we do not give you the information."

Avery interrupted. "What would be the point then?"

"I'm sorry, we give your identification to the adopted person. We do have a lot of experience with these cases. Assuming we find the person we are looking for, we send him or her a questionnaire. Buried deep among many questions is one which is most important. We ask if there has ever been a question regarding his or her birth parentage. Now, if the questions are answered and returned to us, then we can see whether or not the adopted person has questioned his or her parentage. If so, we assume the person knows he or she was adopted. And, the truth is, most do know."

"This child would be twenty now. An adult. And he is my son." The admission brought instant tears to her eyes, followed by embarrassment. He handed her a tissue.

"Sorry."

"I understand this is an emotional time for you."

She looked at the fish mounted on the wall, his licenses, an award, a half-dead areca palm in the corner.

"Nevertheless," he continued, "we follow the same procedure with children or adults."

"So Mr. Patterson, if he knows he was adopted, what happens?"

"Please call me Pat. Then whatever information we have about the parents is sent to the adopted person. Of course you pay for the search whether it is successful or not. If your son wishes to make contact, he certainly is free to do so, assuming we find him at all. It works the same way when a child is searching for a biological parent. Our policy is not to destroy lives but help people make rational decisions once they have the information they need."

"Let me see if I understand this. I pay for you to collect information I will not receive."

"We can tell you if your son is dead or alive. You are paying to get your information into the hands of your adult son. The decision to contact you or not will be his to make."

"I understand. You try to protect everyone. Sounds like a reasonable way to approach things." Avery relaxed at last. "What else do you put on the questionnaire?"

"Oh, we have a lot of questions, like do you have a relative who might have named you in a will, any bank accounts left behind during a move, have you ever transferred an insurance policy, left a school transcript behind, deeds, stocks, and so on. The idea of course is to confuse, certainly not admit adoption up front. Sometimes, the most important issue is to exchange medical information. We've searched for rare blood donors, things like that."

"I see." Avery asked what the charges would be and how long a realistic search would last before he determined it a lost cause. When she was satisfied, she agreed to begin a relationship with him and asked not to receive his progress reports, thinking it best to put the whole idea aside. Otherwise it could easily take over her mind, and the waiting might drive her crazy.

Avery wrote a check for the retainer and gave him the information she knew. Sex, birth date, place of birth, the name of the doctor and the name of the hospital. Patterson made notes, which didn't fill one fourth of a page. If she had raised her son, she could have filled a hundred pages, a thousand pages, with her knowledge of him. His first steps, his first words, his first day at school. Twenty years lost forever.

The trick would be to forget about the whole thing.

21

When Mars and Frankie arrived for their first visit to Florida, Avery grabbed them both and held them for a long time.

"Dear God, I've missed you," Mars said. When Frankie broke free, Mars kissed her, held her, didn't let go. The sparks were alive between them. She could always count on the magic of their chemistry. His kisses touched the deepest part of her, always had, always would.

Frankie turned into the most enthusiastic tourist Florida had ever had the good fortune to attract. Mars and Beverly had not been travelers, and Frankie had never left the mountains. He talked nonstop about the trip down. They'd made an overnight visit to Myrtle Beach to see the ocean. Mars complained about the distance from Interstate 26 all the way to the beach.

"Would have been faster to drive to London," he said.

"A little damp though." Avery laughed at him. "Actually, London's way north. South Carolina is due west of Africa or maybe Spain."

She held his hands when she told him about Mr. Patterson, thinking the news would monopolize their visit, but again Frankie dominated with his plans and his collection of attraction brochures. He scheduled every hour of every day, the beach from ten to twelve, lunch from twelve to one, Disney from one to six, forgetting it was a two- to three-hour drive away.

Mars thought Disney World was the plastic capital of the world. Avery delighted in Frankie's response to it; it was as if he'd found paradise. The Space Center topped Disney World by a wide margin in the boy's eyes. And the airboat ride on the St. Johns River might have been the best thing this side of heaven, especially when they caught a glimpse of an alligator sliding beneath the surface. A trip to Skeeter's Garden showed Mars just how serious Avery was about her mission in Florida. All of these adventures were interspersed with trips to Jensen Beach and lunch at the sandwich shop on the deck overlooking the ocean. At night, they nursed sunburns.

She worried her cottage would be cramped. Frankie had settled into the small guest bedroom and often fell asleep early. She and Mars walked arm in arm along the river in the evenings or shared some wine before sharing her bed. As the blush of sunburn darkened on his face, his turquoise eyes became brighter. Every glance into his face ignited her desire.

Once Frankie's most urgent plans were satisfied, Mars insisted on seeing her folks.

"It's been so many years. And after all," he argued, "they took me so many places. Remember when we went to Cherokee Village? Remember when they took us to the Biltmore House?"

"Yes, Mars, I remember all of it, and I know they will want to see you too."

She called and wrangled a dinner invitation, expecting the evening to be awkward.

"A swimming pool!" Frankie shouted once introductions were complete. "Look, Dad, they have a swimming pool right inside their house."

"Most everybody here has a pool," Avery's father said, pushing the sliding-glass door aside, releasing Frankie for a closer look.

"Nobody I know has their very own swimming pool," Frankie said.

"Are you going down to see Adam, Mars? I know he'd love to see you again."

"He came up last spring," Mars said. "We had a nice visit then. I don't think we'll have time to drive to Miami."

Frankie proceeded to tell every detail of Disney World, every detail of the Space Coast, and the airboat trip. His improved attitude pleased Avery, and she loved his enthusiastic chatter.

"By the way," her mother said, "I have the copy you wanted of the genealogy report we talked about."

Avery folded the report into her bag and thanked her.

"We've been worried about your financial situation, Avery," her father said. "You aren't earning any money. Do you need any help? Are you all right?"

"You'd be welcome to it," her mother added.

"I've collected some commissions on properties I had listed before. I'll be fine when the house sells. Until then, things are a little tight."

"You just let us know if you need anything."

"Thanks, Daddy. By the way, who is the guy you know who charters his sailboat sometimes?"

"Oh, Captain Mike. You all going sailing?"

"If he's available, we will." Her father gave her the phone number before the evening ended.

Avery hugged her mother, held her. "Thanks so much for having us all here tonight. Your dinner was great. Thank you."

She hugged her daddy too, looked in his eyes, and said, "Thanks for everything. You're the best."

He smiled when he said, "Good night, Budlet."

She called the next day to make the arrangements with Captain Mike.

On the last day of their visit, Avery took them to the marina, and Frankie ran along reading the names of the yachts. "*Papa's Folly. Wind Dancer. Just Reward. Legal Tender. Holy Moly.* I never knew there were so many boats in the world."

"I never saw so many in one place," Mars said, "never knew so many folks could afford a boat."

"They represent a staggering amount of money," Avery said. "There it is, the *Meltemi.*"

"Must be a lot of rich people around here." Mars said as he climbed aboard.

Captain Mike greeted them with a smile. "Some folks got nothing but the boat, like me for instance." He welcomed them aboard his forty-foot ketch and introduced his one-man crew. The live-aboard captain motored out into the Indian River while giving a brief safety talk.

"You ever been sailing before?" he asked Frankie.

"Nope, this is the first time. Dad's too."

"Well, you pay attention and you'll be an old salt by the end of the day. You can be my first mate today." The captain proceeded to give a short course in sailing and then ordered Frankie to steady the helm while he and his helper hanked on the sails. They raised the mizzen, flew the gigantic jib, and sailed downwind wing on wing in a fresh breeze.

The captain guided the boy through a tack, explaining the various maneuvers.

"Now we're on a beam reach, matie," the captain said to Frankie. He threaded his ship through the traffic and began to make his way toward the old Roosevelt Bridge.

"You've got a fine boy there, a promising sailor."

"Thanks, he's a good kid and plumb crazy about Florida. How long you been working on this boat?" Mars asked.

"All the years I've owned her," the captain said. "The *Meltemi* is as demanding as any lady in her mid-twenties. The work is never done."

"The fittings are . . ." Mars started to say.

"All bronze. The cabin's mahogany. The decks are teak." The captain puffed his cigar. "Sailed her around the world, I did, seventy-five to seventy-nine. Four years. From the Caribbean to the Aegean, been to paradise and back with my lady. She's the true love of my life, she is. There's beer and pop in the ice box below. Help yourselves." The man stood at the wheel, caressed the bronze rim with one hand and fingered the curved wood spokes with the other.

The wind shifted and the captain winched in the

sheets a bit. "We're sailing along at six knots," the captain told Frankie as the boy watched with growing admiration and awe.

"Can we go in the ocean? How far is the ocean from here?" Frankie asked.

"Not today, son. It's twelve miles out to the channel. We'll anchor and have lunch and take a swim later. Look, there's a great white heron." He pointed to the gigantic bird.

Avery asked if he'd take them to her canal off the St. Lucie so Mars could see her old house. The captain asked for directions, and a change of course meant a change of sail settings. He ordered Frankie to the helm while he repositioned the sails.

"Before the wind, we'll tack," he said. "Ready about." Then explained what he was doing to his first mate. "Now we're set on a beam reach."

Frankie listened and learned, repeated everything so he wouldn't forget. The captain adjusted the sails, aware, quick, and attentive, he responded to his boat's every whim.

Mars and Avery explored the cabin, and he marveled over the beautiful workmanship, antique bronze fittings, its efficient, compact simplicity. Avery remembered the *Bald Wind*, Ken's twenty-eight-foot fiberglass sloop, which had a little wood trim but in no way compared to the warmth and harmony of the *Meltemi*.

"I hadn't thought about your money problems until your dad mentioned it," Mars said. "Are you sure you're all right?"

"I'll be fine, sweetheart. You'll be the first to know if I need money."

"Now we're on a close haul," Captain Mike told Frankie as Avery and Mars returned to the deck. They dodged some traffic, let other boats dodge them, and passed under the bridge. An hour later captain and mate lowered the jib and mizzen to motor down the narrow canal. Mars and Frankie set the fenders out as the long bow nudged alongside the dock.

The manatees greeted them. The hose was still there, so Avery gave them a fresh-water treat. Mars went up to the house and climbed through the bushes to look in every window. The screen-enclosed pool didn't escape Frankie's keen eye either. She sat on the dock by the bow with the captain, watching the manatees.

"How's your father? I haven't seen him in a long time."

"He's fine, sort of semiretired now, golfing as always." She asked him about the name of his yacht.

"The *Meltemi*? She's the wild wind of the Aegean Sea."

They sailed in the afternoon with following winds. The captain moored in an inlet and served a gourmet lunch. Frankie's red hair had turned blond during the weeks spent in Florida's intense sun, and about a hundred new freckles appeared on his face. The sun set behind them as they sailed back to the marina.

"Avery, please come back with us." Mars implored as the day and the visit came to an end. In an effort to delay the separation, Avery suggested they drive to St. Augustine in caravan and spend a day or two seeing the sights. Then he could head north, and she could see Lissa before returning to Stuart.

"I'm coming up in October, no matter what," Avery said at the end of their visit. "I wouldn't miss leaf season for anything. So it's only a couple more weeks."

"I want you to come to stay, not just to come for a visit."

"I know you do, I want the same thing." She held him, kissed his neck and his ears and his mouth. "I want you to set me on fire every day of my life, Mars. I know what we have together is amazing. Trust me a little longer."

"I'll trust you forever," he said as they parted.

Avery was sitting alone in Skeeter's shack leafing through an avalanche of bills she couldn't pay when the owner of a large wholesale nursery, who did business with Kessler Properties over the years, came to visit. She knew him by reputation only. Still, she delighted in showing him around and sharing her plans.

"I want to help you," he said. "We are interested in investing in this venture. Perhaps we can work out a partnership. Am I right to assume you could use some financial backing?"

"A partnership? I'm surprised. Of course I need help. I have many volunteers but few investors, more to the point, no investors. Ken mentioned a number of problems I have yet to address, insurance, public parking, and other things. This seems to be a gift from heaven. I'd love to have you involved, especially considering your expertise with plants."

An instantaneous thought crossed her mind, perhaps Ken had somehow initiated this unusual encounter.

"We have experience with these issues. We have acres of greenhouses and are interested in developing greenhouses here to propagate the native plants. We would expect to supply developers across the region and of course, sell to the public."

"Oh, I see, I didn't realize you wanted to make a commercial venture out of this. If your only goal is business, I would have to decline. This is a memorial garden. I have no interest in turning it into a business." Avery started to turn her back on him, paused and then added, "Thank you for the offer and for your interest."

After he left Avery mulled over the strange encounter. Her financial situation had begun to erode. She was paying rent, all her own expenses for the first time in her life, and trying to support the garden. She'd hoped the house would have sold by the end of summer. Mr. Patterson sent his bills on time and she was happy to pay them. Still, after four months there had been no news. There were a dozen ways he could take advantage of the situation and profit from her emotional stake in the search, but she had no choice. She trusted him.

The second strange encounter in as many weeks occurred when Ken requested a meeting with Avery in his office.

"Why don't you come out here?" she asked.

"I need to see you in my office, Avery. I'm sorry to inconvenience you, but it's important."

She drove to the Kessler offices wondering what he had up his sleeve this time. Whatever it was, she expected not to like it. On the other hand, maybe he'd sold the house.

She was ushered in after several employees gathered around to welcome her.

"Thank you for coming," Ken said stepping around to the front of his desk.

"You don't have to be so formal."

"I have an idea I want to run by you. I have some drawings here, preliminary to be sure, but I wanted your opinion."

Avery was confused.

"I thought maybe you'd sold the house," she said.

"We have an offer. The prospects are trying to get financing, interest rates are high. We'll see what happens." He unrolled architectural plans and put some professional schematic drawings on the easel. "We are proposing to use some of your ideas in this project, so I was hoping you'd look at it."

"Go ahead."

"What would you think about an environment for a community which is all natural? No landscaped lawns, no paved roads, no tract houses."

The drawings he displayed were beautiful. Homes clustered around curving lanes. The drawings included recognizable native plants, sawgrass, palmettos, loblolly pines. The houses were drawn with natural materials, wraparound verandas, and steep tin roofs. Avery was speechless.

"We found an architect who thinks along the same lines you do, Avery. He has done these preliminary drawings for us. He's very excited to find a developer interested in a project where the environment will be handled with extreme care. I thought you'd be interested."

"I am. This is just beautiful."

"We feel it's time we addressed these issues. The environment is very popular these days. It's a bit of a gamble, and certainly something new for us, but we think it has commercial value. In other words, we think we can sell it."

"Where? What land?"

Ken grimaced.

"Oh, I see."

"Avery, please don't walk out the door."

"I'm not. I'll listen."

"Do you like the look of these drawings?"

"Yes, Ken. I like it very much. The architect shows a sensitivity I've never seen on a Kessler project before."

"Okay, here's the deal," he said. "We would be developing our land, which really surrounds your garden and the other undeveloped land you own. We need the original Kessler portion, but we would leave Skeeter's land completely natural. It would remain open to the public and we would agree in writing to support it forever. How does that sound?"

"I'm listening."

"It wouldn't be much different from setting land aside within a development for a golf course."

"A golf course generates revenue," she said.

"True, but the native garden might be worth something in goodwill. Okay. Good. We will pay you for all of it and agree legally to proceed as I've outlined."

"No paved roads? How?"

"The roadways will be natural materials as well, gravel or shell. A new process has been developed, I don't know exactly how they do it, but it winds up looking natural. I can show you a sample."

"And native plants?"

"Absolutely."

"No sod lawns? No specimen imports?"

"None."

Avery studied the drawings. "These are wonderful houses, Ken. I think you're on to something. This could work. People would love to live in a community like this. Especially with Skeeter's Garden right in the middle of the whole development. How did you come up with this?"

"I saw some drawings this architect had done. Then I contacted him and went around to see his other work, even his own home, which is a river house you would kill for." Ken paced a minute. "I was very impressed. I put two and two together and thought maybe you would agree."

"I do agree. It's clear I can't continue to support the garden. Without help, without expert advise, without funds, it's beyond my means. And I want to be in North Carolina, not here."

"Will you sell us the land? All of it?"

"With the restrictions you suggest and if it's all legal, of course."

He grabbed her into a hug, realized he'd taken a liberty, and pulled away. But Avery hugged him.

"I didn't want to fight about this land anymore. This seems like the perfect compromise."

"And it'll put some bucks in your pocket."

She laughed. "Tell me, Ken, how did you really come up with this scheme?"

"I thought a lot about us, you and me, and decided I needed to think about it like a business problem, not an emotional one. When I have an opponent in business matters, the solution is always in figuring out what the other fellow wants, what is important to him. I began to focus on what would be the best resolution for you. Now, it seems to be very good for us as well. Wouldn't it be something if Kessler Properties becomes known for environmental sensitivity?"

"Yes, that would be something."

"All due to your influence, my dear."

"This idea of yours is good and I wish you every success with it. You're okay, Ken. By the way, how are you doing? Are you married?"

"You know, Avery, odd as this may sound, I kinda like single life. I like my condo and I love my freedom."

"I'm glad to hear it." She started to leave.

"What about you?"

"Me? I'm going back to North Carolina. Have the papers drawn up and give me a call."

"I will. I'll be in touch. And, Avery, thank you."

Mars suggested she take a machete to hack away two hundred years of neglect when Avery went to look for the ancient graves of her ancestors. She put the menacing thing in the trunk. While Mars worked and Frankie was in school, Avery studied the maps to the cemeteries. She expected to be trudging through wilderness to find them.

Instead, the first cemetery she and Sylva visited was right in the town of Weaverville, just an hour drive from Mars's house. The manicured grounds surrounded the graves, and vases of plastic flowers adorned the headstones. A monument three feet tall with BALDWIN chiseled into stone was visible from the road. A wrought-iron fence enclosed thirty or so graves in the Baldwin family section. Avery opened the gate and went in to photograph the headstones, planning to send copies to her distant cousin in Kansas who had done the research.

They wandered around the cemetery beyond the fence and way in the back found Avery's great-great-grandfather's grave. Jacob Wells Baldwin 1824–1907. His wife's grave was adjacent, along with a daughter who'd lived only a year.

"I was born in the wrong place," Avery told Sylva. "I'm lucky my cousin found out all about this and shared it. This is a real-life image of my history." She sat on the ground in front of the Jacob Wells head-stone and looked his name up in the documents. "I wonder where his house was, what his life was like, what he did for a living. The records say he had five children, the one died in infancy."

Giant oaks and maples shaded the hill, sunlight created little prisms on the headstones. Sylva snapped a picture of Avery in front of his grave. They sat together in a stack of leaves someone had raked and left.

"I'm glad you came with me to see this, Sylva."

"Your family probably has deeper roots in these mountains than mine does."

"I still feel like you are my family."

"I'm thinking you're going to marry Mars," Sylva said, "and then we'll be real sisters."

"You told me once being friends was the best thing."

"It's still true."

"I can't wait to be your best friend and your sister," Avery said. "What if you'd married Adam?"

"Perish the thought!" Sylva grabbed a handful of leaves and pelted Avery with them. Avery scooped up an armload and peppered Sylva. They rolled and tumbled in the leaves, wrestling and laughing, and chased each other around the markers, kicking leaves, blaming each other for the mess they'd made.

Sylva fell into the pile of leaves, gasping to catch her breath, and Avery took her picture with red maple leaves caught in her hair. They stretched out, side by side, looking up into the branches of the tree, its leaves glimmering against a clear and cloudless sky.

Later, twilight drifted over the mountains, casting shadows through the woods and turning the bright autumn colors into soft muted tones of sepia and bronze. Avery joined Mars on the deck after dinner and settled into a rocking chair he'd built.

"Look at the sky, all pink and pretty," Mars said. "Man, I love this place."

"You're not the only one." Avery got up and kissed him. "I'll be right back. I need a sweater. You want anything?"

"Holler at Frankie for me, okay?"

When she came back, Mars was in the middle of a discussion with Frankie, ". . . blocking the creek, so this weekend let's clear the stream down in the ravine where the tree fell."

"Gonna be a big job, Dad. It's a mess."

"I know, but if we work together we can do it. If we don't clean it up, we might get ice jams this winter, even flooding."

"I'll help too," Avery said.

"You can make sandwiches. We'll have to cut that tree out of there with a chain saw."

"You know what, guys," she said, settling down, rocking the rocker. "You should have built this house on Crowfoot Ridge instead of all the way over here in Crooked Creek."

"What makes you think it's not on Crowfoot Ridge?" Mars asked.

"Because it's miles over there. Ten miles to Mac-Kinsey's Farm at least, isn't it?"

"Yes, but it's the same ridge. You can't drive over it, you drive around it. This is the other side of Crowfoot Ridge."

"I didn't know that."

"We could write a book about all the stuff you don't know about these mountains, Avery." Mars laughed at her. "We started out on Crowfoot Ridge and we end up on Crowfoot Ridge."

"Good," Avery said. "I like that."

Saturday morning, they dressed in their work clothes and went down to tackle the job. Mars wore his bandanna to keep his hair out of his eyes. The tree had clogged the stream so much, a pool of silt and mud covered everything. They began to pull gobs of leaves and debris away, which had caught in the branches. The stream had been reduced to a trickle and the water backed up a muddy pool around the tree. The old southern pine was at least fifty feet, its roots stood ten feet in the air.

"This is worse than I thought," Mars admitted. "It's gonna take us all weekend to clean this out of here."

"Dad, just cut those branches first, so we can get to it," Frankie suggested.

Mars cut away as much as he could to expose the trunk.

Avery and Frankie began pulling the branches out of the stream as Mars cut them.

Within an hour, all three of them were drenched and dirty. Frankie threw a clump of mud at his dad and laughed when it hit midchest. Mars howled and threw some back, which hit Avery. Then the mini-war escalated into a mud-slinging fit of laughter.

A car pulled into the driveway.

"You expecting someone?" Avery asked.

"Don't recognize the car," Mars said. "Anybody you know, Frankie?"

"No."

"Go up and see who it is."

"I'll go," Avery said. "He's got those branches to pull free."

Mars started up the chain saw again while Avery

climbed up the incline to the driveway.

A man got out of the car, hesitated when he saw her, and then walked toward her. The October sun caught like diamond dust and sparkled on his car. Avery stopped, watched him walk for a second. She tried to wipe the mud off her face.

Something about his gait seemed familiar.

She climbed on up to the driveway, pulling herself up by some vines. She realized she was covered from head to toe with mud and wiped her face with the back of her hand, just smearing the mud more, making it worse. He was tall and his chestnut hair reminded her of Adam when he was younger. She felt odd, weak somehow, faint. Breathless. Something about his walk, the way he carried himself . . . something.

"I'm sorry I'm such a mess," Avery yelled trying to be heard over the roar of the chain saw. "We're clearing the stream. A tree fell. It's a muddy job."

He stood in front of her. Must have been about twenty. Neither of them spoke. Strange, Avery couldn't speak.

Mars let the saw die, shouted up at them, "Who is it, Avery?"

He had eyes the color of a lagoon, turquoise eyes. Her eyes were riveted on his face. Still they hadn't spoken. Avery realized he was looking at her with intense interest. Curious interest. She felt herself tremble.

"Are you Avery Baldwin?" he asked. His voice, too, sounded familiar.

"Yes. I am." She wanted to ask him something, but the question quivered in her throat, her heart raced, her eyes were on his face. Tears formed, didn't spill, just formed in the back of her eyes. She realized she didn't know his name. "Are you . . . ?"

"I think so," he said.

He stood before her looking into her eyes. His expression was mischievous somehow, as if he knew something she didn't know.

But Avery did know. She knew who this young man was. She knew his smile. She knew his walk, his hair, and those extraordinary eyes.

She couldn't speak but her mind was screaming. Screaming for Mars. She heard Mars and Frankie climbing up the steep slope from the creek.

She should have recognized him at once.

He smiled an oh-so-familiar smile. His smile made her knees weak, made her hands tremble.

Then his arms were around her and she held him, cupped her hands around his face. He had his father's smile, the same smile she'd kept in her heart all her life.

She'd always loved his smile.